"If thou gaze long into an abyss, the abyss will also gaze into thee." —*Nietzsche*

"Abyss: The primeval chaos. The bottomless pit; hell. An unfathomable or immeasureable depth or void."

—*T̶h̶e̶ ̶A̶m̶e̶r̶i̶c̶a̶n̶ ̶H̶e̶r̶i̶t̶a̶g̶e̶ ̶D̶i̶c̶t̶i̶o̶n̶a̶r̶y̶*

You're holding in your hands one of the first in a new line of books of dark fiction, called Abyss. Abyss is horror unlike anything you've ever read before. It's not about haunted houses or evil children or ancient Indian burial grounds. We've all read those books, and we all know their plots by heart.

Abyss is for the seeker of truth, no matter how disturbing or twisted it may be. It's about people, and the darkness we all carry within us. Abyss is the new horror from the dark frontier. And in that place, where we come face-to-face with terror, what we find is ourselves. The darkness illuminates us, revealing our flaws, our secret fears, our desires and ambitions, longing to break free. And we never see ourselves or our world in the same way again.

Specters

J. M. DILLARD

A DELL BOOK

Published by
Dell Publishing
a division of
Bantam Doubleday Dell Publishing Group, Inc.
666 Fifth Avenue
New York, New York 10103

ISBN: 0-440-20758-4

Printed in the United States of America

Published simultaneously in Canada

May 1991

10 9 8 7 6 5 4 3 2 1

OPM

*For George, with love
and a vow never to mention
that yellow school bus again*

ACKNOWLEDGMENTS

My deepest gratitude goes to those who read the manuscript and offered their valuable comments and expertise:

Russ Galen
Jeanne Cavelos
Leslie Schnur
Martha Midgette
Rik Faith, M.D., and Melissa Clepper-Faith, M.D.
Kathleen O'Malley
George

AUTHOR'S NOTE

Although many sites mentioned herein are based on actual physical locations, some details, such as those concerning the layout of the "Catacombs" in Old Hyde Park, have been altered.

New Orleans

DECEMBER 27, 1965

1

Hot. Sticky hot.

The fan blew directly on Bruner, sculpting the sheet against his skin into billowing dunes, but he could not sleep. Two days after Christmas, and the afternoon temperature had soared into the eighties, falling back to a breezeless seventy-four at night. He despised warm weather. Two years after leaving Minnesota he still wasn't used to it—especially at night. Nights were supposed to be cool, not balmy. Yet even if the temperature had been more to his liking, he would still not have been able to sleep. Not in this aged, creaking house on the Rue de St. Charles. He would still be staring up into blackness, watching without seeing, waiting.

Undaunted by the hot weather, the woman next to him began snoring, a soft wheezing little sound that made him smile. Even asleep, Marie was delicate—a pale, dark-haired woman, so thin that when she slept with her back to him as she did now, her white shoulder blades reminded him of angel's wings—though at times she slept so soundly that it was impossible to waken her. Especially after making love. After sex tonight she had dropped off immediately.

The act had done little to relax him. He was still awake, and the fire within him was growing. He had tried to drown it with cognac from the bottle next to the bed, but tonight liquor only inflamed him further. Marie hadn't touched a drop herself; she never drank, but provided the bottle without a condemning word.

A good woman. He'd known her now for a year, and if she'd found fault with him, she kept it to herself. She had never contradicted him, never uttered a word of disappointment. He admired that in a woman.

And she deserved someone to take care of her. When her husband died three years ago, the insurance money barely met the funeral expenses. Marie went to work as a file clerk and also took care of her two young daughters. She was always exhausted—just as she was tonight—yet he had never heard her complain. Unselfish, hardworking Marie.

The opposite of his spoiled first wife, Elsa. She'd always had money, never worked a day in her life, but her complaints were constant and bitter. Most nights she drank until she passed out, and he would carry her to bed. When she had finally left him, Bruner had only one regret: she had taken their infant son with her. He had grown somewhat attached to the child, despite the fact that he had so desperately wanted a girl.

He felt lucky to have found Marie. And her beautiful daughters.

It was time to think about marrying again. Within the past month he had begun to stay the night as a matter of course. But in the South—even in a town as laissez faire as New Orleans—it was only a matter of time before people started talking. That was bad for a young doctor's practice.

Bruner sat up in the bed and swallowed with difficulty. The cognac had been a mistake. It only dehydrated him more in this weather, making his tongue feel like cotton. And after the peppery *légumes à l'étouffée* Marie had served for dinner, he wanted water, cold water . . . something cool to soothe him to sleep, to let him forget the compulsion that was filling him, pounding slow and steady as a heartbeat deep within.

"Marie?" he asked the pale form next to him, and gently shook the yielding flesh of her arm. Her hair was pinned up; dark tendrils curled against her white neck. "Are you awake, darling?"

No response. Marie's snores were still coming regularly as Bruner pulled on his boxer shorts and made quietly for the bedroom door. He knew the moment he opened it that fate was with him.

The kitchen light was on.

He tiptoed down the high narrow stairs, flinch-

ing at each creak. When he arrived at last at the
bottom and peered into the kitchen, his heart almost stopped.

The kitchen looked the same as always: small
and cramped, but clean. The dinette set was at
least ten years old. The white Formica tabletop
was scratched and stained, the vinyl on the matching chairs was split.

But *she* was there—his blue angel.

It was the title of a 1930 German film, *Der blaue
Engel*, that had obsessed Bruner's mother. Unable
to find anyone to look after the boy, she had
dragged him with her countless times to see it. He
remembered little of it, except the title and the
skeleton of the plot: a professor's unrequited love
for Marlene Dietrich destroys him. The Blue Angel was the name of the cabaret where she performed. But when Bruner had first laid eyes on
Avra, she had been dressed in blue—always in blue
—and the title had popped into his mind and remained thereafter every time he looked at her: blue
angel.

She sat at the table, her delicate arms twined
around her knees, her feet up on the seat of the
chair. A halo of dark hair fell in waves to her waist.
Her pale blue nightgown was made of the thinnest
fabric imaginable, so that when the light shone behind her, the effect was gossamer. Yet she remained blissfully unaware of her nakedness, like
Eve in the Garden. She looked up at him, and her

expression upon seeing him was one of sweet surprise . . . dared he hope, one of quiet joy?

He had been smitten since their first meeting almost a year ago, when Marie had brought Avra and her sister in for a routine checkup. He had examined the sister first, under Marie's calm, watchful eyes.

Magdalen. Magdalen didn't trust him. She squirmed, scowled, resisted. When he was finished with her, he felt nothing but relief. And then he had laid hands on Avra.

She had smiled up at him like an angel. Avra emanated beauty: the classic, delicate features, the wide gray eyes—but her beauty went deeper than the physical, for Avra's face shone with an inner light, and her smile held the promise of unspeakably celestial secrets. . . .

No, it was not just a physical attraction. Of that he could be sure, because of the identical twin whose face was the mirror image of Avra's—that lovely face—and if the sisters sat side by side one could not deny that they looked the same. And yet he saw a difference—Avra possessed an inner sparkle that her twin lacked. Without that brilliance Magdalen was merely pretty, but Avra . . . Avra was a goddess.

Yet for all her radiance it was clear that Avra yearned for more, needed more. He had hoped to be the one to stir her passion, the one she chose to teach her of love. If there were consequences to bear, they were worth it. The past year had been hard, very hard, for him, being so near to her and yet having to exert such strict self-control. There had only been a few times where he had been alone with her—secret, delicious moments, tempered with the fear of being caught. The rarity of those moments had only fed his passion.

He had forced himself to be gradual with her. It was the only way, Bruner knew, to win her trust, to guarantee her silence. But tonight she would be ready for more. . . . And he could hold himself back no longer. He'd been waiting for this night for almost a year. Control had become increasingly difficult. Too often he had pushed too far, too fast, and made her cry . . . hurt her, and been forced to stop and soothe her tears away.

Don't cry, darling. Sometimes it hurts, but you want to get better, don't you?

Yes, it was destiny that Avra was here in the kitchen tonight, and not the sister.

The air in the kitchen was stifling. A faint breeze stirred at the open window, then faded abruptly, leaving behind the damp, rotten-fish smell of the Mississippi. Bruner wiped perspiration from his forehead. "Hello, Avra. You're up very late. Couldn't you sleep?"

Despite the heat Avra seemed fresh and cool. So innocent . . . yet here she was, teasing him in that diaphanous gown with those long legs tucked up in front of her. She leaned to set her chin on her knees, and a long lock of hair fell over one eye.

She did not move it, but sat staring intently at the glass of milk on the table. "No," she whispered.

Was it because she thought of him too? "Neither could I. Avra . . ." His voice quavered. Did she have any idea of the power she had over him? "I think that it's probably time for another examination."

For a moment she kept staring at the table, but then she raised her head and looked up into his face. "You said I was getting better, Doctor."

"Rolf," he corrected.

"Rolf," she repeated automatically. He had always thought his name ugly, until he had heard her say it. Now he made her say it at every opportunity.

"You *are* getting better, but you aren't well yet," he answered firmly, though his heart was pounding so rapidly now, he felt like gasping. "The kitchen is not the place for an exam." It was too open, too exposed to anyone coming down the stairs, and the café curtains were too small to cover the large open window over the sink. "Will you come with me into the bathroom, please, Avra?"

There was another pause.

At long last she picked up her doll from the table and with one hand clutched it to her chest. The other she held out to Bruner.

A thrill of such intensity clutched his abdomen that his legs nearly buckled. He would be very slow, very gentle.

As he led her into the bathroom, he thought for an instant of Marie. She had done an admirable job of raising the child; Avra was very well behaved for a five-year-old.

2

The footsteps coming down the stairs were so soft that at first Avra thought they were Magdalen's. By the time she realized whose they were, it was too late to run.

He had never caught her in the kitchen before. She had thought it was safe. . . . She'd come down every night this week. And she had been very quiet about getting the milk out of the refrigerator tonight.

She put her arms around her legs and hugged herself tight. Sometimes she wished she could squeeze herself into a tiny ball and disappear. She stared down at the glass of milk on the table. Maybe if she didn't look at him, he would go away.

But he didn't. He stood at the other end of the table and smiled at her. "Hello, Avra. You're up very late. Couldn't you sleep?"

"No." She couldn't sleep too well anymore. She had been having bad dreams and seeing scary things in the dark ever since the examinations began.

The first time it had happened was in the living room. Mama had taken Magdalen to the dentist, and the doctor stayed at home with Avra. Avra had been glad then that Mama liked him . . . but that was a long time ago. That day he had been very nice to Avra. They had been playing one of her favorite games on the couch . . .

He bounced her on his knee. *Ride a little pony into town, ride a little pony, don't fall DOWN* . . .

. . . and he straightened his knee, and down Avra went, shrieking and laughing.

But then he had begun to act strange. He got a funny look in his eyes as he gathered her up on his lap and told her that she was sick.

"But I don't feel sick," she protested.

"You *are*, you just can't tell yet. But if we don't help you really soon, then you'll get very, very sick. You could even die."

Avra started crying; she burrowed her head against his big neck. It smelled clean, of soap and after-shave. He stroked her back with his huge hand as he talked. "Don't worry. You'll get better, but you have to do as I say."

"Okay," she said into his neck.

"You're such a good girl." He made her sit up and blow her nose into a tissue. "Now, you have to promise not to tell your mother about this."

"Why not?"

"Because your mother will feel she has to pay

me, and you know how worried she is about money."

"Yes," Avra said. Mama talked about not having enough money all the time, especially when the girls asked for new toys.

"And if I tell her about your being sick, she'll be terribly worried. It would kill her. You don't want that, do you?"

Avra shook her head. She certainly didn't want Mama to die from worrying. The doctor made her promise not to tell Magdalen either. That was the hardest, keeping something from her sister. It made her feel that she was somehow being very bad, and yet she didn't want Mama or her sister to get upset either. Mama loved this man, and said that soon he might be the twins' new father.

Avra knew it would happen, though she dreaded the thought. Just the day before Christmas, when she'd been snooping in Mama's closet, looking for presents, Mama and the doctor had entered the bedroom.

Avra had hidden behind Mama's coat and held very still until they left. But she had listened carefully to what Doctor Bruner said.

Marie, there's something I must talk to you about. . . .

Maybe now, Avra thought with relief and hope, the doctor would tell Mama about Avra's sickness. Maybe now the exams would stop.

But he said: *I've been thinking about the girls lately. It's important for them to have a father, don't you think?*

Mama's answer was so soft, Avra couldn't make out the words. But she sounded happy.

I love you, Marie. And I love the girls. I want to be sure they don't grow up without a father, the way I did. I've never told anyone— His voice broke; for an instant Avra thought he was going to cry. But then it grew strong again.

My parents never married. I'm

And here he used a word that Avra didn't understand, a word that sounded like he was sick. *Illi—* something.

Maybe he'd caught it from Avra.

She didn't remember the rest of the conversation; she'd been too knotted up with fear. Disease or no disease, she would die if Mama married this man.

The grown-ups talked a little while longer, then there was a silence that probably meant they were kissing. And then she heard the sound of their footsteps on the stairs.

All through Christmas she waited for them to say something about it to her and Magdalen, but they never did.

In the meantime Avra did as the doctor said, and kept silent. And she worried.

Worried that she might die. Or even worse, that she might give the disease to Magdalen.

The examinations continued every time he managed to get her alone. At first they weren't bad; she even sort of liked them. Then they began to hurt and she did everything she could to avoid them. But tonight there was no getting away.

Bruner moved closer to the kitchen table. Avra kept her eyes down, but she could feel him staring at her.

"Neither could I," he said. She knew that his face was getting that strange look she had grown to hate so much. "Avra, I think that it's probably time for another examination."

She looked up at him, feeling a sudden surge of defiance. "You said I was getting better, Doctor."

"Rolf," he said softly.

"Rolf," she repeated. She hated the sound of it. It reminded her of an ugly wolf.

"You *are* getting better," he said, moving even closer to her. "But you aren't well yet. The kitchen is not the place for an exam. Will you come with me into the bathroom, please, Avra?"

He held out his hand.

She shrank from it. She didn't mean to be a bad girl . . . she wanted to do what was right, but she hated the examinations so. And somehow she knew that tonight would hurt worse than the other times. If only she could tell Mama, and ask her what to do. . . .

She stared down at her doll on the table. It was the best of all the Christmas presents this year. Gran had made a small cloth Avra with black yarn hair and embroidered gray eyes, and dressed it in bright blue. Maybe, if Avra kept her mind on the doll, and tried not to think about the exam, it wouldn't hurt so much.

Sometimes Magdalen said Avra was chicken. Well, she didn't want to be chicken; she wanted to be a big girl, not a baby. She didn't want Magdalen to get sick, and she didn't want Mama to die. The doctor said Avra was almost well. Maybe this would be the last time, and then she would be all right. Then she could tell Mama all about it.

Doctor Bruner was still holding out his hand.

She grabbed her Avra doll and clutched it tightly to her chest with one hand. The other she held out to the doctor.

He led her into the bathroom just off the kitchen.

The light was off. To Avra's five-year-old eyes the darkness pulsed and swirled with hidden evil. She balked in the doorway and, when he tugged gently at her hand, burst into tears.

"Shh . . . Avra, what's wrong?"

"The dark," she gasped between anguished sobs. "Please, *please*, turn on the light. I'm scared."

Bruner smiled indulgently, then snapped on the light. "All right now?"

"And leave the door open," she said tremulously.

He left it half open. "There, now. Nothing to be afraid of, is there?"

She didn't answer.

He sat down on the lid of the toilet. "Now come here, darling. Come sit on my lap."

She walked over to where he sat, but came no farther; he had to lift her up onto his knee. She sat sideways, and caught a glimpse of her own pale, frightened face in the mirror over the sink. When she saw Bruner's, she squeezed her eyes shut.

"Put that down, darling." She could feel him trying to pry the Avra doll away from her.

"No!" Without opening her eyes she clutched the doll desperately with both arms.

"Hush, darling, it's all right. You can keep it, then." He bent his face down to hers, and she caught the sharp smell of liquor. He kissed her hard on the lips. His own were open; she felt his warm spit on her face. He was shaking all over when he pulled away.

What is he so afraid of? That Mama will find out?

She squeezed the doll tighter as she felt the doctor's sweaty hands on her. She decided to pretend she was the Avra doll—made of cloth, because it didn't feel anything. You couldn't hurt a doll made of cloth.

3

Avra was gone.

Magdalen woke knowing it, even before she opened her eyes to the feeble glow of the plastic owl night-light and saw Avra's empty bed. Magdalen had been dreaming, far away in some strange but familiar place full of strange but familiar people, when all of the sudden the dream stopped like somebody turning off the TV and she could hear someone saying, "Avra's gone."

Radar, Mama called it. Twins have got radar about each other. A sick sense, she said. Magdalen could always tell when Avra was in trouble—like the time in nursery school when the Winslow girl picked a fight with Avra and made her cry. It was Magdalen who knocked the bully down. Or the time Avra wandered into the neighbors' backyard last year and jumped into the deep end of the pool. Magdalen called the grown-ups so they got there just in time to see Avra hit the water. And just a week ago Mama left them in the car for just a minute and Avra hit something near the steering wheel and made the car roll backward—it was Magdalen who pressed the horn.

Maybe, Mama had said, it had something to do with the fact that Magdalen was older. Three whole minutes older, and so she acted just as an older sister should.

But sometimes it seemed Avra tried too hard to get into trouble; sometimes it made Magdalen mad, though she never said so. She couldn't remember a time when Avra took care of *her*—but then, Magdalen never needed anyone's help. She was always too busy looking after Avra to get into trouble herself. Mad or not, Magdalen would always be there when her twin needed her.

Like now, when the radar was telling her something was *wrong*.

Maybe Avra just went downstairs for a glass of milk, something she did a lot lately. It worried Magdalen. Avra was upset about something, but whatever that thing was, she wouldn't tell. Every time Avra went downstairs, Magdalen would wake up after a while and go down to check on her, just to be sure . . . but this time Magdalen felt funny-strange, as if she had just been running and couldn't catch her breath. When the radar felt like that, it always meant trouble. Real trouble.

So Magdalen got up from her bed and made it past the humming floor fan and the child-sized red table and chair without bumping into anything.

She was very good at finding her way in the dark. She wasn't afraid of it. Avra had a real good imagination, so sometimes she got scared of the dark. She would cry and tell Magdalen that the dress on the chair was a monster or something. Magdalen might be just a *little* scared, but not much. She knew the dark couldn't change anything. She'd get up and move it, just to show Avra that it was only a stuffed animal or a jacket, and Avra would feel better and go to sleep.

Magdalen moved into the hallway and put her hand against the wall, so that she would know when to turn the corner. When she got to the top of the stairs, she could see that the kitchen light was on: Avra, with her crackers and milk. But the radar wasn't satisfied.

Magdalen held up the hem of her lavender nightgown (purple for her, blue for Avra, the colors they had worn since they were both babies and Mama couldn't tell them apart) and moved silently down the stairs.

The stairs led down into the living room, where the Christmas tree still stood, though all the presents had been cleared away. The icicles reflected the light coming from the kitchen. Halfway down Magdalen heard a strange sound, one that made her run down the stairs into the living room and peer through the doorway into the kitchen.

The kitchen light was on, and there was Avra's glass of milk on the table . . . but the room was empty. Where could Avra have gone? Magdalen turned toward the shadowy hallway. The door to the bathroom was half open and someone was inside. Avra. Magdalen felt relieved—until she realized that her sister was not alone.

Dr. Bruner sat on the toilet lid with Avra in his lap. He wasn't wearing a shirt, but he was covered with sweat, and he was clutching Avra tightly to him. Magdalen knew that he had come earlier that night, to talk to Mama . . . but she hadn't realized that he was still here. Was something wrong with Avra? Was she sick?

Avra looked as if something were hurting her terribly. She was sobbing, hands covering her eyes and her long dark hair tangled over her face. She had dropped her doll, which was pressed between her and the doctor.

Neither of them saw Magdalen. The doctor's eyes were half open, but his attention was focused entirely on the sobbing child in his lap. It occurred to Magdalen that the doctor might be punishing Avra . . . but he didn't look angry. He looked *happy* to be hurting her.

It was the expression on the doctor's face that frightened Magdalen. She ran back up the stairs and burst into her mother's room.

Mama was sleeping so soundly that when Magdalen jumped onto the bed, she didn't stir.

"Mama," Magdalen whispered harshly into her mother's ear. "Avra's in trouble."

Mama mumbled something into her pillow.

"Mama," she said, this time louder and a little angrily. "It's *Avra.*" She tugged Mama's arm.

"What?" Mama lifted her head a little and looked at Magdalen as if she didn't understand. "What's the matter, honey? You sick?"

"The doctor's downstairs in the bathroom with Avra. She's crying. He's doing something funny to her!"

Mama sat bolt upright in the bed and grabbed Magdalen's wrist. "*What?*"

"He's not wearing clothes, Mama."

Mama's eyes got huge.

Just then a soft sound came from downstairs, sort of like crying, like someone being hurt. Avra.

Mama leapt from the bed and grabbed her robe. She stopped just long enough to shake a finger at Magdalen in the darkness. "You stay here."

And she was down the stairs and in the kitchen before Magdalen could talk back.

Normally, Magdalen would do what Mama said; but of course she couldn't stay now, not with Avra downstairs, maybe hurt. She followed quietly down the stairs, staying behind in the safe darkness of the living room.

From where she was, she could see Mama fling the bathroom door open and freeze in the doorway. Her whole body tensed at what she saw. Mama's hair was pinned up, and Magdalen could see the muscles stand out in the back of her neck.

"Mama!" Avra sobbed gratefully, out of sight.

Mama roared and screamed, all at once. Magdalen knew from the terrible sound that her mother was going to kill the doctor, and was frightened and glad at the same time. She clutched at her own nightgown and started to cry, calling Avra's name.

Mama rushed inside, and suddenly Magdalen could see everything. Bruner was sitting with Avra on his lap. Mama went toward them, her hands stretched out as if to strangle the doctor or rescue her daughter. Startled, Bruner jumped up so that Avra fell onto the white tile floor with a thump.

The doctor tried to push past Mama; his face was very scary. Mama was screaming at him, clawing at him, punching him. Doll tucked under one arm, Avra started crawling out of the bathroom. Magdalen ran to her and pulled her into the living room. "Avra!"

While the doctor jerked up his shorts, Mama ran to the kitchen and grabbed her big knife from the block on the countertop. He followed. She lunged at him with it and stuck him on the arm. He looked surprised but stayed on his feet.

"Don't move." Mama's teeth were clenched. "I'll kill you. I swear it, Rolf. . . ." She backed slowly toward the kitchen wall. And then she looked behind her as she reached for the phone.

Bruner grabbed Mama's wrist, and his other hand took the knife away.

He was going to cut her with it.

"Don't you hurt my mama!" Avra dropped the doll and threw herself on Bruner like a shrieking little monkey. She clamped her teeth down hard on his leg.

"No!" Magdalen ran after her, tried to pull her away.

Bruner howled and flailed at Avra with the knife; she raised her arm to protect herself and pulled it away bloodied. She stared curiously at it while Maggie pulled her back into the living room.

Mama threw herself onto him, roaring with rage, but she was no match for him. The knife came down hard and went into her back with a wet *thunk*. She took two wobbly steps toward the living room and sank facedown on the floor, deflating with a gentle hiss of air. Magdalen knelt next to her, crying. "Mama . . ."

"Run," Mama gurgled; blood bubbled at her lips. She half propped herself up. "Take Avra. Run. For God's sake, RUN. . . ." With surprising strength she gave Magdalen a one-armed push.

Magdalen jerked up like a puppet and found Avra shivering in the darkness. She threw both arms around her sister and pulled her through the dark living room, out the front door, turning only long enough to see Mama dragging herself forward on her elbow, the doctor coming up behind her with the knife. . . .

Magdalen slammed the door behind them.

She was young and fast and knew her way in the dark, but Avra seemed stunned and helpless. "Run, Avra. Mama says we've got to. . . . We have to get help."

Avra stared blankly at her sister.

"Hold on to me. Tight!" Magdalen barked, pulling Avra's uninjured arm around her.

Avra held on tight, her legs pumping mechanically. She was trying her best, but the doctor's legs were much longer. If he followed, he would catch them.

For God's sake, RUN

The door opened behind them. Magdalen could hear Bruner a few steps behind, but she didn't dare turn her head to look. He was breathing hard; Avra was sobbing for breath, and Magdalen could hardly breathe herself, out of fright. He was too close. Any second she would feel his huge fingers on her. . . .

RUN, Avra

No answer

Do you even hear me, Avra?

No answer

They almost fell as the yard ended and the grass changed to dirt, cool and soft against Magdalen's bare feet. Then she remembered: the Lamberts' front yard was all dug up. They were fixing some sort of pipes. She remembered where the pipes were and where the deep hole gaped open. She'd been playing there most of the afternoon, had jumped over it a million times in the daylight. In the dim light of the streetlamp she could just make it out, only because she knew it was there.

Just then the doctor's sweaty hand reached out and brushed them both. Avra screamed, and Magdalen pulled away as if she'd been seared by a lighted match.

Even pulling Avra along, Magdalen was running faster than she'd ever run in her whole life, breathing air like fire into her lungs. Still, she didn't slow down.

"Avra," she said, just loud enough for her sister to hear. "Avra, get ready to jump. NOW!"

They made it over the pipes and the hole without losing a beat.

Magdalen heard the pipes clank together behind them, followed by a soft thud in the dirt. Bruner cried out loud and moaned. Through it all the girls kept running. Magdalen knew he'd climb out in a hurry.

They didn't stop until they got to the Lamberts' door. Magdalen threw herself against it, unable to stop. The Lamberts didn't have a doorbell, and the door was heavy wood with thick panes of glass. She pounded on the door as hard as she could, feeling that she was hardly making any noise, so she started yelling, too, tears running down her cheeks. Avra leaned against the house and moaned softly.

Behind them the doctor's bare feet crunched against the oystershell driveway. He was right behind them, and any minute now those big hands would be around Magdalen's neck. . . .

It took forever for the outside light to come on, but when it did, there was instant silence. Magdalen quit screaming, and the footsteps behind her stopped suddenly, as if the light had made the doctor dissolve like one of Avra's nighttime monsters.

Mr. Lambert looked sleepy and mad, in striped pajama bottoms without his glasses. But then he saw her, really saw her, and yanked the door open. Magdalen glanced down and saw Avra's and Mama's blood splattered all over her nightie, and the blood dripping from Avra's forearm. The oyster shells in the driveway had cut the bottoms of Magdalen's bare feet, but she didn't feel them; she just stood there, looking. Finally she whispered, "Help my mama, please."

There was a flurry of activity as the neighbor called for his wife and son. The girls were pulled inside the safety of the house. Avra sat very still and refused to speak to anyone, not even Magdalen, while Mrs. Lambert wrapped Avra's injured arm in a towel, then called the police. Mr. Lambert and his oldest boy, Donny, ran next door with shotguns. The heavyset older man was an ex-Marine who said he wasn't afraid of anything, but when he came back, he looked sick, and sad.

He didn't have to tell Magdalen anything; she'd already figured what had happened.

It was in all the papers.

Gran adopted the girls and changed their last names. Magdalen liked it in Florida, especially the beaches, and no one had oystershell driveways that cut your bare feet.

When the girls were a little older, Gran told

them that Dr. Bruner had been killed later that same night while resisting arrest. Other than that, she never spoke of the incident at all.

Neither did the twins, until almost twenty-five years later.

Tampa

AUGUST 1990

4

A full four months after it happened, almost three months after he had left D.C., the incident still haunted Feinman. Not in his waking hours, of course—at least, not usually, unless he happened to be strolling down the street, trapped a few seconds too long by a passing policeman's curious gaze—but in his dreams. At night it was harder to disremember the past; asleep, he found it harder to deny the panic that had fueled his southward flight.

The dream began mundanely enough—more an accurate recollection than a dream, really. Feinman in the silver Mercedes, surrounded by darkness, hurtling westward on Route 123 near the claustrophobic cluster of high-rises and malls known as Tyson's Corner. Another two hours of back roads to Harpers Ferry and the lonely stretch of Appalachian Trail, where he later abandoned Celia.

Stab of headlights in the rearview. In the dream Feinman remembered that he did not panic, did not react at all; just another car on the road. The late April night was unusually cool, almost cold. Feinman's Burberry coat was buttoned, but he had rolled down the car windows partway; the chilly air helped him stay awake, kept his head level. On the stereo a Haydn concerto played softly. The digital clock glowed: twelve forty-five A.M.

It was raining. Not the usual spring drizzle, but a solid, steady, soaking rain. That would work, Feinman knew, to his benefit. Rain washed away traces.

The headlights loomed larger in the mirror. Feinman lifted his foot from the accelerator in the hopes that the other car would pass, but it slowed, matching his speed. . . .

Then flashed, red and blue lights.

Feinman drew in his breath with a small, wordless cry, and for the first time since he was a child felt a rush of nauseating fear. Over the past twenty-four years he had never felt fear, never been stopped by the police . . . never been interrupted at this most critical moment.

All that had changed. He had been discovered. He was finished, lost, ruined, dead. For an instant he considered pressing the accelerator, trying to outrun the police cruiser on the dark, slick road.

Despite the terror his rational mind took possession of him, as it always did:

No reason to assume they know anything. Slow down. Gently, gently.

Pull over. Turn on the overhead light. Find the registration in the glove compartment.

As Feinman dreamed, fear distorted the interior of the Mercedes, first larger, then smaller, as if viewed through a fisheye lens. Outside, the dark landscape loomed cartoonishly.

All was lost; yet his mind worked with clinical efficiency, recalling the most successful method of dealing with the police: disarm them by admitting that you are wrong, so very wrong, and they are so very right. It puts them at a disadvantage, for they are psychologically prepared to disagree with you.

If they examined the Mercedes, he was a dead man.

Feinman stared into the rearview at his pale, shocked face and forced an insincere, spastic smile, then let the grimace fade until his expression appeared helpfully polite, vaguely pleasant. He stepped from the Mercedes into the rain, into the glare of the police cruiser's headlights.

The policeman (perhaps a highway patrolman; Feinman had been too terrified to notice the difference) met him halfway between the two vehicles. The blue light flashed against a backdrop of dark, anonymous high-rises.

Between the two men long, sharp drops of rain sparkled, backlit by the cruiser's headlights. The cop's breath formed small clouds of mist.

"May I see your license, sir?"

Feinman fumbled in his wallet and handed it over, amazed to find that his hand did not tremble. "Officer, you have me dead to rights. I was speeding, sir. I'm afraid I didn't even realize it until I saw your flashing lights. Thank you for stopping me."

The policeman—young, Caucasian, nondescript save for a trimmed dark moustache—frowned at Feinman's Virginia license, then stared up at him with courteous hostility. If he was taken aback by Feinman's fawning, he did not show it.

"Is this your car, sir?"

The older man nodded and handed over the registration before the cop had a chance to ask. Cold rain stung Feinman's bald crown and dribbled beneath his collar. He had left his fedora on the car seat with the thought of seeming . . . pathetic, open, honest. With the hope of making the policeman feel sorry for him and let him get out of the rain sooner.

The cop squinted through raindrops at the Mercedes's registration. "You were doing fifty-five in a thirty-five-mile-an-hour zone, Mister Feinman."

Doctor Feinman, Feinman wanted to correct him —such idiots, these police; the fact was right there, on his license—but the instinct for self-preservation kept him silent. At the same time he struggled to keep from sagging with relief against the locked trunk of the Mercedes with its illicit cargo.

The policeman did not suspect a thing. Feinman

had been stopped for speeding, nothing more. It reaffirmed his faith in the absolute stupidity of all law-enforcement officials.

Feinman knew people in an instant. He *sensed* them, the core of their being, their darkest motivations, their point of greatest weakness, all within seconds. And he had contempt for those who lacked this ability.

The only other person he had known to possess it was his mother. Long dead, thank God.

The cop did not know who stood before him. The cop looked at Feinman and saw the Mercedes, the Burberry raincoat, the waterproof gold Rolex collecting beads of rain on its crystal face. Caught the scent of success, not murder.

"I don't doubt it for a moment, Officer. I'm afraid my mind was on other things."

The policeman glanced sharply at him. The fear returned, stronger this time. It occurred to Feinman that he'd had two cognacs less than an hour before. Courvoisier XO. Usually he drank the Napoleon, but he saved the XO for special occasions.

He wasn't drunk. He hadn't even felt the cognac in his exhilaration. But if the cop smelled liquor on his breath . . .

(Ran him in for DUI, impounded the Mercedes, searched it, for God knows what reason opened the trunk)

Easy. Easy. Just imagination running wild. Feinman forced a tremulous smile. If the man thought he was drunk, he'd ask Feinman to walk a straight line next. . . .

The cop produced a clipboard and slid Feinman's registration and license underneath the clamp. "I'm going to have to run a check on your license, Mr. Feinman."

"I understand, Officer."

The cop returned to the cruiser. Rather than retreat to the comfort of the Mercedes or, God forbid, sit inside the police car, Feinman remained standing in the rain, holding vigil beside the trunk.

Another distressing thought occurred to him: He was going to get a ticket. The fact that he had been speeding down 123, headed west at twelve forty-five A.M. on a Wednesday morning, would be forever recorded. Anyone who ever investigated Celia's disappearance could stumble across that fact. . . .

Paranoid. He was being paranoid. There was absolutely nothing to connect him to her. At least, nothing concrete. . . .

But for the first time in nearly twenty-five years, he had made a mistake. Left a trail that might be followed at some future time.

Feinman began to shiver in the damp.

The cop came back out of the cruiser. There was nothing in his demeanor or expression to suggest he was in the least bit suspicious, or that he was going to do anything other than hand Feinman the ticket. . . .

He paused. Feinman saw the look in his eye. He

studied Feinman, the way Feinman stood protectively in front of the Mercedes's trunk, and then—Feinman would have sworn to this—he gazed *at* the trunk. Then back at Feinman. Then at the trunk again.

The blood left Feinman's face. For a wild instant he considered the gun hidden in the Mercedes's glove compartment. He wished he held it now. He waited, still shivering, for the next obvious step.

Could you open the trunk, please, Mister Feinman?

Mister Feinman, could you open the trunk?

In actuality the cop had never asked the question, had hesitated and possibly glanced at the trunk . . . then given Feinman the ticket and let him go. But in the dream, reality dissolved at that instant, at the very height of Feinman's terror. In the dream the policeman spoke the very words Feinman dreaded hearing.

Open the trunk, Mister Feinman.

Image: The policeman drawing his service revolver.

Open the trunk.

Feinman opened the trunk.

He woke to the drone of the air-conditioner laboring endlessly in the heavy August night. He was alone in his bed, but terror had disoriented him. Slowly, memory returned, and he reassured himself: His name was Jacob Feinman. *Doctor* Jacob Feinman. He was in the expensive home on Riverhills Drive that he had recently purchased in

Temple Terrace, a northern suburb of Tampa, and it was a weeknight, a Thursday.

Feinman turned his head against the down pillow and glanced at the glowing digital readout on the alarm clock.

Correction. Three fifty-seven A.M. Friday morning. He needed to return to sleep—he had more than a full load of patients scheduled for today—but his pulse was still racing, even though the panic had begun to ease.

He let his head roll back on the soft pillow and sighed as he closed his eyes. This was happening far too often lately, his awakening at three or four o'clock in the morning and then being unable to sleep. It was in danger of becoming a habit.

And it was utterly ridiculous. He had never feared the police, never in his life. Never, certainly, in the past twenty-four years. And there was no reason to fear them now.

Despite the fact that, shortly after the incident on Route 123, he had closed his practice in the District, announcing to his patients and acquaintances that he was retiring and heading out West, probably to Arizona.

He did not go to Arizona. He had good reason to avoid the state, just as he had good reason to avoid Nevada, Washington state, and California; later Illinois, Ohio, and Wisconsin; and still later, Massachusetts, Connecticut, New York, and Vermont. He had hunted there often, and while he took great pains to avoid a pattern, it was best to leave

an area before suspicion was aroused (as he had left
Monterey, then Chicago, then Boston) or he made
a mistake.

Of course, he never made mistakes. *Had* not, until he let his excitement get the better of him and
allowed himself to speed on 123. Yet Feinman's rational mind knew that a single speeding ticket on
the night of April 24, 1989, was not enough to tie
him to Celia's murder.

He came to Florida. He had not hunted in the
southeastern states—at least, not Florida, Georgia,
Alabama, South Carolina—so Florida seemed a
logical choice. He had sat in the living room of his
split-level home in a Virginia suburb of D.C. and
stared at a color map of the U.S. in the heavy atlas
open in his lap. Florida seemed to leap out at him.
On its west coast a crooked finger of land dipped
into the Gulf of Mexico. And at its base, Tampa.
. . . He knew nothing of Tampa, but he trusted
his instinct, which never failed him. The name had
a vaguely familiar ring. Tampa it was, then.

It took almost a month to make the necessary
arrangements. He promised himself that when he
got to Florida, he would not hunt. At least, not for
a good long while. If he hunted here, he would
have to be more careful than usual. After Celia
he'd been too frightened to think of it . . . but
months had passed, and now the need was starting
to build in him again.

Careful. He was getting old, old enough to think
about retiring. Old enough so that he did not want

to have to move again, even though he despised the
weather here. Florida in August was as bad as D.C.
in August. Except that D.C.'s August lasted one
month, and Florida's a minimum of six. It reminded him of Louisiana. Oppressive, sultry, ugly
weather.

He hadn't thought of Louisiana in years. Or of
Marie and her beautiful daughters.

Marie's death had been a revelation to him. Sex
with women had never satisfied him; and even
with the children who inflamed him so, the anticipation was always far better than the consumma-
tion. The act itself left a vague ache, a need unful-
filled.

And then, when Marie died

(when he killed her)

(Marie, wasn't it? She had been his first victim,
hadn't she? Marie, yes. Marie)

he experienced revelation, knew what had been
missing all along. Society's dictates meant nothing
to him. He had learned long ago that everyone and
everything lied: people, words, appearances.

Even children.

Celia had been his last victim. In a way he had
come close to feeling remorse over her death. She
had been pathetic, a clinging, quivering little
thing. Her sense of guilt had been so great, her
trust in adults so total, that to the very end she
submitted unquestioningly to the punishment and
death he had chosen for her. She did not cry out,
did not accuse or complain, as the others did. She

had only wept, as if she judged herself deserving of this fate and had always glimpsed its coming.

Feinman had felt a tug of compassion. Not for her suffering, but because she reminded him so much of himself at her age. So trusting, so eager to obey, so ready to believe in her own wickedness, to accept that *she* was to blame.

Afterward, filled with sadness at the sight of her, he had wept as well. Or at least his eyes had teared slightly, and he had dabbed at them once, with a clean silk handkerchief. For himself, for the child he had been—not for Celia.

His memory of the entire event was spotty, clouded as if seen through a mist, but he had no doubt that another part of himself, the part he thought of as Bruner, the actual perpetrator, re-membered. Even so, Feinman remembered the child herself clearly: the triangular pale, sickly face, the great, sorrowful dark eyes.

He drifted into the outskirts of a dream. Some-where in the unseen darkness before him—beyond the bed, beyond the open doorway, in the hallway that led to the kitchen—a Presence hovered. As if someone were standing there. A small and melan-choly Presence.

Celia.

The thought alarmed him, enough for Feinman to pull himself back to full consciousness, enough for him to open his eyes. In the darkness he could see nothing, but still he sensed the waiting pres-ence just outside the open bedroom door.

Ridiculous, his rational mind countered. You are tired, under stress. You must reduce your patient load. This is the cause for your panic, the cause for the disturbing dream. Nothing more.

And to reassure himself he reached out and switched on the nightstand lamp.

Celia stood in the shadowed hallway.

He could see her distinctly in the lamplight. There were bruises circling her thin child's neck— yellow, greenish-purple bruises, as if she had some- how survived these past few months, as if the bruises were only a few days old. Her dark hair fell, thin and straight, to her shoulders, her neatly trimmed bangs framed a white forehead. She was naked except for a small stuffed animal clutched in her right arm and nestled against her right cheek. A white Gund bear, face upturned, smiled at Fein- man with undeniable charm. Celia's left thumb was in her mouth, hand a fist, knuckle resting un- der her nose. Her eyes, dark and wide open, stared directly at him.

Feinman gasped and shut his eyes.

In the split second of terror and disbelief before he opened them again, an image flashed before his closed eyelids: Celia, in extremis; the way her head had lolled helplessly in his large hands.

The image melted, changed into an until-now forgotten memory from his childhood. Darla's small black puppy. Its head had rolled limply in his hands, the same way, as it had died.

Feinman opened his eyes again, cautiously.

The apparition remained. It was Celia, and it was real.

A voice in his head then: throaty, faintly accented, feminine.

Someone needs to be punished, doesn't he?

"I haven't done anything wrong," Feinman whimpered. "Please, leave me alone." His own voice sounded small and thin, wavering . . . much the same way Celia's had sounded as she submitted, weeping, to death.

She had been clutching the sunnily smiling bear then too. *Please, it hurts. It hurts. . . .*

Just as Feinman, his bare skin slick with sweat, had pressed her against him. His fingers around her neck, a memory at once sensual and terrifying.

Someone must be punished, Celia.

For your own good.

Each time, the moment of satisfaction, of utter, deep, and urgent release, came then, at the moment the child recognized the approach of death, knew that his vengeance could never be escaped. And at the moment of death:

Triumph. Victory. Transcendence. An explosion of light in his brain.

Feinman perspired now in his bed. Alternating waves of self-pity and fear washed over him. Certainly he was not to blame. Certainly he had done nothing to deserve *this*. Unlike others he did not yield to weakness, did not try to run from his destiny, despite the risks, the potential terrible consequences to himself. No, he *cooperated* with fate.

Celia watched him calmly, soundlessly. It seemed to Feinman that she required something of him

Someone must be punished

but he could not understand what, or why.

Not me. She can't mean me. Certainly not me.

After several minutes of tearless sobbing he relaxed into a state of weary but cautious alertness.

Celia remained with him an hour. From time to time Feinman allowed himself a sidewise glance at the digital clock, saw the numbers change. 4:01, 4:07, 4:10. He was exhausted, but he did not doze.

At four fifty-two she seemed to recede into the kitchen, to sink backward into darkness as soundlessly as she had appeared. First silver body into shadow, then face, then eyes, which seemed to glow from some interior illumination. . . . And then the two small lights winked out, and she was gone.

Feinman did not dare follow. He remained huddled in his bed with the lamp on until morning.

5

That night Avra dreamed as well. She was now twenty-nine, but each time the dream transformed her into a five-year-old. It was one she'd had since childhood, one she worked hard to forget.

In the dream she wandered alone and frightened in the streets of an empty city. A ghost town, right out of an old Western, nothing but a strip of decaying ramshackle storefronts. Around her ankles wind-borne sand swirled.

Night. Avra ran down the silent street crying for fear of the dark, crying because she was lost. At last, desperate, she sought refuge in one of the storefronts, thinking that there might be help there, that adults might be asleep inside. She stepped onto a crumbling wood porch with a rusted-out tin roof and headed for the doorway that led into darkness.

But something blocked her way; something malignant and unspeakably cold. Avra felt rather than saw it. The darkness itself stirred. It coalesced into a figure, draped in a black cloak: the figure of a tall man. Yet not human at all, but the presence of Evil personified: the Shadow. It had no face, but Its eyes glowed like the dimming embers of a fire.

She tried to run and found she could not move. The Shadow held her immobile in Its invisible grasp; approached silently, relentlessly. It drew open Its cloak to consume her, to draw her into Its heart, into cold starry blackness, annihilation, death.

Avra woke at the moment It engulfed her.

The instant of terror clutched her, released her, subsided. Within seconds the image of the Shadow faded, consigned to oblivion. Over the years Avra had become adept at forgetting.

Her eyelids fluttered. She sighed, vaguely aware of the sky lightening outside the wide-open jalousie windows, of the droning ceiling fan and the uncomfortable heat. The sheet beneath her was damp with humidity and sweat.

She rolled toward the wall and went back to sleep.

It was hot the day that Avra saw Bruner. Abysmally hot, and the air-conditioner in the white frame house on Willow Street had labored to a groaning halt two days before. Gran had passed away ten years ago and left the place to the girls, who'd installed central heat and air with what was

left of her savings. Willow Street had been a work-
ing-class neighborhood, modest and unassuming,
Old Florida before the advent of Disney ("the
Rat," say natives). The narrow street was lined
with live oaks; front yards were full of sand and
shade and a few struggling patches of grass. But it
lay only a few blocks west of the bay, and a few
blocks east of the shopping district of Hyde Park.
The young upwardly mobile professionals had
moved in, and Gran's cracker house was worth almost fifteen times what she and her second husband, Den, had paid for it in 1947.

The summer of '66, the year the girls moved in
with Gran, had been a hot one, too. Avra had no
memory of the brief time spent recuperating in the
hospital; no memory, in fact, of the period from
Christmas '65 through mid–'66. It was as if spring
had never come that year. Her first memories were
of summer and heat. Late summer, probably August; an August no doubt very much like this one.

Even her memories of that summer were spotty:
she and Maggie sitting on the screened-in back
porch with the fan going full blast, rocking in old-
fashioned metal lawn chairs and drinking sweet
iced tea. Daytime reruns of *I Love Lucy* and *You Bet
Your Life* with Groucho Marx. She and Maggie
would sit on the floor glued to the TV set, an ancient Motorola you could turn on and off by the
push of a round white button. Sometimes Avra
wore pajamas all day long. She was sick a lot that
summer—or maybe not quite sick, but she and

Gran and everyone else had known that there was something *wrong* with her.

Things were wrong and would never be the same. Even the twins' names had changed. With Mama no longer there to chastise them for using nicknames, Magdalen had taken to calling her sister Ave. And it was Maggie now, not Magdalen; Gran insisted Maggie was a more appropriate name for a young girl.

Gran had just turned sixty that summer. She had never been a talkative woman; after her daughter died, she was even less so. She was a tall woman, spare, with prominent hip bones, large teeth and hands. Quiet, and proper. Except for her large gray eyes she bore little resemblance to her daughter. Marie had taken after her father: dark haired, laughing, given to behavior Gran judged scandalous. Marie had been an artist, self-taught. She never made any money at it, though her paintings once took second place at a statewide art show.

She'd had to give it up when the girls came, of course. And when their father died, she'd gone to work and was always too exhausted to paint. But some of the oils still hung on the walls of Gran's house. One of them—a self-portrait of Marie, smiling, dimpled, wrapped in nothing but a fringed paisley silk shawl that Gran said made her look like a gypsy—hung on Avra's bedroom wall. As time passed, Avra was amazed at how Maggie had come to look more and more like Mama.

There was a portrait she'd done of her shy young husband, too, but Gran had hidden it in the attic. She had hated the girls' father, who had deserted them shortly before dying in an automobile accident. So much so that she'd had their names legally changed to Kallisti, their mother's maiden name, the name of Gran's first husband. When Mama was alive—

Avra tried very hard to forget those times, because when she remembered back when Mama was alive, she also had to remember that Mama was dead

—when Mama was alive, she used to shake her head and laugh, saying that Magdalen took her quiet ways from Gran. Of course, Mag was never as concerned as Gran was about appearances and proper etiquette. There was nothing soft about Gran, except perhaps her silver hair, and that she kept wound tightly into a round bun.

It wasn't that she didn't love the girls. She did, and Ave sensed that Gran wanted to help but didn't know how. Gran simply wasn't demonstrative. Oh, she hugged when the occasion called for it, but Avra could tell she was deeply embarrassed by it. Just as she was too deeply disturbed, ashamed, shocked, by Avra's "trouble" ever to say a word about it.

After all, Gran had taken the girls in out of a sense of duty; the same reason, Avra figured when she was depressed, that Maggie took care of her. Gran died Christmas 1979, when the girls were

nineteen, and it occurred to Avra that Gran
planned it that way—lasting long enough to be
sure the girls were old enough to look after themselves.

Avra scrupulously tried to forget the incident
with Mama and Dr. Bruner and almost succeeded
until she was seventeen, when the memory resur-
faced full force. It left her incapacitated. While
Mag was attending her high-school graduation cer-
emony, Avra was in the hospital. This time she
remembered her stay and felt shame.

That had been another hot summer.

In retrospect Avra might have decided that there
had been hints, that August afternoon in 1990, of
the evil to come. More than just the heat—though
certainly it was hotter, more humid and oppressive, than she could remember—and she had spent
many summers here as a child without the benefit
of air conditioning. It got bad in Florida in August, but this August was somehow worse, and this
particular day was the worst of all.

It was a Friday. The repairman couldn't make it
until Tuesday, if then. The heat had kept Ave up
most of Thursday night—heat, and a forgotten bad
dream.

And something else had disturbed her sleep—a
feeling of . . . foreboding? Most likely due to the
week she'd spent alone in the creaky old house.
And maybe the fact that she'd known something
was going to happen with Maggie and Murray
fairly soon. She knew what Maggie was thinking,

most times before Mag knew it herself. She'd seen the wheels working behind Maggie's perennially calm expression, had sensed the guilt there.

It was very simple. Maggie loved Murray. Murray loved Maggie. They'd spent their semester break together and had recently returned from a two-week trip to North Carolina, where Murray's brother owned a cabin in the mountains.

The signs were clear. It was a matter of time before he moved in . . . or Mag moved out. Either way Avra lost. She'd been anticipating this for months; Maggie was just now thoughtfully considering it. There was no question about the money—if Ave left, Maggie would do the right thing and buy out Avra's half of the property, and if Maggie left, she'd probably *give* Ave the whole house without a second thought.

Money wasn't the problem. If Murray moved in, Avra would not stay. (Not, she told herself jokingly, that she was averse to a ménage à trois—though in Murray's case the thought was revolting.) And if Maggie moved out . . .

Jesus. Almost thirty years old, and terrified of living alone. Of living without her sister. It was sick; and though Avra was ashamed of her fear, knew it was irrational, childish, unwarranted, she couldn't break free from its control. The worst part was that she'd never said anything to Mag about it; but of course, Maggie knew, just as Avra sensed Maggie's guilt.

So there was the heat, the dream, and the anxiety that she'd blamed on Maggie and Murray, on old M & M. The anxiety wasn't bad during the morning, which she'd spent in the air-conditioned university library, researching an article on organic farming. Avra felt a pressing need to enlighten the public—not that the public *wanted* enlightenment all that much. She couldn't understand how people remained indifferent to critical issues: pollution, nuclear war, animal rights. . . . The money she made from the bookstore and occasional free-lance articles wasn't much, but she contributed to all the foundations she could afford, and even some she couldn't: Greenpeace, EarthSave, the Union of Concerned Scientists, People for the Ethical Treatment of Animals. . . .

In the library she napped and did research until three o'clock, then went home to get ready for work. The anxiety worsened. Maybe it was because M & M were there, and she kept waiting for the two of them to drop the bombshell.

She was sweating by the time she stepped from the shower. She dressed cool: blue cotton gauze sundress, as lightweight as possible without being indecent. The cotton gauze was limp against her skin. She twisted her damp hair into a tight knot, held in place with a lacquered chopstick.

In the kitchen she got a spoon and a container of cherry yogurt, then went out back to say hello to M & M before she left. No point in postponing the inevitable.

The screen door banged shut behind her. "Any cooler out here?"

It was. Two ancient live oaks covered the back-yard in shade, and a breeze was coming off the bay.

"If you stay far enough away from the grill." Maggie's voice, glum and soft, filtered through wisps of white smoke. "The a.c. really had a great sense of timing, didn't it? If I'd known, I'd have stayed in Carolina." It had broken the day after her return.

In front of her, Murray, his face red and shining with perspiration, bent over a black Weber grill. He wore a tie-dyed dashiki, jeans, and size thirteen leather sandals, and paused while flipping a steak to look up. Maggie, who otherwise avoided meat, was no doubt going to tear into a New York strip just because Murray had brought it. Even though Ave made her read a book on the cruel, curtailed lives the animals led before slaughter. And the methods by which they were killed—Mag knew, yet she would eat a steak to appease Murray. (*Or has she been appeasing* me *all along?* Avra wondered.)

"Hi, Ave." Murray grinned, displaying large, uneven teeth beneath a fringe of brown-and-gray moustache. He was clearly oblivious to the ethical implications of his actions.

"Hullo, Rasputin. Roasting dead animals again?" Murray was big, bearlike, with an un-kempt beard and longish hair; he really did look like Rasputin. Unlike Rasputin, however, he was determinedly cheerful, even in the heat. He and

Maggie taught English to foreign students at the University of South Florida. An old hippie, an ex–Peace Corps volunteer who'd taught English in Africa, then brought home a fungus that occasionally flared and made his toenails fall off. He had a Ph.D. in comparative linguistics and was a slob. You could tell what Murray'd eaten for lunch by checking his beard. He was the total opposite of the man Avra had expected Maggie to fall in love with. In fact, he looked like the type of loser Avra might bring home *(might* have brought home, back when she was drinking)—except that he had a steady job and was kind and funny and nice.

Avra found it difficult not to like him; she found it even harder not to tease him. But the steaks offended her. Maggie knew it and apparently didn't care. Murray liked steaks, and that was that, regardless of Avra's vegetarian sensitivities.

"Nyet." Murray affected a very plausible Russian accent as he squinted at her from behind his round glasses, partially steamed from the humidity. "Cooking Leningrad peasants. Little bit stringy, but delicious."

Avra managed to avoid the clouds of smoke and took the lawn chair next to her sister, in the shade beneath one of the oaks. Maggie's expression was placid, as always, but the heat had given it a grim edge. Friends said the twins' faces were absolutely identical (though Maggie and Avra knew better) and that the only means of distinguishing them was the hair. Maggie's came to where her neck met her collarbone; Avra's fell at least two inches below her shoulder blades.

Maggie held a sweating long-neck bottle of Dos Equis beer and had already changed from her teaching clothes into shorts and a holey T-shirt. The semester didn't begin for another week, but she and Murray had been obliged to attend a four-hour staff meeting at the university that afternoon. She glanced at Avra with a faint look of concern.

"Trouble sleeping last night?"

Avra nodded as she stirred her yogurt. If anyone other than Mag had asked, she'd have said *Why? Do I look like hell?* But Mag had a way of knowing things . . . such as Avra's sleepless night because of the heat (even though Avra had lain quietly in bed and never stirred). Maggie probably even knew about the bad dream.

And the growing feeling that something bad was about to happen. . . .

Jason, Murray's ten-year-old basset hound, rose groaning from the sand, where he'd been dozing. Infinitely wrinkled, he waddled over to Avra and leaned his graying muzzle against her legs and gave her a look that was intensely spiritual. A dark spot of drool formed on the hem of the blue gauze dress. Avra reached down to give the dog's ear an affectionate scratch.

"Jason, you stink." She offered a spoonful of cherry yogurt to the dog, who moved with uncharacteristic speed to lick it clean. Casually, Avra took another mouthful of yogurt, aware and pleased that both Murray and Maggie noticed. Maggie, of course, made a point of not reacting. "Rasputin," Avra asked, "don't you ever wash your dog?"

He stepped back from the smoking grill and ran a forearm over his high, shining forehead. "Not me. I thought they cleaned themselves. He's always licking himself."

"That's cats."

"No kidding."

Maggie interrupted. "Late night tonight?" She was referring to the dinner date Avra had after work that evening. Ave raised her eyebrows and shoulders a millimeter to indicate: *Don't know. Depends on whether he's a washout, I guess.*

Murray had found his beer and was facing them now, apparently satisfied that the steaks could do without him. "Quit talking shorthand, you two."

Maggie smiled up at him. "Avra's got a date."

A look passed between them, one that Avra interpreted as saying:

A date? Thank God! Now, if this one would just work out . . . if we could just get her to stay with this one for more than three weeks . . .

No more guilt, that's what. Old M & M would be free. . . .

"No kidding." Murray set his beer down on the plastic-coated wire table beside the grill. His eyebrows rose above gold wire-rims. "Let me guess. He works for the Humane Society. First drinks, and then maybe neuter a few dogs just for fun." As he spoke, he bent down and cupped his hands over Jason's ears. The basset compliantly slid down and rolled over onto his back.

Avra finished another mouthful of yogurt. She could have made a smart-ass comeback, but instead she smiled wryly and said, "Actually, I think he's an art instructor. I waited on him at the bookstore, and he seemed nice. We're having dinner at Selena's."

Murray feigned shock. "But, Avra . . . for all you know, he could be a—a *dead animal eater*!"

"For all I know, Raz, he could be an ax murderer. It's a chance I'll just have to take. There *will* be other people around, after all."

"Take my car," Maggie said emphatically, as if no argument would be tolerated. The air-conditioning compressor in Avra's old Corolla had blown last week, and she couldn't afford to get it fixed. She rarely drove it, except in emergencies. Since the bookstore was barely a half mile away, she walked on the days it didn't rain. Thunderstorms were a daily occurrence in August, but the past week had brought no rain.

"I'm walking, Mag." Avra paused. "Where's Murray's van, anyway?"

Murray's tone lost some of its cheerfulness. "In the shop, where else? Cracked cylinder. Mag brought me straight from school."

"Well, then, I'm definitely walking. You two were headed out tonight—Maggie told me this morning. You're going to see a movie down on

Hillsborough Avenue. Quit being such a martyr, Mag."

"Then we'll take you." Inspiration shone in Maggie's eyes. M & M could drive Avra—a trapped victim—in the car, announce their engagement or live-in arrangement, then drop Avra off within sixty seconds at Doubleday. Boom. Finished, done, with a minimum of discomfort. Maggie hated scenes. "I don't want you walking the streets at midnight, or God knows when—"

" 'Walking the streets'?"

"Dammit, you know what I mean."

"Look, Mag, it's all of a ten-minute walk, a two-minute ride. I'll get a ride home later with—with old whatsisname. Chuck, I think it is. He seemed decent enough." Avra had thought she was ready to face this . . . but found herself chickening out. Suddenly, she wanted to be very far away from both of them.

Think of it this way: You're not losing a sister—you're gaining a slob.

Maggie persisted. "What if you don't like him? What if it doesn't work out?"

Avra paused and thought. She could have pointed out that old Chuck would have to be a *very* fast operator indeed to cause trouble during a two-minute drive home . . . but continuing the discussion was pointless. There was no arguing with Maggie; she would simply hold tenaciously to her position until Avra surrendered. "Then I'll call you and Rasputin, regardless of the ungodly hour, and make you come and get me."

Mag settled back in her chair, apparently mollified. "Fair enough, then. Call us. I won't go to bed until you do."

A barely visible flicker of emotion crossed Murray's face, but Avra caught it before he turned his attention back to the grill. There it was: disapproval. He thought Maggie was coddling Avra.

He didn't know, of course. Ave wondered if Maggie had told him the lie that Avra herself used when people inquired after her parents.

Car accident. It happened when we were very young.

And it neatly explained the diagonal scar across her forearm too.

It didn't matter whether Murray understood or not. Whether he knew about the dreams, the periodic depression, the trouble (for years) with liquor and pills, the difficulty sleeping. Especially alone, in the dark. For years she'd depended on night-lights, when she was too old, too ashamed to share a room with Maggie anymore.

It was none of Murray's damn business anyway.

And she was fine now. Nearly thirty years old, and fine. She'd beaten it all: the booze, the depression, the fear. She had done just fine those two weeks alone, and she didn't need her sister around to take care of her.

Avra stood up, suddenly furious at them both. She left the yogurt on the ground for Jason to finish. "I've got to go."

It was irrational, this anger—as irrational as the fear it masked—but knowing that didn't lessen either. The memory of last night's dread swept over her. As Avra stalked through the yard into the house (and let the screen door slam behind her with a vengeance), she had but one thought, directed at herself:

Coward.

Maggie sighed and took another swallow of cool (no longer cold) beer as the door slammed. In an effort to stave off the heat she ran the bottle over her forehead and let the moisture evaporate. Avra, of course, had anticipated exactly what was going to happen—though what precisely had set her off this time was beyond Maggie's powers of deduction.

At the same time Maggie didn't blame her. She felt only sorrow in response to Avra's childish anger. And maybe more than a little guilt at leaving Ave stranded for those two weeks. It had been the first time in years. If she felt any irritation at her at all, it was because of Avra's stubbornness. As frightened as Avra was of living alone, Maggie knew Ave would refuse to live in the same house as Murray. Not because she disliked him. The teasing, the insults, were an act. But because she didn't want to stand in Maggie's way, to be a burden, and all that crap. And there was nothing Maggie could say or do to change Avra's mind.

Of course, it'd taken a month to convince Murray that it was time to tell Ave (and even then he was grudging about the idea).

Murray stood staring through the smoke at the back of the house. "What's gotten into her? Is she upset?" He spoke softly so that Ave, in the house, would not hear. His tone was one of wonder rather than hurt; Maggie had never seen him truly angry and tried to imagine Murray in a rage. Impossible. "Did we say something wrong?"

"No. It's just . . . she sees what's coming, that's all. With us, I mean. And . . . there's something else bothering her. Can't put my finger on it. I don't think she even knows what it is."

"Jesus. Can't one of you take a shit without the other one knowing about it?" With a long-handled fork he set the two steaks on a platter, then turned toward Maggie. "She's jealous, isn't she? Don't take this the wrong way—I'm not upset, and I don't take it personally, but—it's pretty clear that she hates me."

He was right, of course, but she clicked her tongue and grimaced at him as if he'd said something ridiculous. "Knock it off. She doesn't hate you."

"Then you're going to have to explain this jealousy thing to me, because I don't get it. Of course, I've never dated a twin before. Is this what's supposed to happen? Is this normal? Do you get jealous of Avra's men friends?"

"No." Pause. "Actually, I don't know. She's

never dated anyone long enough—or seriously enough—for me to find out."

"I don't think you would." He sat down in the chair Avra had abandoned and set the steaks on the white plastic parsons table between them, just out of reach of Jason's curious muzzle. "Frankly, I'd think you'd be relieved if she started seeing someone. Why do you think you have to act as her caretaker? I mean, it's not like you're her *older* sister. But you act as though she's helpless without you. For crying out loud, she's twenty-nine years old, practically thirty. And so are you."

She was silent for a time, staring down at the steaks, which glistened with liquescent fat and blood. This was not the first time Avra'd been jealous.

Maggie had dated other men, of course, even brought some of them home to meet Avra (a ritual, she knew, similar to others' "bringing them home to meet Mother"). And Avra had despised them all. As she was introduced to them, shook their hands, she would get this look—the same look she used to get when she was in her teens, when Gran would lecture her on some finer detail of grooming or demeanor. The lower half of Ave's face would smile, a small, polite and frozen half-smile; the upper half of her face would not. Her large gray eyes would narrow infinitesimally, as if they viewed something distasteful, or absurd, or stupid. A mocking expression, yet so subtle it was often

missed. Gran had never detected it; Maggie always
did.

Yet when Avra met Murray for the first time, it
was different. There had been the frozen, polite
smile as she took his hand, but her eyes had widened slightly instead of narrowing, and the look
there had been . . . puzzled. Perplexed. And she
had glanced over at Maggie.

As if to say, *What the hell are you doing bringing
home someone I approve of?*

Maggie had never dated anyone like Murray.
She had never loved anyone the way she loved
Murray.

And she had hoped that now—now that Avra
was doing so well . . .

She did not know how to answer him, so she did
not try. "The meat's getting cold."

"You're avoiding the question, Maggie. Not that
you have to answer it; it's personal, and you're free
to tell me to go to hell if you want to. But I'd like
to try to understand. I have this funny notion
about loving you and wanting to help. And it
seems to me you're being taken advantage of. I
don't like to see anyone do that to you. I think
Avra needs to start acting her age."

She jerked her head up to scowl at him; her tone
was quick, tight, angry. "I'm *not* being taken advantage of! It's something you wouldn't understand—"

His reply was soft. "Try me."

"It's not something I can talk about, Murray.

Not something Ave would appreciate my talking about. . . ."

Her face and voice must have told him more than she'd intended. He cocked his head curiously; his expression became sympathetic. He leaned forward to rest a hand on her arm. It touched her to be on the receiving end of comfort for a change.

"So there is something."

"Nothing you can do anything about." She hesitated until she was sure her voice would not shake. "Don't ever say that about Avra again. About her taking advantage of me. It's not that way at all."

"Okay, I won't. But I'm still trying to understand you two. Sometimes I get this weird feeling that there's something you're not telling me. Like you're protecting her." He moved even closer and studied her face closely for a reaction.

She'd always prided herself on her strength. Avra was the one most deeply affected by Mama's death, by

(that other dark, unspeakable, unthinkable thing done to her)

but Maggie had remained (she thought) unshaken by the past; she had needed to, for Ave's sake. But she'd expected that someday she would finally tell Murray the truth. Maybe after they were married a few years. She didn't like keeping secrets, not even this one, from him. She wasn't by nature devious. And she had known that, when she did tell him, she would be able to discuss it with him calmly, unemotionally. After all, it had happened so long ago

(twenty-five years this December, but who's counting?)

that thinking about it, discussing it, really didn't bother her anymore.

Murray was still talking. "Does it have something to do with your parents' death?"

Heaviness settled onto her chest, followed by a mild wave of nausea. It became difficult to take a deep breath. She pressed the cool bottle against her forehead again to stop the dizziness. The heat, that was all. "I . . . can't talk about it just yet, Murray. Please. Not now."

To her relief he didn't press; he stared at her for a while, almost seemed to understand. He patted her arm. "All right. Sorry, Magpie. Didn't mean to upset you." He drew back and lifted the platter of steaks from the parsons table. "Ready to eat?"

"The plates and everything are inside."

They walked together up the concrete steps to the wooden porch, with Jason snuffling after them.

6

Feinman rose at dawn, feeling groggy and hung over from lack of sleep. Not, for once, from cognac—though he had desperately craved a drink throughout last night's harrowing ordeal. But the bottle of Courvoisier was located in the living-room bar, and that required him to cross through the hallway, past the kitchen . . . past Celia.

The last few hours he'd spent dozing restlessly in a twilight anxiety. There could be no doubt: he had been visited by a phantasm, a ghost. Not some hazy, half-remembered image, but a perfectly formed, three-dimensional eidolon. And her appearance had some great and dreadful significance that Feinman, in his semidelirium, had been unable to fathom.

Now, morning, the fear had lifted. His certainty vanished; he very nearly managed to convince himself that he had not in fact experienced a waking vision, but a type of unnaturally vivid dream.

Still, he returned to consciousness with the image of Celia foremost in his thoughts. For several minutes after waking he was afraid to open his eyes, afraid to find the small, solemn phantom awaiting him.

Tentatively, Feinman blinked, then allowed himself to stare. In the gray light the hallway was barely distinct—but clearly empty. Celia was gone. He drew in a long, wavering breath.

He snapped off the alarm fifteen minutes before it was set to go off, then rose stiffly. His muscles and joints ached from tension and lack of rest. He was becoming an old man, too old for the likes of this. As usual he wore only boxer shorts; in Florida pajamas were too hot. But this morning he felt oddly chilled, and wrapped himself in the thin cotton paisley bathrobe that hung on the door. He had a brief spell of anxiety as he neared the doorway to reach for the robe, but he was stern with himself, and it passed.

Feinman padded into the bathroom, urinated, and turned the shower on full blast. Normally, he would have headed straight for the coffee—but the automatic coffee maker was preset so that it would just finish brewing by the time the alarm buzzed.

Besides, to get to the kitchen Feinman had to pass through the hallway—and he was not ready yet. Not yet. A shower first.

Feinman was obsessive about cleanliness. He

often showered twice, sometimes three times, a day. In his profession (not to mention his avocation), cleanliness was critical. And after last night he was sticky with perspiration. He stood before the mirror in the opulent, unnecessarily large bathroom with its long expanse of counter and two washbasins. He was sixty years old. His flesh was pasty, not as firm as once it had been, but it was still lean. His face was that of a man in his late forties. Like his mother he had aged well, but genetics were only a part of it. Secretly, he credited his youthful appearance to the amount of time he spent with children.

And appearance was of utmost importance, if he wished to continue to attract them.

He waited until the shower stall was full of steam before he undressed and got in.

In the shower he managed to direct his thoughts to the day ahead. A full load of patients today; he would be in the office until seven, seven-thirty that evening. Afterward, dinner with Helen, an attorney in his professional building, an intelligent and attractive enough woman . . . and her daughter Amelie. Today was Amelie's sixth birthday. Feinman brightened at the thought, and at the memory of the present he had bought for her: a Madame Alexander doll, Scarlett O'Hara, green eyed, like Amelie, with long dark ringlets, dressed in flounces of green-and-white-plaid organza over dark green satin.

And under the billowing skirt, white lace bloomers. . . .

A very expensive doll, a fact calculated to ingratiate himself with the mother and delight the daughter. Oh, he had no immediate designs on either . . . but he was getting old, after all, and considering settling down. He had promised himself he would not hunt—at least, not for some time. A small family now might be pleasant and not too much in the way. He enjoyed Helen's company and was already developing quite a crush on Amelie. And she, in turn, doted on him. Who knew? Perhaps, if Amelie were amenable, she could be taught. . . .

Of course, harming her was out of the question. As a very wise man once said: *Never kill anyone you know.*

Feinman had learned once, the hard way; he now held faithfully to that axiom.

He stepped dripping from the shower. The air-conditioner had cut on, and as the cool air evaporated the water on his skin, Feinman shivered. He toweled off quickly, pulled on the robe and knotted the belt at the waist, then picked up the boxer shorts and dropped them in the hamper on his way through the bedroom, pausing to slip into a pair of finely made leather slippers.

He strode through the hallway to the kitchen firmly, without hesitation. Yet despite his intent not to yield to the previous night's anxiety, he found he was trembling with cold. Chilled to the bone.

Fatigue, no doubt. From loss of sleep.

He made his way to the coffee maker and saw that he had timed it just right. The glass carafe was full. He fetched a mug from the cabinet, made of pine covered with white Formica. Everything in Florida was shiny, new, white because the sun bleached out all other colors. Buildings here lacked history, a sense of permanence. Feinman preferred solidity: hardwood, brick. But wood tended to warp in the humidity here, and brick retained heat.

He filled his cup. No sweetener, no cream. Feinman took his coffee stronger than most people could stand. He had a taste for espresso without sugar, a fondness for bitter things.

He stood in the kitchen for a while and nursed his coffee. With each sip he became convinced that last night's horrors—the dream about disposing of Celia's body, followed by her appearance—had all been a peculiarly intense nightmare. He'd been working too hard lately; the other, younger pediatrician in his building had been on vacation for the past three weeks, and Feinman had been obliged to accept the overflow of patients. He was unused to such a frenetic schedule. At his age he was accustomed to seeing patients until two or three in the afternoon. It allowed extra time for his avocation; he often spent his afternoon and weekend hours scouting out new hunting terrain.

Nothing more than anxiety and stress . . . coupled with his growing (but still firmly repressed) desire to hunt again.

He drank an entire cup of coffee standing by the sink, then refilled his mug and walked from the kitchen into the vast open area the realtor had called the Great Room. The Great Room had a large stone fireplace on its north wall, sliding glass doors that opened onto a cedar deck along its south. The bay window on the east wall faced the Hillsborough River, a fact which should have been a strong selling point for the property; Riverhills Drive was one of the most prestigious addresses in town. But the view of the river was almost entirely obliterated by the large oaks and cypress in the backyard. The realtor, an inappropriately cheerful blond woman, had been stupid enough to bemoan the fact as detracting from the value of the property, but quickly pointed out that the trees could be easily removed. Apparently the previous owner had been an off-kilter recluse who worried about boaters being able to see into the house.

And about thieves. There were dead bolts requiring keys at every exit and window, and a sliding glass door custom-made of thick triple-pane glass. And on the house's exterior every window was equipped with aluminum hurricane shutters. Being new to the area Feinman was fascinated by them. They were motorized; one press of the control, and the shutters descended, making the house impregnable to wind—or anyone trying to break in.

Or out.

A fortress, the realtor had remarked apologetically.

Feinman had merely smiled. All these things suited him; if anything, they made the property even more desirable. The driveway and the front of the house were shielded by a copse of trees and thus invisible from the road. But Feinman used the fact the realtor gave him, as well as the house's size —he was single, all alone; what did he need with four bedrooms, all this space?—as a negotiating chip.

He moved closer to the bay window and stared out at the backyard as he sipped his coffee. His morning vigil here had become a ritual; he loved watching the birds. There were herons, kingfishers, egrets. And hawks. Especially hawks. This morning, one was hunting. A red-shouldered hawk dived from the highest branches of a big oak and swooped low after a rat. Feinman watched, captivated by the bird's fierce grace. Inches from the ground, talons extended, the hawk seemed on the verge of catching its prey when it became distracted by a quick movement to its right. A second rat scrabbled through the grass.

The hawk's instant of confusion cost him. Both rats fled into the low boxwood hedge surrounding the deck. The hawk reascended with two pulses of its great wings.

Feinman sighed and remained at the window several minutes more, until the bird was successful and captured a young black snake. It flew off with its prize writhing in its beak.

Satisfied, Feinman headed back for the kitchen. Normally, he would have made breakfast—oat-bran cereal, or a poached egg on whole-wheat toast (never more than two eggs a week; he believed in taking care of his health). But this morning exhaustion left him slightly nauseated. After he got to the office, he would send Barbara down to the snack bar for a bagel.

He headed back toward the hallway, the butter-soft leather soles of his slippers sticking slightly to the vinyl flooring. He'd spilled some orange juice the week before and thought he'd gotten it all up. Time to wash the floor. It was to Feinman's advantage not to employ a maid; he did all his housework himself, and he took pride in the fact that his home was always clean.

But the past three weeks there had been no time for that. Besides, the house was large, difficult for one person to keep up. Feinman clicked his tongue in self-reproach. It would be at least another week before he could tend to the floor. No matter; he did not anticipate guests any time soon.

Not so long as he could restrain himself.

Feinman had made it as far as the bedroom door-way when he stumbled over something small, soft, and yielding. His left foot came halfway out of his slipper; he stuck his arms out, waving them in circles in a comical effort to regain his balance, to no avail. He lost his footing and fell on the vinyl hallway floor.

As his right elbow struck the floor, the mug slipped from his fingers, sloshing hot coffee on the floor, the off-white walls, Feinman himself.

He was too startled to swear. He ended up on his back, and a few seconds of confusion passed before he had regained enough self-possession to take inventory and learn he was not seriously hurt. His elbow was bruised, and coffee soaked the front of the paisley robe, leaving his chest and stomach mildly burned. The worst of it was the coffee stains on the wall.

Feinman rose gingerly to a sitting position, then to his feet, intending to return to the kitchen for some paper towels to sop up the mess. He crouched down to retrieve his mug. Unbroken, but the handle had a chip. It would have to be thrown away.

Before he straightened, his eye caught sight of what had caused the fall. It lay no more than a foot from the emptied mug; something small and white. Without thinking Feinman reached out for it, his fingers brushing up against its softness. Abruptly, he jerked his hand away.

The Gund bear lay with its obscenely cheerful little face gazing toward heaven. The same as the one Celia had clutched to herself. But that bear, Feinman knew, had been incinerated months before in the fireplace of his home in McLean, Virginia. This was not, could not be, the same toy.

He gaped at it. And then, very slowly, he reached out a hand and picked the animal up.

It was of recent manufacture, no more than several months old, but its white fur was dingy, smudged in spots. It had a stain on its belly that appeared to be grape juice. It looked exactly the way it would if a not-so-fastidious child had dragged it around for a few weeks. Feinman ran a hand over it, stroked it, felt its soft synthetic fur beneath his fingers.

The bear was no hallucination. It existed, it had weight, it was solid. He had stumbled over it; he held it now in his own hands. Which could only mean one thing: that Celia had been real too.

Someone needs to be punished, doesn't he?

The toy dropped from Feinman's trembling fingers. He raised his hands and covered his face.

The newly renovated area of Hyde Park lies just northeast of Tampa Bay. Its fashionable shops and restaurants line pedestrian-filled Snow and Swann avenues; at its heart rests a small park with a tiered fountain whose floor gleams copper from pennies donated by the wishful. In temperate weather the sidewalks and outdoor cafés are normally crowded, and merchants keep the shop doors propped open. But by late Friday afternoon, as the temperature climbed over one hundred degrees, business slowed; sidewalks and cafés were deserted, the shop doors closed. Inside Doubleday Book Shop it was air conditioned and comfortable, and for the next four hours Avra forgot about the heat.

She remembered it only when she stepped outside the shop door at nine P.M. and crossed the street to Selena's. The air was cloyingly humid; the softened asphalt beneath her shoes radiated heat. In Tampa, summer nights never cooled off.

She felt only a mild apprehension as she approached the pink stucco exterior of the restaurant. She had been on dozens of near-blind dates. She had seen the man in question once before, at the bookshop. She had sold him a hardcover copy of *What They Don't Teach You at Harvard Business School*. It had almost made her dismiss him; and a pity, she thought, because all outward appearances indicated he was her type. Late twenties, longish light brown hair, clean-shaven California type. A young Jackson Browne. The white lettering on his pink-and-turquoise T-shirt said RINGLING SCHOOL OF ART, SARASOTA. He wore baggy white cotton pants with no belt; they hung loosely around his narrow, flat waist. His running shoes were an off brand and he slumped like a teenager. When he laid the book down on the counter next to the cash register, he smiled up at her with eyes that were a light grayish brown, like a weimaraner's.

Lust at first sight.

Which wavered a little as her gaze fell upon the book. Maybe she didn't have the strictest morals in the world when it came to men, but she had *some* standards: no stockbrokers, no lawyers, no MBAs. To Avra's mind Big Business and Prime Evil were synonyms.

His smile became sheepish; he gave a little shrug. "It's for my sister, the overachiever."

Avra brightened. "You've got one of those, too, huh?"

He nodded, tossing his straight brown hair. "She's an investment banker. Drives a BMW." He hesitated, as if too shy to continue, then risked it anyway. "Sometimes I think one or the other of us is adopted."

Avra smiled as she rang the sale up on the register; they exchanged brief glances that made it clear this was a bona-fide flirtation. To keep things rolling she inclined her chin toward his T-shirt. "You a student?"

He glanced down at himself. "What? Oh, you mean at the school. Actually, I teach."

Even better. "So you live in Sarasota?" Not so bad. A ninety-minute commute, at most.

He nodded again, hair falling across his forehead. He swept it to one side (rather charmingly, Ave thought) with his hand. "Came up a little early for the weekend. Jan's birthday—that's my sister." He extended a hand. "My name's Chuck. Chuck DeSantis."

She took it. "Hello, Chuck DeSantis. Avra Kallisti."

His gaze was so pure, so trusting, she was reminded against her will of Jason, the basset.

"Avra," he repeated softly. "What a beautiful name. Does it mean something?"

She did her best not to blush at the compliment. "I'm not sure. I thought my mom just made it up, but someone once told me it was Greek for sea breeze."

"It's very unusual. How about dinner tomorrow night, Sea-breeze?"

"I thought it was your sister's birthday."

"That's Saturday. Friday she can find her own date."

"Tomorrow night, nine o'clock. Selena's, across the street."

"I'll be there, Avra."

Avra entered the restaurant. Just inside the door was a dark-paneled foyer opening onto a narrow hallway. To the left was the bar; to the right, the restaurant. Neither was visible from the foyer, which was jammed with people: three couples, and a man, woman, and child. The ceilings were high, paneled with the same dark wood as the foyer. The carpet was burgundy. The wallpaper in the hall was a Victorian floral print, more burgundy flecked with salmon and cream.

Chuck wasn't there. If he was like other artists she'd known, she didn't expect him to be on time. She patiently waited her turn until the hostess approached, then explained: party of two, but he hadn't arrived yet. She would wait for him. The hostess nodded, then directed her attention to a pair who had arrived seconds behind Avra.

Two couples occupied the carved wooden bench. Avra leaned against the wall, next to the couple with the child, and distracted herself from her slight nervousness by watching the other people. The child caught her attention: the little blond girl must have been about seven. She wore a green party dress and was enormously excited. This was clearly some sort of special occasion. The man who held her hand looked to be in his early fifties. The grandfather, Avra thought at first, then changed her mind. His relationship with the woman was evidently not father-daughter; the amused looks they exchanged each time the girl said something cute held a faintly sexual charge.

The little girl kept plucking at the hem of his jacket and whispering urgently at him. He bent down to offer his ear, then replied pleasantly, "Patience, Amelie. When we get home, darling. When we get home."

He was a handsome man with silver hair and a large bald spot on his crown. His face was well sculpted, with strong cheekbones atop deep, shadowed hollows. His nose was straight, narrow, prominent. He was obviously not a native, for he wore a very expensive navy three-piece suit, raw silk, despite the heat. And even though he seemed to enjoy the child, his air was distinguished.

There was something elusively familiar about him. Avra resolved this by deciding he looked enough like Laurence Olivier to be his surviving brother.

The woman was gazing appreciatively at him. Her forest-green Ultrasuede dress matched both her eyes and the little girl's frock, not to mention her sling-back suede pumps. She was in her forties, obviously professional, obviously the girl's mother (they shared the same coloring) and the man's lover. She was also clearly exhausted and grateful for the man's assistance.

Despite the signs of wealth Avra found her likable; perhaps it was the obvious affection with which she watched the child and the man. Avra smiled at them. The woman smiled back a little wearily (the man and child were too distracted by each other to notice), then spoke with the casual familiarity toward strangers common to those born in sunny climates. There was more than a tinge of pride in her voice.

"It's her birthday."

"Happy Birthday!" Avra told the girl. "How old are you today?"

The little girl burrowed into the man's flank, then peeked around at Avra and gave her a smile broad enough to reveal dimples and a missing canine. "Six."

"No kidding! I'll bet you're going to start first grade next month. Are you excited?"

The girl nodded, pleased.

Avra looked up to find the man studying her curiously, with the intensity of a predatory animal.

She shifted her weight uncomfortably, but the scrutiny lasted only seconds before the man smiled.

Perhaps she had only imagined it.

Yet on a deep level something chill brushed against a dark, forbidden spot in her memory, but she did not allow herself to register it consciously. Not until several minutes later.

The girl tugged at the man's jacket again. Again he bent down to allow her to whisper, her plump child's hand cupped around her mouth, into his ear. This time he laughed.

As he did, the hostess arrived with three menus and led them away. Avra thought no more about them, about the vaguely disturbing man.

She waited in the foyer another ten minutes. She was beginning to think that (a) Chuck had stood her up or (b) he was the type to keep her waiting. In either case, that meant he was (c) a major asshole.

Then it occurred to her: Chuck might have arrived early. He might be waiting in the restaurant, wondering why she was late. When the hostess returned from seating yet another couple, Avra got her attention.

"Did you seat a young gentleman who was waiting for a date? Say fifteen, twenty minutes ago?"

The hostess frowned. "I don't remember anyone like that—of course, I only came on duty at nine. If he got here before then, it's possible . . . Would you like to go in and take a look for him?"

"I think I will, thanks." Avra made her way down the dark hallway and turned left into the large open dining room. One wall consisted of arched beveled glass windows that let in a view of the night; she could see Doubleday and Sharper Image across the street. It was a busy evening. The room was filled to capacity with diners and the sounds of conversation, the clink of glass and silverware. As she squinted in the dim lighting, she got an impression of lazily turning ceiling fans, potted palms, candlelight flickering behind lead crystal. Two wide archways led into another dining room.

Chuck was in neither of them. But seated by the window in the second dining room was the trinity of man, woman, and child. Some instinct made Avra pause and watch them, unobserved, in the archway.

Salads for the adults were already on the table. There was a snifter of brandy for the man; the woman held a wineglass. Although the woman's back was to her, Avra could tell she wasn't eating, just watching the man and child, no doubt with the same fond expression she had worn in the foyer.

The man's food was untouched. He was far too occupied trying to entertain the child. The girl sat on his knee, chewing on a piece of bread.

Something about the tableau distressed Avra

deeply, though at that precise instant she could not have identified what it was.

Until, as she watched, the girl began to bounce up and down. The man was jiggling her on his knee. He began a singsong chant. Avra couldn't hear it clearly across the noisy room, but she knew from the movement of the man's lips and the rhythm of his knee exactly what he sang:

> Ride a little pony into town,
> Ride a little pony, don't fall
> DOWN!

. . . and he straightened his knee, and down Avra went, shrieking and laughing. . . .

Across the dimly illumined room Avra saw the strange light in the man's eye. Recognized it and knew it was not the glow from the candle.

It was as if she had been sucked into the very center of that dark spot in her memory, and the darkness grew until it was a bottomless, whirling vortex of fear that pulled her down, farther down. The sensation was that of drowning; she struggled to breathe, but no air came. For several seconds she stood rigid, and then she began to tremble.

A touch on her forearm made her whirl around with a frightened gasp. A face, a voice, made blurred and indistinct by terror.

"Ma'am? Are you all right?"

Don't cry, darling. Sometimes it hurts, but you want to get better, don't you?

Avra did not answer. *Could* not answer.
She turned and ran.

In the dining room the waiter served Feinman
his main course. The game with Amelie was over;
she sat expectantly, shoulders barely higher than
the table (she refused to use a child seat, insisting
she was too big) awaiting her fried shrimp. Feinman hardly noticed the waiter, was only peripher-
ally cognizant of the flash of white sleeve as the
plate was set before him.

Even that slight distraction was enough. When
he looked up again from his dish of steaming
shrimp creole, the young woman was gone.

Helen had noticed. Not the young woman, of
course—she was seated with her back to her—but
Feinman's reaction. And as usual Helen was discreet enough to wait until all the dinners were
served and the waiter was gone.

"Jake . . . is something wrong?" Then, in a different tone: "Amelie, put down your spoon, dear.
It's all right to eat them with your fingers."

Feinman smoothed his expression, smiled at her
to show that everything was indeed just fine.
Which was far from the truth. In order to function
he had divorced himself, his terror, from his daily
persona. It was a technique he was familiar with,
and he was managing quite well too; he had been
as cheerful with his patients, as attentive and gal-
lant toward Amelie and Helen, as he had ever
been. Yet behind the façade of the day-to-day Fein-

man, the sophisticated, brilliant, affable Doctor Jacob Feinman, he was consumed by fear.

Celia's smiling little bear still lay in the bedroom hallway of Feinman's house. He had been too terrified to pick it up again, even to get near it; it had taken him several minutes to control his hysterical sobbing that morning. For the first time in months he had been late getting to the office.

A type of breakdown from overwork. That was the excuse with which he soothed himself; poor comfort at best. A loss of control in someone with his avocation could prove fatal.

At lunchtime he spoke with a colleague down the hall in his building and obtained several sample packages of Halcion. That way, whether the visions were real or not, he would be able to sleep through them. And it would help the daytime anxiety as well. . . .

Which was most distressing, especially during those first few morning hours. True, he had stayed busy enough. But while Feinman the professional conducted exams, smiled and joked with the kids, comforted the criers and the mothers and wrote prescriptions, the *real* Feinman

(the deepest part of him, the part he almost never dared to think of by its real name: Bruner)

the *real* Feinman was obsessed by thoughts of Celia. She had not harmed him; she had merely wanted to communicate. There was a message there, if only he could interpret it.

Someone must be punished

But who? In his calmer moments Feinman convinced himself that he was certainly *not* that someone. Celia was trying to direct him to another person. . . .

Then why had she left the stuffed bear, if not to torment him?

By seven-fifty P.M. when he got home, he had half convinced himself that the bear would be gone, that it had never existed. Gone, and he would take the Halcion for a few weeks, get more sleep, and all would be right with the world.

The bear lay exactly where he had left it.

If it had been winter, he would have incinerated the damn thing a second time in the fireplace. But this was Florida in summer. Smoke coming from the chimney would attract the attention of neighbors. Instead, he took the bear out into the secluded backyard and buried it. Afterward he took a very long shower.

When he went to pick up Amelie and Helen in the silver Mercedes, he was once again the charming Doctor Jacob Feinman.

Now, sitting across the table from Helen, he smiled reassuringly at her. "Nothing's wrong, darling. Do you remember the woman in the foyer . . . the one who wished Amelie a happy birthday? She was standing over there just now—"

Standing, as Celia had stood in the shadowed hallway.

"—and I got the oddest impression that I know her from somewhere. It seemed she recognized me, too, but couldn't place me. But of course, that's impossible. . . ."

Helen's heart-shaped mouth turned up at the corners, revealing dimples identical to Amelie's; in the candlelight her pale skin was incandescent ivory. Even so, her forty-year-old beauty was a wan reflection of her daughter's. Amelie watched the two adults with wide eyes as she chewed on the shrimp. A fantail protruded from between her lips, then disappeared.

"Amelie, darling, the tails don't taste very good, do they?" Feinman asked.

Amelie was chewing furiously; her expression became one of distaste.

"It's all right to spit it into your napkin, then put it on your plate. That's a good girl. Just like a grown-up."

Helen had picked up her wineglass and paused before lifting it to her lips. "Wouldn't it be funny if she turned out to be an old patient of yours from someplace?"

The entire incident was disturbing, for reasons Feinman could not quite put his finger on. The young woman was a sign of sorts, related in some way to what Celia was trying to tell him.

Such a familiar face. He must try to remember her.

"Yes," he answered uneasily. "Wouldn't it be funny. . . ."

7

The radar.

Maggie opened her eyes to a noiseless thrumming in her brain, a sensation of growing anxiety. She had not felt the radar—the flat, gray fear—for a very long time.

She turned her head, which was nestled in the crook of Murray's bare arm, to glance at the clock on the bookshelf.

Nine twenty-three. Night. Avra had finished work by now, should have been settling down to dinner at Selena's with the mysterious Chuck.

Only something had gone wrong, something far worse than Avra's being stood up or deciding that Chuck was a jerk.

She pushed herself to a sitting position, no easy feat with Murray's heavy limbs resting on hers. The places where their flesh pressed together were damp with perspiration. They were in Maggie's hot little second-story room, lying naked on the bed—Murray nearest the wall, Maggie on the outside edge. Murray had thrown the sheets and bedspread onto the floor (a habit Maggie hated, since they got dirty that way, and the dog always wound up on top of them; and of course, there was Jason lying on them, snoring sonorously). The windows were open wide, not that it helped. Outside, the air was still and heavy with moisture; above them the ancient ceiling fan revolved with an occasional alarming lurch.

She snapped on the bedside lamp.

Murray stirred and put a hand to his eyes. His voice was thick with sleep. "I must have dozed off. Jesus, is it *hot*." He rolled over and put his arms around her. He was stocky, not fat, and thick limbed; he was also the hairiest man Maggie had ever seen. He had a thick growth of hair that began just below the hollow of his collarbone and continued all the way to his pubic hair. He had hair on his shoulder blades, even fine, straight hair on his ass. "But I'd like to thank you for a memorable evening, Ms. Kallisti."

She tensed against him, struggled to get out of the bed. He withdrew his arms and watched her with concern. "What's wrong, sweetheart?"

Sweetheart. When he'd first said it to her, she'd thought he was being sarcastic. So corny and old fashioned, not like Murray (she had thought then, anyway) at all. Something right out of a Humphrey Bogart movie. And she loved it. Yet tonight she was far too upset to be moved by it.

She rose, found her T-shirt and shorts tangled in the sheets beneath Jason. She tugged; the bassett woke and gave her a hurt look, then grudgingly moved aside. "It's Avra. Something—I don't know. I'm going to pick her up."

"What time is it?" he asked, even though he only had to turn his head to glance at the clock. Murray could be impossibly lazy sometimes.

"Almost nine-thirty."

"I thought her date was nine o'clock."

"It was."

"And I thought she was going to call if she wanted a ride. What're you gonna do, go in and pull her out of the restaurant?"

There was no time to explain things now. "Something's gone wrong. Ave's in trouble," Maggie said simply. "I'm going to pick her up."

"You're kidding, right?" He half smiled, his mouth open with disbelief.

"No."

"Come on, Maggie, this is getting *weird*. . . ." When she did not react, he paused, stymied, then tried another tack. His tone grew serious. "This protectiveness thing has gone too far. I don't think even Avra is going to appreciate this."

"I'm going, Murray. Whether you approve or not."

"Can't you see how you're encouraging her dependence on you, doing crazy stuff like this?"

"I thought you promised not to bring that up anymore."

"*Mag*gie . . ."

She pulled on her T-shirt, then stopped her dressing to stare gravely at him with such utter, stubborn conviction that he fell silent.

She stepped into her rumpled shorts, pulled them up and tucked in the shirt, then started looking for her flip-flops. Murray watched for a while, then got up with a sigh.

"Wait a minute, I'm coming with you."

He had to hurry because she was already half-way down the stairs.

Enclosed in the stall in the ladies' room, Avra leaned suddenly over the toilet and was sick. It didn't last long; she'd had nothing to eat since the cherry yogurt, nothing to drink but water. The nausea passed as quickly as it had come. She sat on the floor and leaned back against the cool tile.

Until this moment she had consciously forgotten what had brought on her sudden nervous collapse in her last year of high school, what had caused the memory of Mama and

(him)

to come surging back. It was the recitation by a fellow student in her twelfth grade advanced English class of T. S. Eliot's "The Hollow Men." Avra was no student of poetry; she rarely understood it, but it had seemed to her that day that the poem spoke directly to her.

Those who have crossed
With direct eyes, to death's other Kingdom

Mama, Avra had thought. *He's talking about
Mama.*

Remember us—if at all—not as lost
Violent souls, but only
As the hollow men

Hollow. That was exactly how she had felt. Hollow inside, and cold. . . .

Between the idea
And the reality
Between the motion
And the act
Falls the Shadow

Avra knew very well what the Shadow was. She had lived with It every day of her life since she was five years old. It had begun to visit her then in a dream, the dream she had taken pains to forget countless times. She had never thought of it before in her conscious moments, but in the dream she knew Its name: the Shadow. Most of the time she was able to push It back, publicly deny Its existence. . . .

But today she had seen It face to face, had confronted the Shadow in the form of a living man.

Trembling, she closed her eyes. There had been another line:

> Eyes I dare not meet in dreams
> In death's dark kingdom

Eyes I dare not meet in dreams.
Eyes I dare not meet—
All those forgotten dreams.

The dream last night; and today, the feeling of foreboding. . . .

She had met those eyes, seen down into the bottom of them. Seen them last night in her sleep. Pale eyes, inhuman eyes that belonged to Rolf Bruner. Of that she had no doubt.

Gran lied, dear God, Gran lied

There was no question of her making a mistake after twenty-five years. This was not a man who simply resembled Bruner. The nuances of speech, of gesture, his dress, those eyes—

Those eyes. The ride-a-pony game. That fleeting, hard, predatory look that had come over his face when he saw her face—

My God, if he recognized me—

She leaned her forehead against her knees.

That was it, Gran had lied about Bruner being dead. They hadn't killed him, and here he was, out of prison. . . . Gran had lied so the girls wouldn't be frightened. Had lied, perhaps in a desperate attempt to get Avra to sleep nights. To help her get better.

Still, he didn't look at all like a man who had spent any time in prison. Maybe he had never spent any time there at all. He was a doctor; he'd been rich enough to afford good lawyers. Maybe they'd gotten him off.

And there he sat with that woman, and that little girl.

The thought made her head swim so that she was nearly ill again, but she steadied herself. *I've got to find a way to warn them. Find a way so they'll believe me, so they won't think I'm a nut. So that he won't find out and . . .*

She didn't finish the thought.

She rose shakily to her feet, flushed the toilet, and came out of the stall. In the outer lounge area she went over to the old-fashioned washbasin and splashed cold water on her face. Half bent over the sink, she glanced up, hands still cupped full of water, and caught herself in the mirror. A madwoman, wild eyed and pale, water dripping down her face.

She had faced the Shadow; she had seen Rolf Bruner and knew he lived in places other than her memory. What was she going to do about it? What *could* she do?

Nothing. Not a damn thing.

Yet she couldn't just walk out of the restaurant and pretend she hadn't seen. What if he lived here, in the very same city? What if she were going to run into him, not once, but again and again?

The memory of him both repelled her and drew

her closer. She had to find out—had to *know* that he had at least spent time in prison. Had to *know* that he had suffered.

For Mama's sake. For Mama's sake, her mind repeated nonsensically, though some deeper part of her knew it was just as much for her own.

She straightened and patted her face dry with a paper towel. She looked awful, like someone who had just seen a ghost.

Well, I have, haven't I?

She drew in a deep breath to compose herself, then released it and stepped out into the noisy hallway. She was a little surprised to find that everything worked, that her legs supported her weight and carried her smoothly down the corridor, that her body magically ceased trembling. When she arrived at the hostess's station, she was amazed to find that she could smile.

The crowd in the foyer had thinned. The hostess was leisurely scanning her list of names at the lectern. She looked up as she sensed Avra's presence at her elbow.

"No luck finding him?"

The question caught Avra completely off guard; she had completely forgotten about her date with Chuck DeSantis. Thank God he was not among the people waiting. She regained her composure and answered the woman.

If you only knew what I did find . . .

"Afraid not. I'm giving up."

The woman made a sympathetic noise. "That's a shame."

"Oh, I'll live. But I *do* have a favor to ask. The couple with the little girl—the ones that were here when I first came in. Do you by chance have their name on your list? He's an old professor of mine. I saw them in there eating and wanted to say hello, but I'm too embarrassed. I just can't for the life of me remember his name. . . ."

"That should be easy. I don't get many parties of three on Friday night. They were the only ones around the time you came in. Let me see. . . ." The hostess squinted down at her clipboard and ran her finger up the column of names. "Here it is. Feinman, party of three."

Avra frowned, disappointed. She had expected to hear another name, not this one. "Are you *sure*?"

The woman nodded. "Positive. The one with the little girl, right? I even penciled in 'Doctor' next to his name. He kept telling me, 'It's doctor. *Doctor* Feinman.' You know how some of them make a big deal about their titles."

"Doctor Feinman," Avra repeated blankly, staring down at the name beneath the dull point of the woman's pencil. She glanced up. "There wasn't anyone named Bruner tonight, was there?"

The woman shook her head.

"Thank you," Avra told her. "Thank you very much." She turned and headed for the exit.

"Hey," the hostess called after her. "I thought you were going to go say hello."

Avra didn't answer. She stepped out into the dimly lit street and headed back for the house. Oddly, this time she wasn't afraid of the walk home alone in the dark, of the potential thieves and rapists hiding in the shadows. Being outside was a relief, despite the uncomfortable mugginess. The worst of her fears was inside, having dinner at an Italian-Creole restaurant.

The name given her by the hostess disturbed her. Feinman. She had expected to hear the name Bruner, had expected confirmation of what she knew beyond any doubt to be true.

This was the same man who had killed her mother, but he had changed his name. Why? Perhaps he *had* served time in prison, and changed it to avoid the taint of the past.

After all, the hostess had said he was a doctor. That, at least, was no surprise. The bastard probably still practiced medicine. The change of name could be his protection against being found out—

I remember now. He was a pediatrician—

Avra released an angry, tearless sob. She had made it to the end of Snow Avenue, with its well-lit sidewalks and empty shops, and turned right onto Swann Avenue. She had walked this route so many times in broad daylight that she retraced it automatically. Her stride was rapid, possessed.

A pediatrician. What if the bastard was *still* a pediatrician? All those mothers, entrusting their children to his care . . .

Just as Mama had done.

He had changed his name so that no one would ever find out. The disclosure would ruin him, whether he'd been in prison or not.

Avra stopped abruptly and stood, fists clenched, gasping in the sultry air.

It had taken hellish years to pull herself up from depression, painfully, one step at a time. And she had never known what the struggle was for. There were times even now, as she lay in bed, skirting the gray edge of sleep, when she wondered why. Why living was so goddamned important; why it was always necessary to be brave.

But she had gone on living for Maggie's sake. Out of love, because she knew her sister would have been devastated otherwise. Suicide would have been easy . . . but it would have also been the ultimate cruelty.

Now, suddenly, there was another reason besides Maggie. A reason that didn't make up for the past twenty-five years, but at least clothed them with a tattered bit of meaning.

Revenge. For Mama. For herself. For Maggie. If Bruner was still a pediatrician, she would find him. Find his office, hunt him down. Find a way so that every one of his patients would *know*. So no one else would have to suffer. . . .

But if he had seen her, he might very well kill her to keep her silent. A small shiver of fear passed through her, but she reassured herself: *Doesn't really matter, does it? Just so people know. Just so no other little girls have to go through what I did. . . .*

Maggie, of course, would disagree; despite her guilt Avra sometimes had flashes of insight where she understood that Maggie *needed* to take care of her, perhaps more than Avra needed that care. And so it was important that Maggie not find out. Avra doubted that she could prevent Maggie from guessing that something was wrong. That didn't mean that Maggie would automatically know *what*, and Avra didn't have to tell her.

It would be worth it. She started walking again. And along with the terror, felt a crazy, twisted sense of triumph. She had faced the Shadow—but this time she would win.

Feinman's eyes caught a blur of movement outside the restaurant window: the silhouette of the young woman, backlit by street lamps. He watched briefly as she continued down Snow Avenue and disappeared into the darkness.

He turned away from the window and returned his attention to Amelie. Right now she was trying unsuccessfully to guess what he had gotten her for her birthday. Feinman shook his head at her and smiled absently without registering what she had just said.

Several moments passed, moments during which Feinman tried to converse and eat his dinner—but found himself increasingly troubled by the incident with the young woman, for reasons he did not understand.

At last he raised his fork halfway to his lips. Paused. Set it down.

"What is it, Jake?" Helen's face, concerned, in the candlelight.

Feinman rose and put his napkin on the table. "Would you excuse me for a moment, please?"

He exited the dining room and headed down the corridor toward the entrance. He was still uncertain why the woman disturbed him so, why she had reacted toward him as she did. Yet his instinct recognized danger, even if his conscious mind did not.

Whoever she was, there was no chance of catching up to her on the dark street . . . and Feinman's dignity would not have permitted him to chase after her. Discretion was best.

Halfway down the corridor he watched as a scruffy, long-haired young man in jeans and a T-shirt entered the restaurant and began to converse rather loudly with the hostess. She was a thin, vapid thing, dressed overelegantly for her station in life and her age (fresh out of high school, Feinman judged), in a flowing dress of heavy cream-colored crepe.

"I'm sorry, but dinner jackets are required—"

"Required? In *this* heat? You've got to be kidding!"

"No, sir, I'm afraid that after eight on weekends—"

"Well, look, don't you have an extra jacket or something?"

She shook her head. "Sorry."

Feinman stood patiently off to one side, to await the moment the hostess's attention would be free.

"Well, my date's probably waiting inside for me. Could I at least go find her?"

Wariness crept into the hostess's eyes. Feinman agreed. Judging from the man's demeanor, his poor posture, his clothes, the run-down heels on his dirty jogging shoes, he was a poor risk. Feinman would not have trusted him to return.

"I'll find her for you," the hostess offered diplomatically. "What was the name?"

"Damn, I don't remember. It was Italian or Greek or something. Do you have any names like that—party of two?"

The woman scrutinized her clipboard, then shook her head. "Doesn't sound familiar. . . . Nope. I don't see anything that looks like that."

The man sighed and took a step forward, as if to see for himself.

"Wait a minute," the hostess said. "There *was* someone. I mean, she didn't give her name, but she mentioned she was waiting for a date—"

The scruffy young man lifted his chin, brightened. "What did she look like?"

"Tall. Pretty. Sort of exotic looking—Italian, maybe. Long dark hair."

The young man smiled and opened his mouth to speak; Feinman took the liberty of interrupting him. Perhaps here was an opportunity to solve the mystery.

"Excuse me. I believe the young lady you're looking for just left."

"*Damn.*" The young man moved toward the door.

"It's too late to catch her," Feinman said quickly. "It happened a few moments ago. She's quite gone. You said her name was . . . ?"

The young man turned his head, hair swinging, and narrowed his eyes at Feinman. "I said I didn't remember. Why do *you* need to know?"

But the hostess smiled. "Oh, you must be the professor. The one she asked about."

Feinman's tone remained carefully pleasant. "Did she?"

"She wanted to speak to you, but she was too embarrassed; she'd forgotten your name."

A ripple of panic, firmly controlled. Feinman's expression never altered. "Ah. So you gave it to her."

"I hope you don't mind."

Feinman showed teeth. "Not at all. I'm pleased, in fact. At least now she'll be able to look me up. I must admit, *I'd* forgotten her name as well. It's been some time, you see, and—"

The rumpled young man interrupted.

"Look, thanks anyway. I'll check across the way. . . ." He squinted at one of the shops on the opposite side of the street. Feinman tried to follow his gaze, but it could have been one of three: Sharper Image, Doubleday, Victoria's Secret. ". . . But it looks like they're all closed up over there. She said she got off work at nine. . . ." He gave Feinman a curious, somewhat friendlier glance. "So, you know Avra?"

It seemed to Feinman then that the room changed: became warmer, brighter, in some subtle way more *intense.* And absolutely still. The background noise of piped-in music, diners chatting, busboys clattering dishes, melted away into silence; evaporated, like dew under a desert sun. Motion ceased as well. Certainly, people entered the restaurant, stepped around the young man and Feinman to give their names to the hostess. But Feinman never saw, never heard.

He heard only the question as it hovered in the air, approached him, enveloped him. It reverberated in his ears, grew louder with each passing second.

More than the room. The world had changed, irrevocably.

So, you know Avra?

The face, the dark hair, the eyes. No wonder the sight of her had unsettled him; he had looked at her and seen, not the child she had been, but her mother, Marie.

So great was his will, so total his control, that throughout it all his kindly smile never wavered.

"Yes," Feinman answered softly. "Yes, I know Avra."

8

 As Avra turned right onto Willow Street, she found herself trapped in the glare of an oncoming set of headlights. The car slowed obviously as Avra neared, but she was unafraid; she knew the identity of the driver. Still, she feigned confusion for an instant. It gave her time to collect herself, to prepare for deception.

She stepped from the sidewalk into the street and raised a fist to rap on the driver's side window of the little brown Datsun. Maggie was already rolling down the window. She wore what Avra called "the Look"; an expression of almost maternal concern, brow puckered, mouth tugging down at the corners. Murray sat in the passenger's seat, looking dazed.

God. It was bad enough trying to hide things from Maggie, much less trying to hide *this* when she was still so shaken. Maggie must have known something was wrong even before setting eyes on her. Avra did her best to affect an expression of surprise, mixed with mild annoyance. Anything but the horror she felt.

She leaned down and put a hand on the window's glass edge. "What's up? You two going to catch that movie?" She knew damn well, of course, that they were not.

"Jesus," Murray said in quiet, awe-hushed tones, "You were right, Mag. I wouldn't have believed it if I hadn't *seen* it." He spoke less than a split second before Maggie (with the Look still in place) said:

"You okay? You look really upset."

"Yeah," Avra lied. "Mister Wonderful didn't show. Left me hanging around the restaurant watching everyone else eat dinner. I guess I'm a little pissed about it, that's all." She tried her best to sound natural, but the words came out a little too quickly, making her catch her breath.

"If you're hungry, there's leftover steak at the house," Murray said.

"Fuck *you*," Avra replied, not at all nicely. "You know what you can do with your dead animals, Murray. I'm not in the mood." She put her hand to her forehead and rubbed the beginnings of a headache. A mistake; her fingers shook.

In the light from the dash she saw the crease between Maggie's brows deepen. Maggie took her time responding, a sure sign that she didn't buy Avra's act. Didn't buy it at all.

"Get in," Maggie said. "I'll take you home."

"I'd rather walk. Work off some steam. You two get to your movie." Not good; her voice was becoming uneven.

"We fell asleep and missed the movie, okay? Get in."

"No," Avra said. She didn't dare say more. If she did, her voice would break, and she would be tempted to tell Maggie everything. *Christ*, a snide little voice in her head jeered, *not in front of Murray*. . . . She took her hand off the window and began walking rapidly toward home.

After a moment's hesitation the Datsun B210 backed into a driveway, changed direction, and followed.

In the shifting light and shadow of the car, Murray said, "Maggie. If I break my promise, will you kill me?"

Maggie stared at Willow Street before her; her expression was morose, unreadable. Murray waited for an answer until they were in the driveway in front of the old house. Sometimes Maggie could be painfully slow in answering, particularly if the topic disturbed her. Murray looked through the windshield at the old house and saw the lights come on as Ave made her way up the stairs to her bedroom. Maggie put the car in park, turned off the headlights and the engine, pulled the keys from the ignition, and sat.

"Look," Murray said finally, "she's upset, but it's not about the date. I even think it's possible she stood him up. Do you think—do you think she's still upset about us? That's she's trying to make us feel guilty?"

He hesitated, certain he had made her mad. But when she turned and faced him in the darkness, her voice was perplexed.

"I'm not sure what I think," she said.

By eleven that night Feinman was alone in the big house on Riverhills. There'd been a party at Helen's condo for just the three of them, complete with ice cream and cake and balloons and the grand unwrapping of Scarlett O'Hara. It was hard to say who had been more charmed by the gift, mother or daughter.

He'd pleaded exhaustion and a headache shortly thereafter; quite unlike him, giving up a chance to play with the girl, and Helen knew it. He took one token bite of cake, no more. Helen had noticed. Noticed not only the cake, but his unusual silence, his preoccupation. And she assumed, just as he had hoped, that he had taken ill in the restaurant.

There had been real concern in her eyes when he admitted feeling unwell. After all, he was almost twenty years her senior, and she was seeking a husband, a father for the little girl. He could read her face, knew in advance the questions she was going to ask: Was he sure it wasn't serious? Shouldn't he call one of his colleagues from the clinic, just to be safe?

No, he had told her wearily, he wasn't really ill,

just tired. Tired from overwork and suffering from
a headache. She had offered then to rub his neck
for him and he had submitted to her attentions,
sensing that a refusal might offend her.

And there was Amelie in her emerald party
dress, her eyes welling with tears at the thought of
his leaving so early. It was, of all days, her birthday. But it was more than simple childish disappointment, Feinman knew; she was beginning to
return his love. Why, when her mother was out of
the room, she often flirted with him, gave him sly,
coy glances.

With Amelie it was only a matter of time.

But tonight he left her with her mother and the
exquisite green-eyed doll and retreated to the
safety of Riverhills. As he passed through the
kitchen and into the bedroom hallway, he noted
with great relief the absence of the white stuffed
bear.

The relief was momentary. There was Avra to
deal with. Avra, who had so obviously recognized
him; Avra, who could go to the police. There was
no statute of limitations for murder.

Or raping a child.

He would have to flee again. Change his name,
get the falsified IDs, the certificates, the diplomas.
Find a part of the country where he had never
hunted before. Texas, perhaps. Or perhaps it was
time to leave the country altogether. Leave the
house on the river, the hawks . . . and Amelie.
He felt very, very old. Tired and full of self-pity to

the point of weeping. He went into the bedroom, snapped on the overhead, pulled off his jacket, and lay down fully dressed on the bed without turning down the royal-blue Ralph Lauren bedspread. It was unfair. Grossly unfair, that he should have to relocate again. His eyes closed over unshed tears.

He would simply have to stop Avra from going to the police. Otherwise, she would haunt him wherever he went. He would be hunted down, followed, as long as there was a living witness. . . .

He sat bolt upright on the bed, startled by a horrifying thought.

What if she had already gone to the police? What if she was there right now, had gone there directly from the restaurant? They might be looking for him, even now. They might come *here*. . . .

He rose from the bed and strode through the kitchen, into the great room. At the wet bar he stopped to turn on a small fluorescent lamp above the counter and pour cognac into an oversized crystal snifter. His hands shook; liquor sloshed over the rim of the glass onto his fingers.

As he raised the snifter unsteadily to his lips, Feinman paused to snap off the lights. This time the darkness soothed him, seemed to offer protection, anonymity. He stepped down into the carpeted living area and pulled the cord with his free hand. The vertical blinds covering the large bay window opened to reveal an occluded view of the river. At that exact instant a long, jagged bolt of lightning streaked through the blackened sky; seconds after, he heard the thunder.

An electrical storm brewing, not uncommon this time of year. Some nights the noise was bad enough to wake him from a sound sleep. It occurred to him that he had been subliminally aware of the thunder for some time, but had been too distraught to register it consciously. He stared through the thick plate glass as fat tear-shaped drops of rain sparkled in the outside floodlights. The drops became thinner, elongated, began to come down faster, heavier, until he was staring at sheets of water soaking the backyard. Feinman sipped his drink and felt the fire move from the tip of his tongue down the back of his throat.

It had rained the night of the dream. The night Celia died.

The wind picked up until the water was hurled sideways. It pelted noisily against the window, rippling down in waves. Feinman watched the rain and the lightning for a long time. He felt trapped, powerless to take action. Avra had to be eliminated before she contacted the police; yet if she had already spoken with them, killing her would implicate him. He had no way of knowing whether she had already gone to them. But if he hesitated, took the safe way out and let her live . . .

Then he would have to flee, and be followed for the rest of his life. There was simply no logical resolution to the problem. And so he stood in the dark room, staring out at the storm.

Suddenly, a pale shape formed outside the window; a small hand pressed against the glass. Feinman almost cried out, startled by the presence of an intruder, until he recognized the child. His grip on the snifter loosened. It fell, landing silently on the plush gray carpet. The heady fragrance of cognac permeated the air.

"Celia," he whispered. In spite of his dread he felt drawn to her. He moved closer to the window and touched his fingers to the glass. Perhaps his fear had been misplaced. Perhaps she offered help, not madness.

This time she was not alone. Behind her bare right shoulder stood a second pale form, blurred by waves of water sloughing off the outside pane. A girl, three inches taller than Celia, lean and willowy, with a dreamy expression. Her golden, waving hair, lifted by the wind, spilled over one side of her face, fell past her elbows. There was a sultriness in her heavy-lidded eyes, a seductiveness that at once attracted and repelled him. A young Lauren Bacall; one of Nabokov's nymphets. Feinman thought he remembered her as a girl he had once killed, but her name and the place and method of her demise eluded him.

She remained behind Celia. Amazingly, neither of them seemed touched by the rain, but the wind beat their hair against their faces. They seemed to float.

Feinman touched the window and thought: *Why have you come, Celia? What do you want of me?*

Their skin flickered blue-white in the lightning. The rain beating against the house, the thunder, the wind, seemed to merge into a single incoherent sound, a sound that culminated in Celia's sweet voice, whispering in his head.

Revenge

Feinman snatched his hand away from the window.

Someone must be punished

"It wasn't my fault," he whimpered, taking a step backward. "Not my fault—"

Not his fault the girls had to die. It was simply . . . Fate. He had needed to hunt, and the girls had been available. Not his fault—

He stood gasping, staring out at the rain and the two small wraiths beyond the window for several minutes. To his mind, several hours. Would it be the same as last night? Would Celia keep him prisoner, fearful, transfixed by her presence, until dawn?

Abruptly, the children vanished, dissolved into the wet and the darkness.

Feinman stepped forward and strained to see. As he did, there came a heart-stopping crash of lightning, so close the thunder was simultaneous. The hairs on his forearms lifted.

He blinked, temporarily sightless. When his vision returned, he could see nothing in the backyard but the darkness and the rain.

And something small and pale atop the muddy ground.

The Gund bear, he thought at first, with a start. Perhaps the rain had uncovered it. But he had buried the stuffed animal in another part of the yard, farther down toward the river. And he had done a thorough job, digging far too deep a hole for it to be unearthed by anything so casual as a summer cloudburst.

He stared through the glass. No, it was not the bear; the shape, the coloring, were wrong. As he watched, the rain washed more of the sandy river soil away, revealing a deeper color against the pale.

Whatever it was, it had been left as a sign.

Feinman dreaded going outside into the storm, dreaded knowing what the thing was. Yet if he did not—if he ignored Celia's obvious attempt at communication—he would only hasten her reappearance.

He crossed to the other side of the room, to the sliding glass doors that opened onto the deck. He drew in a deep breath, pushed open the door, and went out into the storm.

The rain had eased; it no longer fell in sheets, but it still came down hard in thin, needle-sharp drops that stung Feinman's head, his face, the back of his neck. The cedar deck was slick. He walked carefully to the deck's edge, then stepped onto the soft muddy ground. The spot where the dead girls had been was dotted with clumps of grass which grew poorly because of the trees and the sandy soil. The object he sought was soaked, half covered with washed-up mud.

He did not recognize it immediately. It was a doll. A rag doll, clad in a muddy blue dress with short puffed sleeves. It was obviously homemade, obviously very old. Its black yarn hair was matted and stuck out at crazy angles; its embroidered features were frayed in spots, completely unraveled in others, showing the tiny holes where the needle had punctured the cotton.

Feinman squatted down and picked the doll up in his hands. He felt himself on the verge of recognition . . . of understanding.

He had seen this doll before, knew instinctively, even before the actual memory surfaced, that it had lain pressed against the bare skin of his chest. As he held it face up, the rain continued to clean the dirt away.

Its embroidered eyes were blue, and it wore a dark blue frock. Blue.

Avra had carried it with her that night.

He held it carefully, almost reverently, as he went back inside the house. He set the wet doll on the ceramic tile hearth in front of the fireplace, snapped on a lamp, and stared at it.

The air-conditioner cut on, raising gooseflesh on the skin beneath his soaked clothes, but Feinman did not permit himself to be distracted by mere physical discomfort. He was too close to understanding Celia's message.

It all had to do with Avra. With his seeing Avra.

Someone must be punished

It had not been his fault. If the blame lay with

anyone, it lay with her. He remembered very clearly now, as if it had been a matter of days rather than years. Avra had cried out that night. He remembered:

Her cries had wakened Marie.

If Avra had kept silent, Marie would never have known, never have guessed, and he could have remained as a happy father and husband, lived in New Orleans and had a quiet life, a contented life.

But Avra had cried out. And forced him to kill Marie. And if he had not killed her . . .

He would never have been released. And Celia and the blond girl, and all the others, would not have had to die.

Revenge.

It was becoming clearer, yes.

The final vestiges of control snapped. A new mind was released, now occupied its rightful place in his body. Bruner's mind.

His body tingled—not with cold, but with a surge of intense raw power. A compulsion. It had come over him many times this way, hard and strong, unstoppable, beyond all his puny efforts to control it. The need to hunt. His exhaustion vanished, replaced by limitless energy. He would not sleep tonight. At times, when the power filled him like this, he could go without rest for two, even three days.

He would not flee; not yet. Not just yet. First, he would give Celia and the blond girl their revenge.

Someone must be punished, mustn't she?

The vision of Celia and the unknown girl had left him fearful, yet in the midst of the fear a new emotion was emerging: anticipation.

There was no need for the Halcion, after all. He knew how to stop the apparitions.

He hurried back to the bedroom and entered the spacious walk-in closet. There behind his hanging suits was a small safe built into the wall. Bruner turned the dial, waited for the tumblers to click, then opened the heavy steel door impatiently, eagerly.

There were two articles inside: a will and a photograph album. Bruner pulled out the album. It was a white vinyl ring binder with gold trim, of the sort used for wedding pictures. The binder was so full that it no longer closed properly. If he took any more pictures, he would have to buy another. The alternative was to put two people to a page, and for stylistic considerations he did not want to do that.

He opened it to the back, to the very last page.

Two photos, both Polaroids. The first caption read: CELIA RYNERSON, APRIL 23, 1989. BEFORE. A little brown-haired girl held a white Gund bear. She was smiling and happy when he had taken it. She had still trusted him then.

The second read:

CELIA RYNERSON. APRIL 24, 1989. AFTER.

Carefully taped beneath the photographs was a

lock of dark brown hair. Beneath that, a clipping from *The Washington Post*.

Bruner turned the page back. On the next-to-last page was a picture of the blond girl. In her "before" picture her smirk was impish, beguiling. The caption said, TABITHA WHITLOW, FEBRUARY 19, 1989.

Strange. He had no memory of her. But here were the last photographs ever taken of her; here, a lock of the wavy golden hair.

Bruner carefully peeled back the protective plastic and ran his fingers over the hair. Its silkiness made him marvel, brought back a dim recollection of another time when his fingers had brushed against something this soft.

Yes. He remembered now. He had closed his eyes when he stroked that hair, and imagined it to be long and dark. He had looked at the girl and not seen Tabitha Whitlow at all.

He replaced the plastic and began flipping through the pages slowly, letting the fever build. It was a ritual he always performed at this stage, before the hunt.

After some time he reached the front of the album. There was only one photograph on the first page, an old one shot back in December 1965, according to the date printed along its once-white edge. The colors were yellowed, untrue, and the entry on the page was incomplete. Yet the picture moved him more than any other. Only one word was lovingly inscribed beneath it:

AVRA

An obviously posed portrait. Her thin, triangular face was framed by dark waving hair, parted in the middle and pulled back at the temples with blue barrettes. It was carefully brushed down onto her shoulders. Her sharp little chin rested on her fist. She wore a royal-blue velvet dress with a white lace Peter Pan collar.

(She had been wearing a blue dress tonight in the restaurant, hadn't she?)

Beneath the plastic two newspaper articles, yellowed with age, were folded into neat squares. Part of the headlines were visible: OMAN SLAIN; SUSPECT read one; the other, URDER SUSPECT STIL. But the lock of hair was conspicuously missing. Each time he reviewed his work, Bruner lamented that fact.

At long last he had the opportunity to correct the omission.

His blue angel. He felt a tug of wistfulness at the sight of the girl, a sorrow that she was gone—the same grief he might have felt for a love long dead. For he had recognized no trace of this beautiful child in the woman she had become.

No trace of his Avra. He had loved her more than any other child. In the twenty-five years since he had seen her, no one had ever taken her place in his heart, had evoked the degree of obsession he had felt for her.

But she would have to be punished, for the sake

of the others. In one way he yearned for it; in another, the thought of killing her broke his heart.

Much as he had done for Celia, Bruner bowed his head and wept. For himself. For his blue angel.

9

Avra slept little that night. When she got to the house she went straight up to her room and closed the door. The last thing she wanted was to talk to Maggie, to face that maddening calm. Maggie would refuse to believe, of course; Maggie would speak rationally in soft, soothing tones and have Avra doubting herself in no time flat.

She knew what she had seen. She did not doubt that she was right. But her resolve for revenge had weakened by the time she reached the house. She knew she could not face Rolf Bruner again to publicly accuse him. She was, quite plainly, terrified. What if he had recognized her, and followed? What if he found out where she lived? He only had to look in the phone book—

Relax, for Christ's sake. He probably didn't recognize you, and even if he did, he wouldn't know your last name.

She listened as Maggie and Murray came in, and dreaded their leaving again, as they often did now that the air-conditioner was broken, to spend the night in Murray's tiny, run-down apartment near the airport. Avra had almost gotten used to sleeping alone in the old house without too much difficulty, but tonight . . . tonight she was grateful to hear the stairs groan under Murray's weight as he, Maggie, and Jason headed up to her room; grateful to hear the rise and fall of their voices across the hallway, through the thickness of two closed doors.

Maggie must have guessed how upset she really was. Enough to convince Murray to stay the night without air conditioning.

Despite the fear Avra was consumed by curiosity. She had to know about Rolf Bruner, about the details of his life. Had he served time in prison? (That was the most important question.) Did he practice medicine here in town? She was drawn and repulsed at the same time, rather like being compelled to stare at a particularly gruesome accident on the highway to know if anyone had been killed.

She did not want to know. She *had* to know.

How long had they been together in Tampa, in the same city, gliding past each other like strangers? How often had he been to Hyde Park, eaten at Selena's, and gazed leisurely through the beveled windows at Doubleday Book Shop?

Perhaps he had already known. Perhaps he had been watching her for a long time.

She thought of going down to the kitchen to get the phone book and look him up, but Maggie might come out of the bedroom and start asking questions before she could get downstairs. And so she sat on the bed, trying to think about what to do.

First, find out if he lives here. Then worry about the rest. . . .

After all, he could have simply been passing through on vacation. Maybe by tomorrow he would be gone, and she would never see him again.

The thought brought a momentary relief, but then self-honesty took over. How many tourists came to Florida in *August*, at the worst time of the year? He and those with him had been dressed as if they were going to a formal party, not in casual tourist garb. Tourists did not wear three-piece suits to restaurants; he had been dressed as a professional.

That's *Doctor* Feinman.

Shortly after midnight, when she thought she heard Murray's low, rumbling snores, she stole quietly down to the kitchen. Near the wall phone, propped up next to the microwave on the counter were the Tampa directories.

She looked in the White Pages first, trying all the possible permutations of the name. F-i-n-e-m-a-n. With two *n* 's. F-e-i-n-m-a-n. F-i-e. Even F-y-n-e-man.

Nothing.

She tried the Yellow Pages next, under "Physicians," by specialization first. He was not listed with the pediatricians. Then she tried the general listing.

Feinman wasn't there.

She vacillated between hope and fear. If he wasn't in the book, maybe he'd been vacationing after all. That, or he had given a fictitious name. Or the woman's name—but then she'd have been listed.

Quietly, Avra picked up the telephone receiver and dialed 1411. The kitchen phone was the only one in the house. If she wanted to know now, she'd have to risk waking Maggie up.

She wanted to know now.

A male voice came on the line. "Directory assistance. What city?"

She kept her voice low. "Tampa. A listing for Feinman. I think it's spelled F-e-i-n-m-a-n."

"One moment, please."

Avra waited. She honestly expected him to come back on the line and say, *Sorry, ma'am, we have no listing.* . . .

He responded sooner than she'd expected. "That residence is unlisted, ma'am. But I can give you a new office listing for a Dr. Feinman. Would you like that number?"

A new listing. My God, he *was* here. He had just moved here, to the same city. . . .

"Ma'am?"

"Yes. Yes, I'll take it, Operator. Thank you."

The computerized voice began. "The number is 555-4085. The number is . . ."

Avra realized she was listening, mesmerized, without writing the number down. She found a purple Post-it that said BEING A TEACHER IS AARD- VARK, with an illustration of an anteater aiming a pointer at a blackboard, then grabbed one of the pens from a cracked coffee mug beside the phone. In her agitation she knocked over the mug; the pens spilled out and rolled across the counter. Avra tried unsuccessfully to catch them as they bounced onto the floor. She glanced anxiously over her shoulder toward the staircase. No one came.

The resultant scrawl looked shaky, as if it had been written by a Parkinson's victim.

There was nothing left to do except wait until morning. She went back up to her room and lay down to sleep, dreaming that when she woke in the morning, all of this would be gone.

An hour before sunrise Bruner drove the silver Mercedes to a three-level parking garage on the southern outskirts of Hyde Park and left it on the unlit second level. It was exceptional for him to risk using the Mercedes when he was hunting, but the urgent situation demanded it. He would re- duce the risk as soon as possible—but for now it was necessary to prepare.

If she worked in a shop in Hyde Park, then it was probable that she worked Saturdays, the busiest day, and he could not afford to let any time lapse. The longer he waited to act, the sooner she might go to the police. He had already decided that if Fate were against him and she did not work today, he would go from store to store inquiring after her. He would obtain her last name and from that, her address. The situation required desperate measures. There was not enough time to be cautious.

He stepped from the car into the unpleasantly humid darkness. The lenses of his spectacles clouded with steam, which slowly cleared. Lit only by the streetlamps outside, the parking garage stank of stale air and diesel exhaust from the Mercedes.

Bruner wore a pair of leather tennis shoes and a pale gray jumpsuit that zipped up the front. He used the jumpsuit occasionally for gardening, though he had done little of that since moving from D.C. The front had a number of roomy pockets for storing gardening tools; the most spacious and accessible of these held a loaded .22, whose shape was hidden by rags stuffed over it. The sleeves, like all of Bruner's clothes, were full length; he preferred them long because it hid the unsightly scar on his left forearm. Even now, in the heat, he kept the cuffs buttoned. The gold Rolex was locked safely inside the Mercedes's glove compartment. If seen, Bruner wished to give the impression of a maintenance man.

He found the exit stairs at the far corner of the

garage and descended them quickly, then pushed the heavy door that opened onto the sidewalk. Outside, the air was only slightly better than in the garage, due to a phenomenon the local weather forecasters called a heat inversion. The high temperatures prevented car exhaust and industrial pollutants from rising into the upper atmosphere. The air's foulness made Bruner gasp for breath.

The darkness, at least, was fading to gray. He was at the far south end of Snow Avenue. Across the street and several buildings down stood Selena's, where he had seen Avra the previous night. Now he stood on the same side of the street as the store where she worked. The single sprawling building incorporated several shops, each with its own entrance onto Snow.

Bruner walked silently down the sidewalk on his rubber soles. He carried the .22 as insurance, but he was strangely unafraid of being challenged or even seen. He no longer felt fear, only a steadily growing excitement, the thrill of the hunt . . . and an unshakable conviction that he was *right* in what he was doing, utterly and totally correct according to cosmic law. An injustice existed, had existed for twenty-five years, but he, Bruner, had been chosen to set it right. Soon he would have peace. He was acting in harmony with the universe; therefore, the universe would cooperate with him.

With barely a glance he passed changing shop-fronts: Brooks Brothers, Limited Express, a photography studio. As he approached Victoria's Secret, he slowed; it was one of the shops where Avra might work. Surprisingly, its interior was brightly lit.

It was fortunate that he had hesitated. Inside, moving carefully around displays of silk bathrobes and ruffled lace bustiers, were human forms: a cleaning crew. A heavyset woman pushed a vacuum cleaner while a thin man dragged black plastic bags full of trash.

Bruner paused for a moment, watching, but the man and woman were far too absorbed in their tasks to see him. He continued past them, past the bookstore, past Sharper Image and its eye-catching displays of needless gadgetry, around the corner and past Ralph Lauren Polo.

At last he arrived at the rear entrance of the building. Employees had to come and go either here or through the front entries. Most likely, here; at the alley's far end was a dirt lot with a sign: EMPLOYEE PARKING ONLY.

He noted three entrances as he made his way down the narrow alleyway. At the building's north end, near Sharper Image and the bookstore, there was a heavy, solid door . . . locked. Not with a dead bolt, fortunately, but a simple spring lock which could be picked. An identical door stood at the south end, by the parking garage.

And, midway—the most promising prospect. An invitation inside: a sliding garage door, half open. Bruner crouched down and peered inside. A spacious delivery area. It contained a large Dumpster/trash compacter, and ample room for a garbage truck plus a couple of delivery vans.

The garage was brightly lit. Bruner waited until he was certain he heard no one, saw no one . . . then slipped under the door. Inside sat a white truck with its windows open. The words AAA JANITORIAL SERVICE were painted in large black letters on the doors.

The garage led to a small unlit entrance. Bruner crossed to it quickly and stood listening, one hand on the doorway.

Silence inside, and darkness. Not even the distant hum of a vacuum cleaner. Beyond lay a huge, high-ceilinged maze of concrete block leading in three directions: north, south, straight ahead to the west.

He chose north, knowing it would lead him toward the suspect stores, the place where she worked. He also knew it would lead him toward the cleaning crew, and so he moved silently, with exaggerated caution.

Unending concrete block to either side; smooth concrete beneath his feet. The effect was strongly claustrophobic. He swore at himself for not having thought to carry a flashlight, but the darkness turned gradually to dimness; the concrete ceiling was occasionally interrupted by skylights.

The corridor ended sharply at a janitorial supply closet, then opened to the east and west. The stores lay to his west. The corridor leading to the east was short and ended with a heavy door—the exit to the alley behind the building.

The closet caught his interest. It was open, lit by a single naked light bulb, large enough to hide one adult. The door had a slatted panel just below eye level to allow for ventilation of noxious chemicals. The bolt was turned so that when the door closed, it would lock. Bruner removed a pair of gardening gloves from his pocket, slipped them on, and undid the lock, careful to leave the door open precisely as he had found it.

He removed the gloves, returned them to his pocket, and continued west, to his left. Farther down on the opposite side of the hallway were double doors marked ELECTRICAL. They were padlocked shut. He ignored them and went on. After a dozen steps the corridor branched off to the left, presumably leading to other stores. Several feet in front of him were two doors. Bruner drew closer, straining in the dim light to read the names lettered on them: DOUBLEDAY BOOK SHOP on the left, SHARPER IMAGE on the right.

If she worked at either of these stores, she would most likely take this exit, passing by the storage closet on the way out.

He followed the left-branching corridor. As he had guessed, it led ultimately to Victoria's Secret and the other stores. He got close enough to the door of the lingerie store to read the name painted there. Amazingly enough, he could only just make out the faint whine of the vacuum cleaner. He would not have noticed had he not known it was there. Bruner smiled to himself. The acoustics of the maze were perfect. Someone could scream in the corridor and it would most likely go unheard by anyone outside or in the shops.

He scouted the area around Victoria's Secret. He saw no closets or obvious places to hide. If she worked there, he would have to wait out in the hallway for her. More of a risk, but one that he would have to take.

He had moved down the corridor with the intent of returning to the garage when a door opened and slammed behind him. He hurried to the right, toward the bookstore and Sharper Image, too late realizing that the cleaning people were heading in the same direction, where the supply closet lay. Bruner withdrew into the short corridor in front of the bookstore, pressed himself against the wall beside the door, and hoped the shadows hid him. A flashlight beam swept the darkness; Bruner held his breath as it came perilously close to him.

But it passed without revealing him. The man and woman, joined now by a young female, moved talking and laughing past him at a leisurely pace. He waited motionlessly until the beam receded. They headed far down the hall to the closet and snapped on the light bulb, rattled around for a time, then turned the light off. Bruner heard the closet door shut—but not *click* locked—then lost track of the three as they made their way to the garage.

Several minutes passed before he dared follow them to the garage. The overhead light was off; the aging truck was gone. Bruner went over to the garage door and studied it. It locked from the outside with a key. The key turned a lever connected to a coiled wire spring; the spring hooked onto a metal bar which, depending on the tightness of the spring, slid in or out of a bolt on the wall. In the bolt, locked. Out of the bolt, unlocked.

At the moment the door was unlocked. An oversight, or perhaps it allowed easy access for other later deliveries. At any rate Bruner decided that the door should remain so. A simple matter, actually. He unhooked the wire spring from the metal bar. Now, if someone attempted to lock the door from the outside with a key, the lever would turn, but the spring could no longer slide the metal bar into the bolt. The door would remain unlocked.

Bruner pushed the door partially open and slipped beneath it. In the alleyway he tested the handle to be sure the door was unlocked, and would slide open easily.

It did. Bruner closed it again, then walked, cheerful and confident, into the first gray light of the morning.

He would return, and by tonight he would have her.

*   *   *

There'd been a thunderstorm the night before, the type that in the old days would have sent Avra (with Maggie not far behind) downstairs to huddle at the kitchen table until the worst of it was over. But Avra stayed in her room, hopeful that the torrential rain would cool things down. It did, for a while at least, until the power went off, cutting off the ceiling fans.

She didn't set the alarm, since she usually woke at seven and didn't need to be at work until ten. When she rolled over in bed to glance at the clock, she saw it was only seven—until she remembered the storm. She called Time & Temperature and discovered it was already quarter past nine. She struggled from the bed with a groan.

The events of last night seemed very far away, and in her current sleep-drugged state she was too groggy to feel fear. The scene in the restaurant seemed no more real than a nightmare.

It's all very simple, my dear. Either Bruner's alive and you saw him last night eating dinner at Selena's . . . or you're going crazy.

She'd take going crazy any day.

Avra forced herself through the motions: shower, makeup, clothes. As she crossed the hallway to the stairs, she noticed Maggie's bedroom door was open. The sheets had been stripped from the bed, and M & M were nowhere to be seen.

With any luck they were gone; the last thing she felt like this morning was a confrontation with Maggie. As Avra headed downstairs, she saw through the front window that Maggie's Datsun was missing, another hopeful sign.

But when she turned into the kitchen, she discovered Maggie, coffee mug in hand, with *The Tampa Tribune* spread out on the table in front of her. In the next room Gran's old washer churned noisily.

On her way to the Mr. Coffee, Avra glanced down at the section Maggie was scouring. The classified section; apartments for rent. She avoided eye contact as she pulled a mug from the cupboard and poured herself some coffee. She drank it standing by the machine. She felt, rather than saw, Maggie's concerned gaze on her; the sensation was irritating.

"Feeling any better this morning?" Maggie's tone was carefully neutral.

"I'm fine. I was just pissed at Chuck Whatsisname, that's all. Christ, it's hot in here." Avra gulped her coffee until the cup was half full, then poured more.

"I've got the dryer going in the utility room."

"Where's Murray?"

"I loaned him the car so he could go get his laundry. His van won't be ready till this afternoon." His dirty laundry, that is, which would soon see the interior of the Kenmore washer and dryer, purchased the year before Gran died. Maggie paused, then drew in a breath to speak again. At the sight of her solemn expression Avra raised her free hand and held it palm out.

"Mag, if this is serious, I'm really not in the mood. I don't have time, anyway. I've got to get to work."

Maggie frowned. "It's only seven-thirty. I was going to ask what you were doing already dressed."

"It's almost quarter to ten. The power went out last night, but I guess you lovebirds didn't notice."

Maggie set her cup down on the paper. "Ave, something's bothering you, and it has nothing to do with your date last night. It's about Murray and me, isn't it?"

She stiffened. "That's what he's told you, right? That I'm in a snit because I'm trying to make you feel guilty. Because I realize you two are going to shack up and leave me in the cold. Or the heat, as it were."

Maggie's gaze was calm and steady. She could rarely be baited into an argument, a trait Avra found infinitely frustrating. After several seconds Maggie asked calmly, "Are you?"

"Am I what?"

"In a snit because we're going to shack up?"

For a moment Avra considered slamming down her coffee cup and stomping out the door. Instead, she drew a breath and answered honestly. "Dammit, Maggie, I can't honestly say I'm thrilled about it. I'll miss you. But I'm an adult, and it pisses me off that Murray thinks you coddle me. Don't think I don't know it." Her anger faltered. "And . . . maybe he's right. Look, I've seen this coming for months. Probably before you did. And I'm happy for *your* sake, at least. Murray's a good guy. But— stop treating me like I'm an emotional cripple, okay? For once, stop feeling so damn guilty."

"Right," Maggie said, with an ironic little half-grin. "I'll never feel guilty again in my life. Thanks for the advice." The smile disappeared. "So if that's not it, Ave—what *is* bothering you?"

"Jesus, Maggie, I told you already." Avra drank what she could of her coffee, then set it down on the counter. "I've got to go."

And she dashed from the kitchen, through the living room and out the door.

Maggie sat watching her from the kitchen. She didn't believe Avra for a minute, of course; and she still felt guilty. Twenty-four years ago she had known Avra was hiding something from her . . . and she had ignored the fact. And never forgiven herself for the consequences.

She was not going to ignore it now. She would talk to Ave again about this; later, when she got back from work.

10

At shortly after ten o'clock in the morning Avra unlocked the northernmost back door that led to the Catacombs. The term *Catacombs* had been coined by Reid, the bookstore's manager, a term his employees enthusiastically adopted. It was an apt phrase; even now, in bright daylight, the Catacombs were dim and shadowy. There were occasional spotlights in the tall, narrow hallways, but the lights came on only at seven in the evening and shut off three hours later at ten. Those who didn't make it out of the shops by then were forced to walk to their cars in the darkness.

The Catacombs. Avra would not have been surprised to find, upon closer examination, that the less-used hallways hid crumbling skeletons covered with spiderwebs . . . tombs of the Unknown Employees. As a kid she would have refused to set foot in a place like this. Of course, she'd had a pretty active imagination back then. Around age six or so she would actually have *seen* the decaying corpses piled up in the corners, would have *felt* the spiderwebs soft and crawly against her skin.

Nope, she would have refused to go inside . . . unless Maggie went first, that is. Magdalen, they had called her then, because Mama hated nicknames. Magdalen would have marched right up to those rotting bodies—

It's all right, Avra. See? There's nothing to be afraid of. I'll show you . . .

—and stuck her hand right in the corner, right into the middle of the festering flesh, while Avra (a good distance away) squeezed her eyes shut and gasped.

If Avra had dared such a thing, the corpses would have come alive, would have grabbed her arms and pulled her down into the slime and stench. . . .

But because it was Magdalen, utterly unafraid Maggie, the ghouls retreated. Disappeared. Maggie never laughed, never made fun of her. Instead, she would turn solemnly to Avra and say,

See, Ave? It's okay. Just some empty cardboard boxes, that's all they are. Just empty boxes. Do you want to come see?

And most times Avra, reassured, would come and see. As long as Magdalen was with her, the skeletons couldn't get her, and she wouldn't see them anymore.

Of course, she was no longer a kid. She was an adult, no longer afraid of the dark, no longer able to turn shadows into skeletons with bits of decomposing flesh stuck to them.

At least if she was, she had learned not to tell.

Now as she walked—a little more quickly—down the unlit claustrophobic corridor toward Doubleday, she wore an ironic, unselfconscious smile as she thought of Maggie and the rotting bodies. It was the one personality trait her sister had inherited from Mama: perfect fearlessness. A quality Avra could have used right about then.

Her smile faded. After last night a stroll in the Catacombs wasn't sitting too well. Normally, she didn't mind them at all during the daytime. Winter evenings were another matter. In the winter, when the sun set early and Avra got off at five or six, she left through the front door of the shop if at all possible.

But today the Catacombs were part of her special precautions. She had driven the Toyota and parked it on the street, only steps away from the alley and the Catacombs' entrance, instead of in the more distant employee parking lot. Reid wouldn't like it if he noticed—the Park's management wanted employees to use the sandy lot, leaving the parking garage and more convenient spots on the street for customers. But today Avra didn't give a damn. Twenty-some steps from the car to the Catacombs, all in broad daylight. Yesterday she'd been annoyed at having to take the ten-to-five shift; she would have preferred noon to nine after working late last night. But today she was grateful.

As certain as she had been last night that the
man in Selena's had been Rolf Bruner, this morning she was vexed by doubt. All of last night's bra-
vado—her decision to find this Feinman, to expose
him for the monster he was—withered in the face
of exhaustion and uncertainty. She had taken
down his office phone number and still had the
scrap of paper in her purse. She had intended to
call today and get the street address. . . .

For what? To go there and confront him? Tell all
the patients in his waiting room who and what he
was?

And if she was wrong . . .

Contemplated in full daylight, last night's encounter took on a dreamlike unreality. When she'd
awakened, her first thought (accompanied by a
deep sense of relief) was that it *had* been a dream.
A nightmare. A monstrous apparition, certain to
melt away at Maggie's touch.

*See, Ave? There's nothing to be afraid of. It's all right.
Just a stranger, a harmless old man. Want to come see?*

She hadn't told Maggie. She wasn't sure that she
ever would. Maggie would think her insane.

Perhaps she *was* insane. Gran hadn't lied; Rolf
Bruner was dead, and Avra had fled in terror from
the sight of a stranger. . . .

She recalled images from the previous night: the
child on the man's knees. The ride-a-pony song.
The swift predatory glance he had given her.

No. No, she wasn't crazy. It had been Bruner.

And yet— It had been a long time. How could

she know for certain after twenty-five years? Certainly, other people played the ride-a-pony game. Seeing the game must have triggered her memory. The memory of the Shadow dream. . . .

(Don't think about it. Not here—)

Avra increased her pace down the corridor. The heels of her leather pumps clicked against the smooth concrete, echoed faintly. Her emotions had been like this all morning—back and forth, back and forth.

There was a way to be sure; a way to know if Gran had told the truth about Bruner dying.

The fall semester would soon begin at USF. Even though it was a Saturday, the library might be open. She had an old friend—an ex-lover, actually—who worked there. Ron, a perennial graduate student in linguistics. They had dated during Avra's drinking days. He mostly just checked out books or reshelved them, but he was good at research, and if he spoke to one of the reference librarians for her . . .

She dreaded talking to him. It would be awkward. Even though they had parted on less-than-hostile terms, it had been months since they had spoken. Still, she had thought about it all last night, and there was no other way. She would tell Ron, make up some lie about doing research on a magazine article . . . and find out what had really happened to Bruner. At least, what the newspapers had reported.

Find out that he was really dead, please. That Gran had told the truth.

Which would mean, of course, that she had gone certifiably batshit the night before. But she could deal with that better than with the alternative. . . .

Don't think about it anymore, okay? Just call Ron on your lunch hour.

Doubleday Book Shop at last. Avra had her key out and ready—it'd been ready since she'd first set foot in the Catacombs. She unlocked the heavy door and gave it a hard push.

The back room was dingy white, lit brilliantly like an operating theater. The sudden change from darkness made Avra squint. Except for cartons of unshelved, uninventoried books, the office was empty, but the coffee maker had just finished brewing, which meant Carl, the assistant manager, was already there. Avra slipped her purse off her shoulder, set it inside the tiny employees' bathroom, then came out into the office. Carl stood in the doorway that led into the store.

He flashed a slightly puzzled smile at her. He was tall, six foot three or four, thin and stoop shouldered. "Hi, Ave. I didn't expect to see you. The schedule says Eunice is on this morning."

"She had to take her kid to the doctor's this morning. We switched."

"You look like you had a late night."

She narrowed her eyes at him, but his tone was only mildly sarcastic. She liked Carl, though they often engaged in teasing. The crueler, the better. "How kind of you to notice."

"And here I thought you'd given up the grape, my dear."

"Don't be such an asshole this early in the morning, Carl. The air's broken at our house. *You* spend the night there and see how *you* look in the morning. I didn't sleep a wink." Avra took a mug from the shelf; the cleanest was a dark blue ceramic with a white starship and the words HE'S DEAD JIM painted on it.

Carl's comment bothered her for some reason, maybe because she really *did* feel like shit, hung over without any of the fun of a drunk the night before. Or maybe it was the fact that the idea of a drink seemed enormously appealing, even now, at ten o'clock in the morning.

"Poor baby," Carl said, his tone somewhat more sincere. "I'll be nice and won't even touch that invitation to stay over at your place tonight. In fact, I'll be magnanimous and let you choose your poison. You want the register or inventory this morning?"

"I'll take the register." Avra filled her cup from the coffeepot. "Please. My eyes are already crossed. I don't want Reid on my case for screwing up the inventory."

"You got it, kid."

He had just said it and Avra had just taken her first sip when a soft doorbell tone sounded in the back office. Someone had just entered the store.

Carl turned, but Avra set down her cup and put up a hand. "No. It's okay. I'll get it. Take my mind off my suffering. Get a cup of coffee and get cracking on that inventory."

She went out into the shop.

Across the street a man wearing a cap and a gray jumpsuit walked slowly down Snow Avenue in front of Selena's restaurant. The street was already beginning to fill with early shoppers. None of them noticed the older man in the jumpsuit; or, if they did, it was restricted to the vaguest subliminal impression of a passing Park employee, a maintenance man, say, or a gardener.

Bruner paused on the sidewalk to squint through the glass storefront of the Doubleday Book Shop. As he did, a smile spread slowly across his face.

Avra. No doubt of it. Incredibly fortunate that she had come to work today, and this early; fortunate that she worked at the bookstore. The fact would make things easier for him.

Most importantly, she had not come in the front door—which meant that she had used the rear entrance, though the concrete maze. Easier indeed.

He stood boldly now and watched from a distance as she came around the register to offer a customer assistance. He was no longer afraid that she, or anyone else, might see him. Everything was working too well, going so *right* that he felt protected by some unseen force, as if Celia and the

others were providing invisible aid. He was working with Fate now, and nothing could hinder him.

He watched her for some time. And then he
went to prepare.

Avra never called Ron at the library; she had
good reason. After Friday's lack of business Saturday was hectic, and on top of it Eunice phoned
from the doctor's office to say her kid might have
infectious hepatitis, so she wouldn't be coming in
at all. Carl tried to get in touch with one of the
part-timers, but no one answered the phone. Carl
then called Reid, but Reid was out, and by the time
he finally picked up his phone, it was only an hour
or two before he was scheduled to come in.

Despite the heat it was almost as busy as a tour-
ist-season Saturday. Avra did all right alone at the
register for the first few hours, but after that she
had to interrupt Carl from doing inventory (which
meant she'd probably get stuck with it Sunday).
They didn't even have time for lunch. At two-fif-
teen, when things eased a bit, Avra dashed over to
David's Cookies for take-out sandwiches. She ate
hers standing up in the back room while Carl held
down the fort, and then they switched.

As much as she complained aloud about how
busy it was, privately she was grateful. There was
little chance to reflect on last night's terrifying vision, even less chance to contemplate what action
to take. She'd been exhausted to begin with, and
after today she might be able to get a good night's

sleep. By tomorrow her mind would be clear. She would know what to do.

By three o'clock, when there was finally time to give the library a quick call, she felt too foolish to do so. Calling Ron would be so awkward. She'd had it all figured out: She would tell him that she needed to look up some old newspaper articles for a free-lance piece she was writing, and he'd never know the difference. Ron was not a person to pick up on details.

But then it occurred to her: What if the newspaper articles mentioned her by name? What if they ran a picture of Mama? She had old pictures of Mama; were it not for the dates and the outmoded hairstyles, they could have been mistaken for photos of Avra. Or Maggie.

The last person she wanted to have to explain any of that to was Ron.

Funny how the physical activity, the exhaustion and daylight, lessened the reality of last night's events. By four-thirty that afternoon Avra was beginning to believe she had never seen Rolf Bruner at all. Better to forget it; better to go home and go to sleep.

Carl echoed her thoughts as the two of them leaned against the front counter. "Go home, Ave," he said, glancing at his watch. "Your eyelids are at half mast. I can't stand to look at you anymore."

Avra didn't protest immediately, but glanced over her shoulder. There were only two customers in the store, a young professional-looking couple leafing through a copy of *What Shall We Name the Baby?* Outside the sky had filled with black thunderclouds. "But I've got a half hour to go yet." She punctuated the statement with a yawn.

"You never got lunch. Go ahead. I'll explain to Reid—he won't mind. Besides"—he nodded at the darkening sky—"it's going to storm like hell in a minute. I won't get any customers with the rain."

"Shit," Avra said. "I'm parked on the street."

"Then you'd better hurry."

"Are you sure . . . ?"

"Get out of here before I change my mind."

She didn't argue. She blew him a kiss, went back to the employee bathroom and retrieved her purse.

This time she headed into the Catacombs without hesitation.

Bruner had been waiting for hours.

The air in the maze was stuffy and warm, though not as miserably hot as the air outside. The supply closet smelled of chlorine and pine. From time to time he risked stepping outside into the hallway to gulp in fresher (though hardly fresh) air. He wore a jogging watch, the type with a blinking luminous dial so that he could check the time in the dark closet quickly.

Avra must have taken the back entrance to the maze shortly before ten. The chance that she would not leave the same way was slight, too slight to give Bruner any real concern. Since her shift began at ten, she would probably work until at

least two o'clock—four hours, half an eight-hour
day, if she was part time. By one-thirty Bruner
was in his hiding place. At two o'clock, three
o'clock, four o'clock, his vigilance increased. She
would be walking through the corridor a few minutes after the hour, whenever that hour might be.

He was well prepared. The delivery entrance remained unlocked. At a mall parking lot he had
stolen a nondescript white van and temporarily
stored the license plate under the front seat, having replaced it with a plate taken from a similar
van parked nearby. The white van now sat in the
parking garage at the south end of the building.

Bruner's left hip pocket held the loaded .22; his
right, an automatic syringe filled with ketamine, a
synthetic drug often used as an animal tranquilizer. Although capable of inducing psychedelic
hallucinations in humans, an unnecessary side effect, the drug was extremely fast acting. He had
cooked it down in the spacious Riverhills kitchen,
to ensure a concentrated dose: he could allow her
no more than thirty seconds' struggle. The syringe
was an automatic injector, the type carried by
those allergic to insect stings. It was normally
loaded with epinephrine. The injector could be
used by anyone and required no special skill.
Merely jabbing it quickly into a thigh, say, or an
exposed arm, would deliver a sufficient dose.

Even during a struggle.

Beside him on the floor of the closet was a large

canvas laundry bag, for when the ketamine took effect.

He had already determined that Avra should not die—not here, not now. Her punishment would have to be carefully meted out; it was important that she know *why* she was being punished for her death to be effective. Important to him; important to Celia and the others.

And he wanted to see her, talk to her again. Wanted to see if there was any trace of the child he had loved in this stranger, this young woman.

Four-fifteen. She would have to walk past him soon.

Of course, he realized that employees often got off in shifts. It was possible that when she came down the corridor, she would not be alone. For that reason he had brought the revolver. He was not afraid to kill, not afraid of being discovered.

He no longer believed that he *could* be discovered. Celia and the others would protect him.

It was fortunate, despite the heat and the boredom, that he had come hours early. His eyes had adjusted completely to the dim light. Earlier he had watched through the vent slat in the door as dark figures passed by in the shadows. Each time his pulse had quickened at the sound of approaching footsteps; each time had slowed as he strained his eyes and saw it was not Avra.

In the twilight of the maze Bruner yawned. Not from boredom, but nervous anticipation. After twenty-five years he would be alone with Avra again; after twenty-five years he would again possess his blue angel.

Avra stepped into the corridor as she pulled the door shut and heard it click as it locked behind her. She hesitated, temporarily blind. With the storm darkening the sky the Catacombs seemed pitch-black until, slowly, her eyes began to adjust. She began walking briskly.

It wasn't that dark. Not really.

Above her thunder rumbled; the first drops of rain began to drum against the skylights. She swore softly. If it started coming down hard, she'd be soaked by the time she made it to the car. Usually, she carried an umbrella when she walked, but today she'd left it at home.

Funny, how in the Catacombs it was easier to remember the fear. To believe that Bruner was alive. That she had seen him

(*Ride a little pony into town*)

in the restaurant.

Jesus, stop spooking yourself. You're perfectly safe. It's just your imagination running wild again. The way it did when you were a kid; the way it did at the restaurant last night.

She wished she had called Ron anyway. It would have been reassuring to see the headline in black and white: ESCAPING KILLER SLAIN BY POLICE. But the library was probably closing up by now. She'd call and find out when she got home, if old M & M weren't breathing down her neck. Maybe she'd go tomorrow, if the library was open Sundays. She didn't have to get to work until noon tomorrow. She'd get up early; in the Catacombs it was easy to believe that she couldn't take another whole day of uncertainty.

Out of habit she paused to fumble in her purse for her keys, found them, and clutched them in her right hand so that the key to the Toyota stuck out like a weapon. Somewhere, years ago, she'd read an article on self-defense in some housewives' magazine that recommended holding car keys at the ready. So you could get into the car fast or, if you didn't make it that far, jab the attacker in the eyes.

Take that, fucker! Now, drop that gun, or I'll really nail you good with this here ignition key—

She grimaced wryly as she passed the electrical closet. Pretty silly, all right. Still, it gave her some pathetic measure of security.

A sudden crash of lightning made her freeze in her tracks. A near hit. In the aftermath the Catacombs seemed strangely quiet. It took a few seconds to realize that the faint hum that normally emanated from the electrical closet had ceased. Probably struck the power line, then. The electricity would be off in the shops, which meant that the computer was down at Doubleday and poor Carl was going out of his mind. Talk about luck; she had gotten out just in time.

As she started walking again, the power hummed back on. She was almost to the end of the long corridor when a horrible thought occurred to her: What if Maggie and Murray had been right? What if she was creating this Bruner thing out of thin air? Maybe seeing him in the restaurant was a crystallization of her fears that Maggie would leave her. Leave poor little Avra all alone in the dark.

Christ, was she really that twisted, that manipulative? She couldn't afford to start seeing a psychiatrist again. There wasn't any insurance—

Behind her the metallic click of a doorknob turning. A small sound, nearly swallowed by the drum of rain against the roof. Yet Avra heard and in some instinctive way understood. Understood, by that one tiny sound, that Maggie was wrong after all, and she, Avra, had been right.

She whirled. Facing her in the dimness stood the figure of a man—a man she once again recognized, though this time his features were hidden by darkness. She paused, unwilling to believe her instincts, for to believe what she saw was to accept an emotion far more intense and horrible than fear.

The Shadow in the doorway.

She hesitated seconds too long. It moved toward her as if to envelop her.

Avra cried out softly, more a moan than a scream. She turned and tried to run. But his hands were upon her, and his grip was fearsomely strong. He caught her from behind, one arm diagonally across her chest, holding her back. The other arm moved low, found the hem of her dress, and yanked it up. She thrashed, arcing her spine, whipping her head back with the hopes of striking his face with her skull.

A swift jab of pain burned her thigh, as if she'd been stung by a wasp. His grip eased slightly; she took advantage and, with a surge of forward motion that used every reserve of her strength, pulled away from him.

For God's sake RUN

RUN Avra

Time froze. Seconds passed with agonizing slowness. Her limbs grew heavy, her movements thick and languid, as if she waded through water instead of air.

She took three staggering steps toward the perpendicular turn in the hallway. By the third step her body no longer supported its weight. Her foot touched the floor, and the downward momentum continued until she sank to her knees, then forward onto all fours . . . then settled the length of her body against the cool concrete.

Do you even hear *me, Avra?*

In her last dimming instant of consciousness she saw the Shadow, swooping low to embrace her.

11

On the couch in her stylish cream-and-pastel-yellow living room, Helen Devereaux sat, legs tucked beneath her, and dialed Feinman's number for the seventh time that day. From the bedroom just off the hall came the high-pitched lilt of Amelie's voice as she played with the Scarlett O'Hara doll. It was a Saturday, and Jake never saw patients on the weekend. Those two days he reserved for Helen and Amelie.

It was now four-thirty in the afternoon, and Helen was honestly worried. During the months she had been seeing Jake Feinman, she had never known him to be ill. True, he was sixty years old, but he seemed younger, and in robust health. Last night, in the restaurant, she had sensed something was terribly wrong. When he had returned to the table after a mysterious absence, he did not eat, merely rearranged his shrimp and rice with his fork. She noticed as well a subtle change in his countenance: in the candlelight his face seemed paler, slacker . . . suddenly old. For the first time since she had met him, he looked his age.

Several years before, her father had died of a heart attack. She had adored her father; he had encouraged her, against her mother's wishes, to attend law school. Her mother was southern, old fashioned, her father a Yankee liberal, a world traveler. Daughter and father presented a united front against the mother. It was Helen who had been talking with him that morning before the attack's onset, before either of them knew what would happen later that day. She had been impressed with how aged her father looked that day, how pale and gray his complexion had become. And the stricken look in his eyes. . . .

Jake's eyes had looked much the same as he had returned to the table in the restaurant. And when he left early from Amelie's little party, Helen became convinced that he was seriously ill. But Jake had no other physical symptoms; at least, none he would admit to. And she could not very well insist on taking him to the emergency room on the basis of his feeling tired after a hectic week. She could only let him go home, and then worry about him.

It had struck her last night for the first time that he was almost two decades older than she. She had always known that he was sixty—he did not lie about his age, as other men did; he seemed proud of the fact that he looked younger—but it had never occurred to her that he would live, at most, another fifteen or twenty years, then leave her a widow.

If he made it that long. Cordless receiver pressed against her ear, she listened as Jake's number rang unanswered for the twelfth time. She had called earlier, at ten and eleven that morning. Each time, she had let the phone ring several times before hanging up. Thereafter, she had called at roughly one-hour intervals, to no avail.

A disturbing tableau formed in her mind: Jake, sick and struggling to answer the phone . . . and, having finally succeeded (too late, alas, to hear anything but a dial tone), now lay dead or dying, receiver clutched in his hand.

All very melodramatic. But too plausible, given his odd behavior last night. He had promised that she could call to check on him in the morning, that he would make arrangements to spend the day with her and Amelie to make up for Friday's curtailed birthday celebration. Helen clicked the control on the receiver from TALK to OFF and set it down on the glass coffee table beside the couch. Childish of her, to let her imagination frighten her like this. She hadn't done so in years.

He was off somewhere running errands. He had simply forgotten.

No, that one wouldn't work. Jake's memory was phenomenal; she had never known him to forget anything.

When she first met Jake Feinman, she had thought immediately of marriage. Initially, she was ashamed by her reaction; she had been raised by her mother to believe she was nothing without a man, but she had rebelled against the notion. She thought she had overcome it.

But the year after she left David had been the hardest of all. Mother had been right—she felt bereft, incomplete. And guilty for Amelie's sake. The girl needed a father. David had visitation rights, but he rarely saw his daughter. For Amelie's birthday he had mailed a gift to the house—*mailed* it, and the man lived in Orlando, less than two hours away. He hadn't even called to find out what Amelie thought of the gift.

No, she didn't need a man. Amelie actually seemed happier now that David was gone (or was Helen projecting her own feelings of relief?). But shame had given way to hope. Jake Feinman was gracious, sophisticated . . . older. He possessed a curiously old-world charm; Helen got the impression that his family was German, though he never spoke of them. He emanated security, and she found it more than a little ironical that he physically resembled her father. Amelie adored Jake, and the feeling was clearly mutual. David had scarcely paid attention to his own daughter.

As for Helen—well, she did love him, but in a far different way than she had loved David. There was little sexual fire, but much affection—the opposite of her and David's stormy relationship. All David wanted from a woman was passion, and when that was spent, he quickly turned to another.

At times Helen wondered why he had bothered to marry her. Perhaps he had wanted a child—or had she been so desperate for the public legitimacy of marriage that she had pressured him into it?

With Jake there was affection, even occasional hints of desire . . . but, like David, he was an intensely private person. In some deep recess of her mind she found certain things about Jake Feinman disturbing.

He was neat to the point of obsessiveness, for example. But such hang-ups, she told herself, were unimportant. In time, perhaps, she could help him over such things.

The way you helped David, right?

And then there was his reaction to animals. For all his affection toward Amelie, Jake showed no trace of warmth toward Goose, Helen's nine-year-old Manx cat. Instead, he had tensed as Goose, yowling for affection, approached for the first time. The cat had stopped an inch short of Jake's ankle, peered critically up at the man, then withdrew with sudden, silent hostility.

Sorry, old boy, I'm allergic, Jake had said charmingly. Helen had apologized. And she had known immediately that Jake was lying. She watched him that evening. Even though poor Goose was thereafter confined to the guest bedroom, he'd left hair all over the couch where Jake sat, and those hairs soon covered Jake's silk suit. If he were truly allergic, symptoms would soon follow.

They never did. For all his good humor there

had been a note in his voice—hard as flint, and as cold. Almost spiteful.

Too polite, of course, to say that he hated cats.

And perhaps she'd imagined it. She was, after all, a trial lawyer, and she'd become too obsessed with judging, evaluating, everyone—facial expressions, body language, tone of voice, and only to a small extent what they actually *said*—so here she was, doing it to Jake. Too critically, of course, because she was concerned that he be a suitable father for Amelie.

Relax, for God's sake. He's a human being. Who gives a damn if he doesn't like cats? He was probably bitten by one as a child. . . .

More than just cats, though. There was the weeknight they were riding in Jake's elegant Mercedes when a squirrel darted across heavily trafficked Fowler Avenue. The car in front of them had crushed its lower legs, and it was trying—unsuccessfully—to drag itself off the roadway with its front paws. Certainly Jake would have avoided it if he could, but the Mercedes was hemmed in by cars in either lane. Jake was forced to drive over the poor creature, which was still pathetically struggling to get out of the way when the Mercedes's wheels went over it.

Amelie burst into tears, and Helen had struggled hard not to join in. Jake never flinched.

For the briefest flash of time the coolness in his eyes sickened her. And then he began to tell Amelie a silly little story about how the squirrel was happy now and felt no pain. He was probably wearing a squirrel halo and little squirrel wings, and clutching a harp in his little white paws. At that very moment he was drifting on a pink cloud toward Squirrel Heaven, where the sun always shone and he would always have all the acorns he ever wanted, already shelled and lovingly presented by adoring lady squirrel angels. . . .

Amelie stopped crying and began to giggle.

Obviously, he had shown no dismay for Amelie's sake. He had been thinking only of the child. . . .

Yet there was no denying he was a very private person. He had invited them to his house only once. Not so strange, really. He had little furniture, and never cooked; it only made sense for the three of them to spend their free time at Helen's house. After all, Amelie's toys were there. And there was something vast and desolate about Jake's house. And oppressive. There were dead bolts everywhere, locks on all the windows. The previous owner had been intensely paranoid, Jake had explained. He'd bought the place intending to remove the locks—until he'd learned about all the break-ins in the area. Oppressive, maybe, but cheaper than installing an electronic security system.

During that one visit Amelie had run in and out of every room, then said:

This house is too big for just you, Uncle Jake!

Jake had smiled. And after a quick, knowing

glance at Helen, had said: *Would you like to come live here with me someday, Amelie?*

The girl had shrugged. *That depends. Which room is mine?*

The adults had smiled at each other. At last Helen was sure that Jake's intentions matched her own. After that comment she had ceased her internal debate over whether she was wrong to want marriage for marriage's sake.

There was Amelie to think of, after all.

After a moment's reflection Helen picked up the phone again, switched it to TALK, and dialed. Not Feinman's number this time, but the operator. A voice, bored and distant, replied.

"Yes, Operator. Can you check a number for me, please? It's been ringing off the hook for several hours, and I know that the party is home. It might be out of order."

A pause, while the operator presumably considered the request. Helen gave the number, then was put on hold. After some time the operator came back on the line.

"That number's in working order, ma'am. No problems reported with the line. Your party must be somewhere where they can't hear the phone."

"Thank you, Operator." She switched the phone off and set it aside. It was not the answer she'd hoped for. As she closed her eyes, an image, unwanted, formed behind her lids: her father's pale, stricken face the day he had died.

Or was it Jacob Feinman's?

For a moment Helen stared through the pale yellow sheers covering the bay window. Outside, the sky was darkening with storm clouds. Soon the rain would start coming down, hard.

She rose and went to tell Amelie that they were going for a ride.

To the drum of rain against skylights Bruner bent low over his prize. He had not expected Avra this soon, not for another half hour; the watch's glowing dial showed four thirty-eight P.M. Yet it was all to his benefit, as if Celia and the others had intervened to ensure Avra would walk down this hallway alone.

She lay facedown, breathing shallowly. With a touch that approached a caress he slid a hand beneath her shoulder, her breast, and rolled her upper torso toward him.

Her eyelids fluttered. She stirred under his hands, groaned, and stilled again. The ketamine had done its work. In the semidarkness her skin appeared a pale silver-gray. Unconscious, she had lost the air of suspicion that had aged her. Her expression was slack, innocent, as she breathed through parted lips. He could see her as she really was now, see traces of his blue angel.

In a rare moment of self-indulgence Bruner reached for the chopstick—how artistic, how stylish, how like Marie—and eased it from her thick coil of dark hair. Gently, he slipped a hand beneath her neck. The skin beneath his fingers was supple, firm, smooth, the skin of a child. With one hand he lifted her head; with his other, freed her hair. Thick, perfumed, soft as down, it spilled onto his arm. His hand trembled as he stroked it. He leaned forward and pressed his face against it.

The brush of it against his skin aroused him. This new Avra, this strange blending of woman and child, was compelling, erotic. He remembered how she had struggled against the touch of his hand upon her thigh.

To possess her at last. His Avra. . . .

(Darla)

Distant footsteps abruptly drew him back to the present. He rose, pulse quickening. But the steps were already receding; they belonged to someone headed in the opposite direction, from one of the southward stores—Victoria's Secret or Brooks Brothers—to the parking garage.

Still, Bruner took the warning to heart. He could not afford to lose time. The ketamine's effects would not last long. He stooped down, pushed Avra into a half-sitting position, and slipped his arms under hers, embracing her from behind.

He was just able to lift her. At first he chided himself for growing weak. Certainly he had lifted others with more ease—and then he realized that he was unaccustomed to the weight of an adult body, especially a tall one, almost his height. With difficulty he got her into the closet and pulled the canvas bag up over her face, her beautiful hair. He did not pull the drawstring taut. He wanted to be sure she could breathe. It would be too heartbreaking to come this close, only to have her suffocate.

He let her sag to the floor of the closet, then shut the unlocked door behind him as he stepped back into the maze.

Three and a half minutes to drag her into the waiting van, then depart. He had timed it all very carefully. The drug's effects would not wear off until well after they had reached the safety of Riverhills.

When the radar struck again, Maggie was sitting next to Murray on the sagging sofa in his claustrophobic living room. They had returned ten minutes before from picking up the van at the shop; Maggie left the Datsun back at Willow Street, and Murray brought them back here. The heat was worst afternoons around four or five, when the white house was like an oven.

Murray's apartment—a tiny second-floor apartment above a garage, separate from the landlady's house—was better, though it had only two ancient window units, one in the bedroom, and one in the living room. Maggie despised the place. The walls that divided it into three tiny rooms were more room dividers than real walls, hasty work done by the landlady's brother. Not long before, Maggie had seen a rat scurrying across the top of the bedroom wall; it was the last night she'd spent will-

ingly over at Murray's before the air-conditioner
broke at the Willow Street house.

Right now the window unit in the living room
rattled at full blast, blowing gusts of mildew-
scented air while Maggie scanned the movie list-
ings in the *Tribune*. Murray was in the bedroom,
putting away his laundry. The Hillsboro Eight
had a five-thirty showing of *Days of Thunder* at a
discount rate. It was on the other side of town, but
they probably had more than enough time—

She glanced up at the laminated cypress wall
clock: four thirty-seven.

In that single instant the room changed. The act
of raising her head seemed to take her breath away,
as if someone had struck her hard in the solar
plexus. She expelled air in a gasp. Her head reeled
as if she'd suddenly pitched forward, though she
knew she was sitting perfectly still. Disoriented,
she put out a hand to steady herself, but could find
no support. For a brief flash the dingy surroundings—the clock, the sagging furniture, the scarred
pale green walls—faded into a shadow-gray void.

Falling. Sinking. Then . . . *nothing*. Nothing at
all: an emptiness that was far more terrifying than
the usual anxiety. In all the times she had experienced the radar, it had never been like this—dead,
cold *nothingness*. Whatever had happened was bad,
very bad.

From some far distant locus in her brain a silent
voice said,

Avra's gone

When she came to herself, she was standing, rigid and trembling. The *Friday Extra* section had fallen from her grasp and fluttered across the floor and the orange crate that served as Murray's coffee table.

Murray stood frowning in the doorway, Jason at his ankles. "Maggie, what on earth—?"

Unable to answer, she stared at him until he crossed the tiny room and put a hand on her arm.

"Avra," she said hoarsely. She realized he would think her crazy, but at the moment she was too stunned to come up with a plausible lie, and far too frightened for Avra's sake to care.

Disapproval and disbelief subtly altered his expression of concern. "Maggie . . ." he began.

Her answer was swift but quiet. "I know what you're going to say, and I don't care. Something's happened to her. You can think I'm nuts all you want, but something's *happened*." Her voice rose on the last word.

His face was always expressive, sometimes comically so, and she could easily follow his thoughts. At first he was going to argue with her, then clearly thought better of it . . . then his eyes brightened as he hit upon the perfect method for reasoning her out of it. And through it all she saw his attempt to hide his shocked reaction:

My God, she's a lot worse off than I thought. . . . How could I have known her all this time and not noticed she was this nuts?

He glanced at the time before finally speaking.

His tone was careful, neutral. "You said Avra works till—what, five o'clock today?"

She nodded.

"It's twenty till now. Call her at the bookstore and see if she's okay." Simple enough. And clearly meaning: *And when you find out that she's fine, maybe I can try reasoning with you. . . .*

"I will," she said, without resentment. In fact, she felt grateful for the suggestion. In her panic she had forgotten Ave was still at work. She moved past Murray to the wall phone by the small kitchenette.

In her agitation it took her a few seconds to remember the number. Carl answered on the fourth ring.

"Doubleday Book Shop."

"Carl, hi, this is Maggie. Is Avra free? I had a quick question for her."

"Hi, Maggie. Actually, she's free as a bird. I let her off a little early today; in fact, she left only three or four minutes ago. Sorry."

"Was she feeling all right?" Uttered a little too quickly, a little too anxiously.

"What? Oh. Yeah. She was just a little tired, that's all. Didn't sleep much last night. I understand ya'll are without an air-conditioner these days. That's rough."

Try to sound casual, not rushed . . . "Yeah. Perfect timing. Well, look, I'll catch her at home. Thanks anyway."

"Anytime, Mag. Say, before I forget, would you tell her someone named Chuck called?"

"Chuck? Sure."

"Thanks. Take it easy."

"You too."

She held down the hook for three seconds, aware of Murray's scrutiny. She was fighting to keep from trembling. For some reason she'd known from the beginning that Avra wasn't at the store, but at some dark, shadowy place. Still, she had hoped. . . .

She dialed her own number and let it ring ten times before hanging up. Avra had taken the Toyota, hadn't she? It would take her two or three minutes, at the most, to get home from the store. She looked over at Murray, who sat on the couch. His expression had become guarded.

"Ave left work early a few minutes ago," she said. "She hasn't made it home yet."

His tone was calm, soothingly rational. "It probably takes her five minutes or so just to walk from the store to the parking garage. I bet if you call again in a little while, she'll be there. And even if she isn't—well, it *is* Saturday night, after all. Maybe she ran into that guy who stood her up and he decided to make it up to her. Or maybe she was in the mood for a little fun. . . ."

She forced her outward composure to match his. "Mur, you remember how it was last night. You didn't believe me at first—but Ave *was* upset. It was more than just the guy standing her up, I know—whatever it was, she still won't tell me. But this is worse than last night. I think"—her voice caught in spite of herself—"I think something's happened to her."

"You mean, like she's hurt? Been in an accident or something?" Said kindly.

She nodded. "Something like that." Her voice caught again, and she swallowed hard before she could speak. "Only I don't know what to do this time, don't even know where she *is*. . . ." The sentence faded to a whisper.

The skeptical expression had completely vanished now; Murray's eyes, magnified behind the lenses of his glasses, regarded her with sober concern. When he finally spoke, his tone was no longer patronizing. "I've known you—how long now? A year? And you've never done this thing with Avra before. I don't understand, Mag. Maybe it's real, maybe there's something to it. I admit it blew my mind when I saw Avra walking home early last night. You obviously sensed *something*—and who am I to say twins can't read each other's minds? But at the same time I'd be a liar if I said I wasn't worried about this—especially since it starts happening right when you're supposed to tell Avra you're moving out. I confess, I'm a jealous son of a bitch, and I don't want Ave or your own guilt talking you out of it.

"Have you considered that maybe you're both upset about it and picking up on each other's vibes?"

"It's occurred to me," she answered carefully, struggling against the sense of frustration that Avra was in trouble *now*, and she had no idea where to look for her. "But this isn't the first time this has happened to me. To us."

"What other times were there?"

"It's been a long time since I've felt it this strong. A long time. Twenty-five years." She stopped, unwilling to continue, unwilling to remember further. Until that moment she had not admitted to herself exactly when she had last felt this way . . . or the exact event that had triggered the feeling.

He rose, took her hands, and drew her over to sit on the couch next to him. His voice was very soft, his gaze intent. "Tell me, Maggie. What happened then? Was that when your parents were killed?"

"My mother." She faltered, looked away.

"You mean, they didn't die at the same time?"

Lips pressed tightly together, she shook her head. To her disgust she realized she was very near tears—she, who prided herself on being strong, on always remaining cool and level-headed in the worst crisis. Though he wept unashamedly at the symphony and sentimental movies, Murray had never seen her cry. She swallowed again and said, "No. My dad left us when we were very little—I think we were about two. He died a few months later in a car accident."

"And your mom?"

"She was killed when we were five." She drew

in a breath and tried to steady her voice. "Murdered. Ave and I witnessed it."

He didn't flinch, didn't stir. His gaze remained steady, but Maggie saw the shock in his brown eyes. She knew he wouldn't press her to continue, but mixed in with the panic was an odd relief at finally telling someone else.

"Mama was seeing a man—a horrible man. He seemed so nice at first, but—"

"It's all right," Murray interrupted. She stared blankly at him until she saw that she had pulled her hands from his grasp and was clenching her fists. She relaxed her hands and let Murray take them again.

"—but he was only trying to get close to Avra. That's how it happened. Mama caught him with Avra. Actually, I caught him first, and went to get Mama."

(and maybe if you'd done something yourself—yelled at him to stop, instead of just sneaking back upstairs—maybe Mama wouldn't have died)

She paused and let the flash of guilt pass. She had expected the revelation to be traumatic, but it was curiously anticlimactic. The urge to weep had passed; she felt nothing now except the anxiety. The radar, she'd called it back then.

And the radar was beginning to blot out everything else.

Murray stirred and was clearly about to say something reassuring. Maggie interrupted him.

"When that man—his name was Bruner—"

Amazing, that she could finally say the name aloud, so smoothly, so easily.

"—when Bruner was hurting Ave, I *knew* it, Murray. I was upstairs asleep when it happened, but I *knew* something was wrong. It woke me up, and I went downstairs and found them. And I know something's wrong now." Her tone lightened. "If I'm crazy, then just indulge me. If Avra's okay, it won't really matter, will it? But if she's *not* okay, and we don't do anything—"

His expression was grim. "All right, Maggie. What do you want to do?"

"I—I'm not sure. Usually, I know where to find her, but—"

"Take it easy. Look, why don't I take you back to the house? I bet by the time we get there, she'll be home. And if she isn't, I'll take a little drive around Hyde Park and see if I can find her. Would that make you feel better?"

"Yes. Yes, it would." She looked gratefully at him as they stood up. "Murray—"

"What is it, sweetheart?"

"I love you." She hugged him so fiercely that he stumbled backward and the two of them nearly fell against the couch.

12

Shortly before five o'clock, Helen Devereaux pulled her black Volvo into the curving, tree-lined driveway at 1123 Riverhills Drive. She was relieved to have found the place without difficulty; she had only been to Jake's once before and wasn't all that good at finding her way around. But the directions were simple enough even for her to remember: right off Fowler onto Riverhills, then keep going until you see the one yard almost totally secluded from the road by all those big oaks.

Amelie sat strapped into the passenger's seat, umbrella in one hand, Scarlett O'Hara in the other. She was humming a little nonsense song to the doll and swinging her legs in time to the music. She wore a pair of bright turquoise Osh-Kosh b'Gosh overalls and a white, lace-trimmed T-shirt. There hadn't been time to change, and she'd been a little whiny about it. She was enormously excited about going to Jake's house, but was disappointed when she learned she couldn't get dressed up for him. She had wanted to wear the green dress again, so that she would match the Scarlett doll.

Before them the long driveway branched in two directions: straight ahead to the garage, and off to the right so guests could park by the front door. Helen turned onto the inlet by the front door and brought the Volvo to a stop, then put the transmission in park and set the emergency brake.

"Give me the umbrella, darling." Helen undid her own seat belt and held out her hand. "I need for you to stay here for just a minute." She hadn't told the girl about her concern for Jake, of course; she'd hidden her worry as best she could, pretending that this spur-of-the-moment visit was just for fun.

Amelie's forehead puckered instantly. "But, Mommy, I want to—"

"You'll get to see Uncle Jake, Amelie. But first I've got to knock on the door and make sure he's home. His telephone is broken, so Mommy couldn't call him. This is a surprise visit. Hand me the umbrella, darling."

"Oh." Amelie seemed mollified; surprises were apparently good things. But a note of disappointment crept into her tone as she asked, "You mean maybe he's not here?"

"That's right. And if he isn't, we'll go get some frozen yogurt at the TCBY near here. Is that a deal?"

"Deal," Amelie said gravely. She handed over the umbrella.

"You just stay here, darling. And don't touch the steering wheel or anything."

"I won't." Amelie returned her attention to the doll.

Helen checked the parking brake one more time, then left the Volvo running so Amelie could benefit from the air conditioning. Helen would have trusted no other six-year-old in a vehicle with the motor running, but Amelie had been born a remarkably obedient child. She would sit quietly and play with Scarlett O'Hara until her mother returned.

Helen stepped outside onto the concrete driveway, then slammed the car door behind her. Outside, the air was an oppressive ninety-five degrees, and cloyingly humid. The rain would be a welcome, if temporary, respite from the heat. She tucked the umbrella under her arm and headed for the front door. The exterior of the house was white stucco and dark stained wood—unremarkable, typically Floridian.

She stepped up to the front door and rang the bell, then waited. She counted silently to thirty before ringing again—give the man some time to answer the door, after all—then repeated the procedure. Count to thirty, ring the bell.

No answer.

She knocked in case the bell was broken. The wood was heavy, and she skinned her knuckles.

She tried the knob. Locked, of course. The next step was to get a look inside, but there were no windows along the front. The paranoid owner again.

The image of her father's face, gray lipped and stricken, came to mind again. It had happened so quickly, so unfairly; there had been no time to brace herself against the shock of losing him. She'd flown home for the Christmas holidays her third year of law school, and the morning her father died, the two of them had sat at the kitchen table, laughing over coffee. At some remark made at her mother, Leila's, expense, no doubt; to the end it was the two of them against her. Leila was still in bed, and father and daughter had risen early so they could at least see each other. That was the running gag that year—Leila dragging her daughter daily to shopping malls, bringing her home in the evening, exhausted. Flown across the country to spend her entire vacation inside a damn mall.

She'd tried several times to recall the exact content of that last conversation, to remember what they had been giggling at. She remembered only that, in the middle of their laughter, her father, still grinning, had rested his hand on her shoulder, briefly—no more than a second—and said,

I'm so proud of you, Helen.

He said it lightly. Of all things he detested sentimentality most. Just the quick touch on her shoulder, and then he was laughing again. But for a moment his eyes had been very bright.

By evening, when she and Leila returned from their shopping adventure, he was sitting alone in the dark living room in his recliner. Helen knew even before Mother snapped the light on that something was terribly wrong. Even before she saw the look of dull fright in his eyes. . . .

(Jake's eyes had looked just like that, hadn't they? The eyes of a man who sees the end of his world approaching)

He'd refused to tell them his symptoms. *Tired*, he said. *Just tired*.

(Hadn't Jake said the same thing?)

But she could guess from his grayish pallor, from the obvious pain he was in, from the way he held his left arm. All he wanted, he said, was aspirin. Leila went upstairs to get it; Helen went in the kitchen to phone for an ambulance. By the time she hung up and went back into the living room, Leila stood shrieking in front of the recliner. The aspirin and water were on the carpet.

The worst of it was, she should have been able to help him, should have done *something*—but she had thought there was enough time.

Jake, are you in there?

Despite the heat she felt an unexpected chill. Jake could be lying helpless this very moment inside the huge, silent house. A sudden, irrational, yet compelling conviction seized her: there *was* someone dead in the house. She *felt* it, just as she had the day she walked into the living room and saw her father sitting quietly in the dark. The

sense of death was strong, almost palpable. It settled over her, as heavy and still as the humid air.

For God's sake, why are you doing *this to yourself?
This isn't something outside you; this is something you're
making up.*

Anxiety, that's all it was. Was she that afraid of
losing Jake? That afraid of the fact that he was
older, and most likely to die soon?

No. He had promised to see them today. And
Jake never forgot.

She was careful to compose her expression before she turned to face the Volvo, but instead of
climbing back inside, she went over to the garage
and tried to peer into the window. It was half obscured by a scraggly rain tree; she scratched her
legs trying to get close enough, but it was pointless. The window was so darkly tinted that she
couldn't tell whether Jake's Mercedes was inside.
The previous owner, again, paranoid that someone
might peek inside his garage. She wasn't sure, but
thought she saw the dim outline of Jake's car.

As she headed back toward the Volvo, she heard
a car pass by on the road and looked up hopefully
—Jake?—but the road was obscured by trees. The
car passed on, unseen.

She went over to the Volvo and opened the passenger side door. Amelie, who had been engrossed
in the imaginary adventures of Scarlett, stared up
at her blankly.

"Amelie, darling," she said. "I'm going to be a
little while longer, okay? I think the doorbell's bro-

ken. I'm going around back to knock on the sliding glass door. This door is too thick for Uncle Jake to hear me knock."

Not the most airtight lie, but it worked. The girl nodded, and Helen closed the door over her.

Knowing Jake, the back door would be locked, if not bolted; he constantly worried about burglars. But if she could get a good look inside the sliding door or one of the windows—

To do what? Catch a glimpse of him lying dead on the floor? And what'll you tell Amelie? "Sorry, darling, but we'll get our yogurt just as soon as I call an ambulance for Uncle Jake"?

As she made her way around the garage to the back of the house, it began to rain.

It was a risk, Bruner knew, driving the white delivery van up to the house on Riverhills. But not as much a risk as trying to get Avra unseen into the Mercedes, which now sat in an open-air-mall parking lot. It would have taken too long, besides; the lot was a good thirty-five minutes out of the way, and by then Avra might be conscious enough to struggle. Oh, he could dose her again, but ketamine was tricky stuff, and he needed her clear and cognizant for tonight's events.

No, better this way. Someone might spot the van on the street, but once he pulled into the driveway, he would be invisible from the street. And once in the garage, he was home free.

Slightly behind him and to his right came a muffled noise, a sound between a moan and a sigh. He glanced down at the laundry bag on the floor of the van. Avra was stirring slightly. No matter. She might not be sedated to the degree required for surgical anesthesia anymore, but she would remain in a twilight state for a good while longer. And the ketamine would keep her conveniently uncoordinated.

As he turned off Fowler Avenue onto Riverhills, the first drops of rain began to fall. First, one lazy, fat drop over here, one over there. Then another, and another, the rhythm quickening until, as he came out of the turn and headed straight down Riverhills, the blackened sky pelted fierce, sharp rain.

By the time he reached the entrance to the driveway, it was pouring. He was unconcerned.

(rain, after all, washes away traces)

He would park the van in the garage and take Avra into the house from there. No one would see.

"Mama?" Avra asked petulantly beneath the canvas, then fell silent. Her voice was high pitched, thin, the voice of a sleepy child.

Bruner smiled indulgently as he wheeled the van onto the concrete driveway. He did not fear her wakening; at the moment he feared nothing. He was omnipotent, invincible, godlike, and no power was great enough to interfere with his perfect plan.

Yet, the shock of what he saw as he rounded the driveway's curve forced the air from his lungs in a single gasp: a black Volvo, parked in the inlet near the house's front entrance. Without thought Bruner jammed his foot against the brake pedal. The van fishtailed slightly on the rain-slicked concrete, then lurched to a stop. A murmur came from the canvas laundry bag.

His first reaction was one of disbelief; this was not happening. Such an unkind reality could not be permitted to interfere with his plan. He squeezed his eyes shut. When he opened them again, the black car remained. And through the veil of rain and the tinted glass of the Volvo's windows, he perceived a small, dark form on the passenger's side. The small head turned to stare. Amelie was alone, which meant that her mother was somewhere nearby.

Fool that he was, he'd forgotten he had promised to visit them today. A simple call this morning, another lie, would have prevented this. What was *happening* to him? He never made such mistakes—

(Easy. No reason to assume they know anything. Gently, gently.)

Despite the initial shock his instinct still operated. He grasped the automatic door-opener—borrowed from the Mercedes—and depressed the control. The garage door rumbled upward, slowly. Too slowly.

As he pulled the van into the garage with as much speed as possible, he caught a flash of movement to his left. Helen, under the shelter of a bright yellow umbrella, had apparently come from the backyard and was following him into the garage. She was close enough so that they passed within a few feet of each other at the garage entrance. Through the glass they exchanged shocked glances as the van shot into the garage. He saw all too clearly her frown of disbelief, and though he could not hear over the rumble of the van's engine and the rain, he read the single word her lips formed.

Jake?

He pulled past her into the garage and cut off the van's engine. His first impulse was to close the garage door and hope that it barred her entry or, better yet, caught her unawares and crushed her—and then he remembered Amelie, waiting outside in the car. Easier to control her if she witnessed nothing.

And it would have been too late to keep Helen out of the garage, at any rate. A glance in the outside mirror revealed her approaching the driver's side of the van, umbrella closed and dripping. He waited, motionless, until she was alongside him again, staring up at him through the window. Her expression was a mixture of curiosity, surprise, and suspicion. As she caught sight of his clothes, her frown deepened.

"Jake? What on earth's going on?"

A cold serenity descended on him. Feinman would not have known what to do; but then, Feinman was dead.

Bruner smiled down at her and pressed the garage door control.

Utterly confused, Helen watched as Jake pulled the van past her. She'd been returning from the backyard, and had succeeded only in getting mud all over her shoes. Getting a look inside the house was impossible. Bizarrely, the sliding glass door and all the windows were covered with metal hurricane shutters.

As if someone were expecting one hell of a storm; or, more gruesomely, as if someone had died in there. Months ago, instead of hours. The place was sealed like a mausoleum.

And then she'd heard a car pull into the driveway. It was definitely *not* the Mercedes; the engine sounded far too rough. Still, she'd half run through the mud, around the side of the garage.

At first the sight of the white van had disappointed her. Not Jake. A repairman or delivery person. She approached the van, ready to explain to the driver that Doctor Feinman was not at home, when the garage door had opened only feet from her. Taken aback, she had peered in the van and seen Feinman. She called to him, then followed him into the garage, holding her breath at the nauseating smell of the van's exhaust.

Inside, the Mercedes was conspicuously missing. Perhaps he had taken it to be repaired . . . but Jake would never accept such a replacement vehicle. When he took his car to the Mercedes dealership on Florida Avenue, he always insisted on another Mercedes. And he was the type to rent a nice car himself rather than be seen in this old, beaten-up delivery truck.

There was an explanation—*had* to be one—but at present it eluded her. Frowning, she snapped the umbrella shut and stepped up to the driver's side of the van.

And saw that Jake was wearing a gray jumpsuit —a coverall, something a mechanic might wear. Almost as if he *wanted* to be mistaken for a repairman. She met his gaze through the van window. His expression was that of a man who has just been caught doing something he is not supposed to be doing.

That look unsettled her. She frowned at him with honest suspicion. "Jake? What on earth's going on?"

Ridiculous thoughts filled her head. He worked for the CIA; he had multiple-personality disorder; he moonlighted on the weekends as a mechanic. She dismissed them all.

A loud rumble startled her. She jerked her head. Behind them the garage door lowered shut, blotting out the rain, the Volvo, Amelie. The sight was somehow ominous.

When she turned back to look up at Jake, he was smiling.

For some reason the smile troubled her even more than his fleeting look of guilt, though she could not have said why.

Still smiling, Jake rolled down the window and leaned toward her. Now the explanation would come. She could not begin to guess what it might be.

"Step back, please, darling," Jake said. Even before she recognized the object in his right hand, she experienced a horrible, insightful certainty: This was not the man she knew. This was not Jacob Feinman. It was Feinman's body, but this was someone else.

She saw now what disturbed her about the smile. The eyes, the terrible coldness there. The look in Jake's eyes at the dull, horrid sound the Mercedes's wheels made as they passed over the squirrel's body. . . .

No. Something far worse than coldness. Something she hadn't wanted to see, hadn't admitted to herself. Something brutal.

"Step back, please," Jake said again. He had raised his arm; he was pointing a gun at her through the open window.

For a moment she was too stunned by the absurdity of the situation to feel fear. And despite the look in Jake's eyes she could not believe he would actually kill her. He just wanted her to get away from the van, that was all. She complied. She took a step back, then another.

Jake seemed satisfied. And then he carefully began to take aim.

She gasped aloud. Of course. He was such a tidy man; he didn't want to get splattered. She had only an instant to be bitter about the depths of her own stupidity. She should have seen. The signs had been there. But she had not *wanted* to see them. She moved away from him until her back was pressed against the garage wall.

"Oh God," she said swiftly. "*Amelie—*"

Jake fired.

13

Get up, Mama said.

Avra stirred. She was floating someplace vast and dark and serene, and didn't want to wake up. She was bodiless, free—and at the same time distantly aware of movement around her, of something vibrating against her back. She opened her eyes and saw . . . Nothing. Grayness. As she stared into it, the grayness began to crawl with colors, red and yellow squiggles. Fascinated, she watched until their motion nauseated her, then closed her eyes.

Get up, Mama said again. She was standing next to the edge of Avra's bed, wearing her blue bathrobe. It must have been the middle of the night, but Mama didn't look like she'd been sleeping. Her dark hair was done up in a French twist, the way she wore it when she was going out, and she had on makeup. She was so strikingly beautiful—pret-

tier than her daughters, Avra had always thought
—that Avra began to weep.

It's not the time to cry, Mama said, not ungently.
She was like Maggie that way; she hated tears,
never wept. At least, not where the girls could see
her. *Get up, honey.*

Avra stopped crying and sat. Her body moved
without effort, as though it weighed nothing.
Mama took her hand and helped her from the bed.
Avra rose and, looking down at herself, saw that
she was wearing her blue-and-white flowered
nightie. She had forgotten how very *tall* Mama
was. . . .

How tall she had seemed to a five-year-old. They
were standing in the darkness in the girls' old bedroom. The bed opposite Avra's hadn't been slept
in.

"Where's Maggie?"

Mama shook her head. *Magdalen can't help us right
now. We've got to get out of here, honey. We've got to go.*

"What for?"

You know why

"No, I don't."

The Shadow's here

Avra tried to pull away, but Mama gave her arm
a firm tug.

Come on

She pulled the girl forward. Avra staggered, off
balance, toward the doorway. This was the house
in New Orleans, all right, surreal and distorted in
size and shape, but reproduced in detail. There

stood the red metal table and chairs with white alphabet blocks painted on them; there, on the carefully made bed, lay the Magdalen doll, resting on the rose print comforter. They passed into the hallway, stepping from the polished wood floor onto pale olive carpet. Avra closed her eyes. The house was dark, yet the colors were painfully vivid.

She did not keep her eyes shut for long. They quickly rounded the hallway and paused at the top of the staircase. Something black and devouring and endless hovered at the bottom of the stairs. The Shadow.

Avra suddenly realized that she was holding a dead woman's hand. She understood then: Mama was taking her down to die. She struggled free from her mother's grasp.

"No—!"

Honey, we've got to go down the stairs.

The stairs led down to the kitchen. Avra knew what waited there.

There's no other way out of the house, Mama said.

She was going to die.

Avra, honey, you're just going to have to trust me. And Mama grabbed her hand and pulled.

At first Avra stumbled, uncoordinated, down the stairs. But Mama's touch brought serenity, comfort. She relaxed and found herself floating easily down the stairs, one hand in Mama's, the other brushing against the papered wall for support.

Mama's right hand glided smoothly over the white wooden banister, scarcely touching it.

Downstairs, the light was on in the kitchen.

Avra could see Bruner now. He sat at the dinette table clasping a juice glass of whiskey, staring pensively at some far-distant point. He looked very young, early thirties at the outside, with thinning blond hair and eyes that were an eerie fluorescent blue.

At the sight of him the sense of movement and vibration against her back ceased. The abrupt stillness brought with it the sense of something ominous about to occur. She stopped on the stairs.

Don't be afraid, Avra. He can't see us.

"I can't go down there—"

He can't see us. We've got to help Magdalen.

"He has Maggie?"

We've got to help her.

"I *can't*—"

Don't be afraid. He can't hurt us anymore, honey. We're already dead. . . .

"No—" Avra began to weep. It was true, then— she was dead after all, and Mama was taking her to face the inevitable. . . .

You can't cry now, honey. You've got to help Magdalen.

From where he sat, Bruner couldn't possibly have seen the two on the staircase. Nevertheless, he looked up, shining eyes unfocused . . . and smiled.

Avra shrank against the wall. "We can't go down there, Mama. He knows we're coming."

Mama smiled herself. *He thinks he knows. Remember, he can't hurt us anymore.* She took Avra's hand; her touch magically dissolved fear. Avra straightened, calmed.

He can't hurt you anymore, honey.

"Because I'm already dead, right?"

No answer.

Yet, even if it were true, the fact no longer seemed as frightening. They began gliding downward once again.

A startling interruption: a sound from outside the house, but somehow very nearby. A stranger's voice, a woman's, crystal sharp. Four musical notes, each sung so clearly that Avra saw them as stabs of changing colors, brilliant oranges and reds. The pitch ascended quickly, hysterically, to a piercing crescendo.

Oh God Amelie

An explosion, dull and contained. The noise triggered a dance of brilliant orange and yellow squiggles against her closed eyelids, then faded to gray silence.

Bruner crawled down from the van and stepped over Helen's legs, then bent down to examine the wound made by the .22. Helen, elegant and refined in life, was reduced by death to the same ungainliness as any corpse. In her last second she had retreated toward the garage wall, as if the extra distance of a few inches might afford her some protection. (He had seen to it that she had no time to run.) At the moment of the bullet's impact she had been thrown back against the wall, then fallen/slid so that she half sat, shoulders and head propped up, legs sprawled wide in front of her. The left side of her head was half turned toward the wall; her mouth and eyes were open.

Bruner turned her chin toward him with the gloved tip of his right index finger. He had touched her in this way before, when he had moved to kiss her, only now the movement seemed to him infinitely more sensual. The necessity of her death stirred no remorse in him. She had been nothing more than a vehicle through which he might reach Amelie.

Yet the act had brought, as it always did, an explosive, deep release, and left behind a euphoria more powerful than that induced by any drug. It had been a long time since he had killed an adult; almost twenty-five years.

There was a small, dark red hole in the center of her left eyebrow. The skin around it was darkened and slightly puffed. Fortunately, there wasn't much blood, the reason Bruner had chosen the .22 in the first place. As far as he could tell, he hadn't a drop on himself, though there was blood obscuring Helen's left eye, blood down the front of her silk blouse, a small spatter of blood on the wall beside her face. Still, the .22 made for a much neater kill than a larger caliber weapon.

And it was quieter. With the help of the closed
garage door and the deafening rain outside, Amelie
would have heard nothing. But he would have to
decide very quickly what to do with the child.

He withdrew his finger. Helen's head lolled
back to rest against her left shoulder and the wall.
The appearance of the Volvo had temporarily
thrown him off balance. He had reacted, as he always did when the situation called for violence,
without a single conscious thought. In the midst of
the deep pleasure triggered by her death, he was
aware that there would be consequences to deal
with.

For he had broken his own maxim: he had killed
someone he knew. What if her disappearance
could be traced to him? What if she had told someone where she was going? Certainly the police
would question him, since he knew her. What if
someone saw the Volvo turning into his driveway?

The Volvo was still sitting out there. And Amelie was inside.

He felt a wave of self-pity. Not Amelie. He
could not kill her, not yet; he could not bear to
squander her, after all the time he had in-
vested. . . .

But if he waited much longer, she would become
suspicious and venture out of the car. She
wouldn't be able to see into the garage, of course,
but if perchance she wandered out into the street
or a neighbor's yard, and drew someone's attention—

As much as the thought of leaving behind a mess, especially such an incriminating one, distressed him, Bruner rose and left Helen where she lay. The child first. That was the most important thing.

He would have to move quickly, before Avra recovered enough from the ketamine to offer resistance. Out of habit he closed the door to the van, fished his keys out of one of the big work-suit pockets and removed his gloves, then let himself into the house.

Seconds later, he stood at the front door with an umbrella taken from a stand in the foyer. The rain had eased somewhat, but was still coming down hard enough so that Bruner dashed instead of walked to the passenger side of the Volvo. The door was unlocked.

He had to remind himself to smile down at Amelie as he opened the door, but her anxious little face brightened so at the sight of him that his smile became sincere.

"Amelie, darling," he said. "Come in out of the rain."

He took her hand as she clutched the doll. Under the shelter of the umbrella they hurried into the house.

He took her to the living room and sat her down on the sofa facing the unused stone fireplace. Had she been a more inquisitive, less obedient child, he would not have risked it. True, he had left nothing incriminating lying around, although there was always a chance she might wander out into the garage.

At first she had inquired rather anxiously about her mother. Helen, Bruner had explained, was feeling unwell. She was in the bathroom and would be returning shortly. His tone conveyed that it was nothing serious, and the girl seemed to accept this. She had brought the beautiful Scarlett O'Hara doll into the house with her, and went back to playing with it. She was so caught up in her imaginary world that he decided it would be safe to leave her.

"Amelie, stay here, please."

She glanced up at him, instantly on the verge of despair. "Where are you going, Uncle Jake?"

He smiled. "Just to check on your mother. I'll be back in just a minute, darling."

She nodded and abruptly went back to Scarlett.

Bruner went back to his bedroom. He felt unclean wandering through the house in the work suit, worried that some incriminating bit of evidence might be transferred from it to the house—but it was not yet time to change. He went into the walk-in closet, and from the highest shelf removed his medical bag and filled a hypodermic syringe with a pediatric dose of Demerol. He capped the syringe and put it in his hip pocket, then went back out into the living room.

He found Amelie on all fours on the carpet, exploring with the Scarlett doll under the coffee ta-

ble. She withdrew from beneath the table—amazingly, without hitting her head—and sat back on
her haunches to direct her bright, intense gaze at
him.

"Where's Mommy?"

"Still sick. Amelie, I'm afraid I'm going to have
to take her to the hospital."

With alarming swiftness her expression metamorphosed into one of anguish; she uttered a wail
and dropped the doll. "Is she going to be okay?"

"Yes, yes, darling. Of course, she'll be all right."
Bruner spread his arms. Amelie ran to him,
clutched his waist, buried her face in his stomach.
The sensation was altogether pleasurable. He
stroked her baby-soft hair. "But you're going to
have to be a big girl and stay here."

Her indignant reply was muffled. "How *come*?"
Real, angry tears now.

"I don't have time to look after both of you. For
your mother's sake I have to hurry. I know you'll
be safe here."

She shook her head, face still buried in his stomach. Bruner took advantage of her inattention to
reach for the syringe in his pocket. He slipped the
cap off with his thumb and, with one swift move,
grasped Amelie's left arm firmly and inserted the
needle into her triceps.

She yowled and tried to pull away, but with
strength and grace born of thirty years' experience, Bruner held her fast until the syringe was
empty and the hypodermic withdrawn.

Outraged, gasping, she raised her dark red, tear-stained face up at him and scowled. "What'd you do *that* for?"

"So you wouldn't get sick too," he replied simply. "It's very contagious. It's bad enough your mother's sick, isn't it?"

She looked away and wouldn't answer him.

He led her back to his bedroom and convinced her to lie down on the bed. In a few minutes she was glassy eyed and breathing regularly. He retrieved the Scarlett doll and laid it gently beside her on the bed. Only then did he dare leave her.

By the time he returned to the van, Avra had freed her head and shoulders from the laundry bag and was struggling to sit. The van reeked of the sour-sweet smell of bile; vomit stained the front of the canvas.

Fortunately, the ketamine hadn't entirely worn off. As Bruner slid open the side door, Avra glanced up at him, but her eyes would not focus. Nystagmus was a common side-effect. As he neared, she withdrew fearfully and moaned, but was still too disoriented and uncoordinated to struggle.

He crouched down and reached for the canvas, ignoring the vomit. He was, after all, a pediatrician, and had long ago learned to accept being vomited, urinated, and defecated upon with good-natured stoicism. He pulled the bag down so that both Avra's arms were free. She lay, panting, against the floor, occasionally able to fix her wandering gaze on him with the peculiar intensity with which a victim beholds a coiled, ready-to-strike viper. Tendrils of her long hair stuck to her face with sweat.

She didn't move when he pressed the auto-injector, loaded with another dose of ketamine, against her upper arm. He did not use the Demerol with her—not yet. For now, it was necessary that she return to consciousness quickly, necessary that she know *what* was happening to her, and *why*.

In the seconds before the drug took effect, her eyes cleared briefly. She looked straight at him and said, with only a slight slur (and a belligerence he found amusing):

"What have you done with Magdalen?"

The corners of his mouth began moving upward —how absurd, her angry accusation, directed at him! Didn't she recognize him? Didn't she realize *he* held her life in his hands? She should be *pleading. . . .*

Yet at the same time, a separate part of his mind reacted to the name. Magdalen. Magdalen. Achingly familiar, but he could not quite—

The sister. My God, the twin! He had entirely forgotten about her existence. She had been eminently forgettable: a silent, sullen, mistrustful child, always jealous of his competition for Avra's affections.

That's right, the suspicious little bitch had come with Marie that night, hadn't she? Marie had al-

ways slept like the dead—she would never have
wakened that night. Not unless someone

(the little bitch*)*

had gotten her up. The sister had warned Marie,
then. It had to have been the sister . . . always
sneaking up on him, always showing up at the precise wrong moment, when he and Avra were finally alone, as if she instinctively knew. . . .

What if she knew *now?*

The revelation stole the breath from Bruner's
lungs. He reached a hand behind him and dropped
backward to a sitting position.

The sister. How could he have let himself forget
her? (Just as he had forgotten about his promise to
Helen and Amelie; he was slipping danger-
ously. . . .) How could he have failed? *How could
Celia not have told him?*

The sister was as much to blame as Avra—perhaps even more so. She, too, would have to pay. He
would need her for the reenactment, yes. Yes. She
must be punished as well. . . .

He stared down at Avra's unconscious, angelic
features. She had spoken of Magdalen. But she was
under the ketamine's influence. How could he be
certain the sister lived in the same area, that she
had not moved across the country? That she even
still lived?

How would he find her and bring her here?

There was a way. In twenty-five years his cun-
ning had never failed him. He would think of
something. Gingerly, deliberately, he turned to-

ward the driver's seat and pulled Avra's shoulder bag from under it. He rifled through it until he located her wallet.

The driver's license—with a photograph that was grossly unflattering—gave her name as Avra E. Kallisti. The address was on Willow Street. So she lived in the Hyde Park area, not far from the restaurant where he first saw her.

Kallisti. The name stirred something in his memory. Greek, wasn't it? Marie's father had been Greek. . . . Her maiden name, yes. So the girls had taken her maiden name—for what purpose? So that he would never be able to find them again?

He smiled grimly, slipped the purse strap over one shoulder, and put the autoinjector into his pocket. Carefully, he lifted Avra under the arms and dragged her clumsily from the van.

It took him longer than he'd expected to get her inside, but at last she lay on the floor of the specially prepared guest room. Like the others it contained no furniture—he'd never intended to have people over—and just as well. No point in providing her with anything that could be used to aid an escape.

Instead, he left her with two items to ponder upon her awakening: the Avra doll and his personal scrapbook, filled with mementos of Celia and the others. In that way her memory would be invoked, and she would be educated as to the role she would play in the plan.

As she would be returning to full consciousness

while he was gone, he closed the bedroom door and locked it from the outside; he'd installed the dead bolt himself that morning. He slipped the key into his chest pocket and reminded himself to stop at the hardware store again while he was out. He'd need another dead bolt for the sister's room.

And a plan, if he could find her, to lure the sister. . . .

He carried Avra's purse and the autoinjector back to the bedroom, changed out of the work suit, and put the three items in the closet safe. After a quick shower and a change into fresh clothes, he went into the kitchen and found the Tampa GTE White Pages. His answer was listed under the *K* 's:

Kallisti, A.
Kallisti, M.

Both at the same address on Willow Street. Bruner tore a piece of paper from the notepad by the empty phone jack (the phones were also locked away in the safe) and copied the number, then folded the paper once and slipped it into his pants pocket.

As he headed back through the living room toward the garage, his thoughts were resolute. He would find a way to bring the sister here; he would not permit his plan to be destroyed.

By the fireplace a flash of white, barely detected by his peripheral vision. He turned, and the sight of Celia brought him to his knees.

The sight of her did not terrify. What terrified him was the silent message he *felt* emanating from her: He had failed. So soon, and he had failed; she and the others were displeased.

Worse than displeased. They were furious, and wanted vengeance.

They wanted *him*.

"No," Bruner whispered. He pitched forward onto his hands, which sank deep into the plush carpet. "The sister. I have to find the sister—"

The realization—whether a direct communication from Celia or the product of his own fevered reasoning, he could not say—struck him with full, cold force then:

He had killed Helen. He had killed someone he knew. And now, even if he killed Amelie—

and yes, he would have to kill Amelie, and very soon. There would be no time to fully enjoy her

—even if he killed Amelie, he would have to leave Florida. Possibly even the country. He was skilled enough at covering his tracks when it came to the death of one stranger, a child with no ties to him. But now he was dealing with the deaths of four people, two of whom he knew.

No matter how perfectly he managed to dispose of all the bodies, all the evidence, the fact was that, because he *knew* Helen and Amelie, the police would question him about their deaths.

Would watch him. Would advise him, perhaps, not to leave town. Eventually, they would find the one small shred of forgotten evidence linking him to the killings.

And if he fled soon after the murders, before the police had a chance to interrogate him, it was tantamount to admitting guilt. They would hunt him down.

He shuddered and lowered himself until he lay facedown, sobbing into the thick wool pile.

So unfair. So grossly unfair. He had done everything in his power to appease the children. He had thought they would *support* him in this. After all, he was trying to bring those truly responsible to justice. But then Helen and Amelie had appeared at the worst possible moment; two more bodies to dispose of. And now, the sister. . . .

Whatever rational, logical part of him was left fled. Getting rid of the bodies, misleading the police, none of that mattered anymore. Fear, misery, and self-pity took him far beyond such petty concerns. He saw now that he had far worse things to worry about than getting caught by the police.

What mattered most of all was finding a way to appease his tormentors, to convince them not to wreak their vengeance on him.

Bruner raised his tear-streaked face and looked straight at Celia's image, wavering as if caressed by an invisible wind, in front of the fireplace.

She returned his gaze. Her manner was remote, distant, so regal that for a moment her plain, sallow face seemed almost lovely. The bruises that ringed her tiny neck had faded. even more so than when he had seen her outside his bedroom door, as if her ghostly body were marking time.

Her lips moved. *Rolf.*

Her voice was soft, lower than he'd expected, strangely seductive. He drew in a trembling breath, astounded that she would speak this *directly* to him, uncertain as to whether her tone held hope or condemnation. He stared, slack jawed, utterly transfixed.

You'd better come with me, Rolf

His heart began to beat wildly, at first from titillation, then from a growing sense of alarm. The words were ominously familiar.

Come with me, Rolf

"No," Bruner sobbed. He covered his face with his hands, but not before he saw her features begin to metamorphose, and pull him down into the dark vortex of his own past.

Baltimore

JULY 1936

14

His mother, Elise Bruner, was very beautiful. He had heard it said many times when he was growing up, yet he could never quite fully believe it. True, she had a pretty face. She was fair haired, with alarmingly blue eyes and porcelain skin that acquired a charming rosy flush in the sun or the cold. Even when they were poor —when things became difficult during the Depression and the Feinmans paid their governess little beyond room and board for her and her young son, Rolf—she dressed stylishly and well. A necessary investment, she said, to catch a man. And if Rolf had to do without in order for his mother to have fine clothes—well, it was worth it. After all, she was doing her best to find the boy a father. Her body was fashionably slender and small breasted, with a singular wiry toughness. There was nothing soft about Elise.

Her voice was throaty, deep for a woman's, but

most men (and there were many men) seemed to find that seductive. Only her son knew how shrill it became when she was angry. And she was almost always angry at him.

At those times she was anything but beautiful.

She had come from Germany to the United States six years before the onset of the Depression, when she was sixteen. From Berlin, Rolf thought, though she never spoke to him of her native country, or of his grandparents, except to say that they were "horrible people" and Rolf was lucky never to have known them. As he grew older, he began to suspect that Bruner was not her real name. She tried her best to forget her native country. She learned English quickly and spoke it with surprisingly little accent. Rolf never heard her speak German, save in ragged whispers to her employer, Doctor Feinman, as the two adults wrestled in the twin bed next to Rolf's as the boy supposedly slept. Or when she swore. Curse words and endearments were the only words he knew in the language.

Doctor Feinman visited their downstairs servants' quarters often—always when his drunken wife and young daughter, Darla, were asleep or away. According to Elise, Feinman was responsible for Rolf's existence. She often mentioned this to the boy.

Feinman's your father. Don't ever forget that. If anything happens to me, be sure to tell them: He's your father. The point, Rolf knew even then, was not to ensure that her young son was taken care of, but to ensure revenge.

And she never failed to mention it to Feinman whenever possible.

Rolf stood in awe of Feinman. To begin with, Feinman was a *doctor,* a surgeon, a fact his mother declared in reverent tones. In other words, Feinman was *rich.* Rich enough to own a big house and car, rich enough to spoil his wife and daughter and support his mistress and son.

Rolf must never, ever forget that.

Feinman was not a handsome man. He was middle aged and pudgy. He had a plain, broad face with a round nose and thinning, slicked-back brown hair. He squinted at the world through wire-rimmed spectacles that he was constantly polishing on the edge of his vest. He always came to Elise in fine woolen three-piece suits, even after everyone else in the house was asleep. He usually came home from the hospital very late, and those nights that he did not come home late, he was often stricken with insomnia. Even if he *had* risen from his bed to come to the governess's chambers in the middle of the night, he would have come fully clothed. Feinman was an exceedingly formal man, cold and passionless—except when it came to Elise. When it came to his alleged son, however, Feinman exhibited no feelings whatsoever. He never addressed Rolf directly; he spoke of him in the third person to Elise, even in the boy's presence.

Elise was charming, Elise was witty, Elise dressed well. But when her son compared her to Feinman, he saw the traces of vulgarity in her speech, in the flashiness of her clothes. Feinman rarely swore, and though he shared Elise's native language (his family had emigrated from Germany when he was a boy), he never spoke it to her, even in the throes of passion. His personality was quiet, even bland—but he was subtly elegant, refined, wealthy. And powerful enough to control his own life, and the lives of those around him.

Though he sometimes had difficulty controlling Elise's.

She became involved with other men whenever she could—that is, whenever she felt like risking Feinman's wrath or felt his jealousy might be useful, or whenever she thought she could get away with it. Sometimes she left Rolf locked in their bedroom and went to the man's place. Sometimes, when the Feinmans were out of town or at a late party, she would smuggle the men into her room. If they objected too strenuously to the boy's presence, Rolf was ejected from his bed and ordered to wait in the bathroom or sit quietly in the kitchen. All too often the men did not object. Most times it was night, and Rolf pretended he was asleep.

It was daytime, a July afternoon, when Doctor Feinman came looking for Elise. Rolf remembered clearly that it was July—either shortly before or after the Fourth, because of the firecrackers. He had three of them in his pockets (the week before

Feinman had inadvertently left several coins on Elise's dresser, and the boy had risked taking a couple of them). He also had some kitchen matches, stolen the night before from the box by the stove. He planned to go to an abandoned field a few blocks away—well out of range of Elise's phenomenal hearing—before setting them off.

His mother had been standing over a large pot on the stove that afternoon, humming to herself. The kitchen was warm and steamy and stank of boiling cabbage. It was a perfect summer's day: the sun bright and warm, the air clean and hinting at coolness. The windows were open to let the breeze through. Elise had been in an excellent mood all week. The Feinmans were on holiday in New England, and she had managed to arrange some encounters with an attorney—a younger, single man who, she kept telling her son, would someday be as wealthy as Feinman.

Because she was in such a good mood, she didn't seem to notice the boy as he slipped past her and headed for the back door. She noticed, of course; nothing got past Elise. Rolf had long ago decided that she was capable of reading minds. Normally, she would have stopped and interrogated him and, if the whim struck her, would have forbidden him to go outside.

But today, she was humming and smiling slightly to herself, and didn't even glance at him as she said: "Be back before dark."

Which meant that she would be going out again

with the lawyer tonight, and Rolf would be locked in the bedroom again. He would dutifully return before dark, of course. Not because he was by nature obedient, but because his mother's punishments could be vicious—and he was punished often enough without understanding why to intentionally try to provoke her to anger.

Buoyed by the prospect of a new experiment with the firecrackers, Rolf dashed out the door, down the wooden steps onto the grass. He had hopes of finding a stray dog or cat—animals often rummaged through garbage cans in the alley near the field—and strapping a firecracker to each hind leg, plus one to the tail. For that purpose he had also secreted three lengths of string and a stale soda cracker in his left hip pocket. It was a new-found hobby, doing things to animals.

From one of Feinman's stolen razor blades and some wire, he had managed to rig a child's guillotine. It worked well on insects and guppies from Darla's fish tank, not so well on toads and larger prey. Experiments, Rolf privately called them. As time passed, his passion for the experiments increased. So, gradually, did the size of his victims. After all, his mother always told him he would someday be a doctor, just like his father. And doctors needed animals for research.

He always found the experiments strangely exciting.

Elise had caught him at it barely a week ago. It had been a similar project, except that he had

strapped only one firecracker to a stray dog's tail.
It had been an ugly dog, anyway—a yellow mon-
grel, part Labrador retriever maybe. It had clearly
been fending for itself a long time. Rolf could see
each vertebra of its curving spine jutting beneath
its mangy coat; its rib cage stood out like fully expanded bellows. Sores oozed on its back and hindquarters.

Yet there was gentleness in its brown eyes,
which brightened with hope when they beheld
Rolf. The dog approached the boy apologetically,
gratefully, head low, tail thumping. At the sight of
the soda cracker, the dog began drooling copiously; long, thick strands of saliva dripped from its
muzzle.

It had been just trusting enough (just stupid
enough, Rolf thought) to allow him to attach the
firecracker to its tail without protest. Perhaps it
was so desperate for human companionship that it
was willing to accept almost any form of contact as
a sign of affection. Only when Rolf struck the
match did it show the first sign of apprehension.

He had been careless. He had lured the animal
into the backyard instead of coaxing it the half
mile to the field, but he had not expected to see
Elise walking back from the market so soon.

She'd arrived, grocery bag slung like a child on
her hip, at the back door. Her timing could not
have been better (or worse, Rolf had feared). She
turned and caught sight of the two just as the boy

lit the fuse at the end of the dog's tail and stepped back.

And as he drew back, Rolf cringed and raised his hands in front of his face—not in anticipation of the explosion, but of Elise's reaction. He fully expected her to swoop down in one of her bursts of temper. Waiting, the boy peered between his parted fingers.

But Elise did nothing of the kind. She stood on the top step in front of the door and watched curiously, bag still balanced on one hip.

Sensing disaster, the mutt began to run. There was a flaring sound as the flame found the fuse's end. The firecracker exploded in a burst of noise and light.

The dog screamed. There came a puff of dark smoke and the smell of sulphur. As the smoke cleared, Rolf saw that the firecracker was gone. In its place was charred skin and what might have been blood and what Rolf hoped was bone. Frenzied, the dog curled itself into a U and snapped and mouthed at its tail, unable to decide whether to attack the source of the pain or nurse its injury. Then, with a second shriek, it raced through the backyard, stopping twice to drop its hindquarters and chew at its wound.

The boy stood, suspended between illicit pleasure and fear, and trembled as he watched the dog disappear past the trees. At any second Elise's hands would be on him. Only a beating, if he was lucky.

Please, only a beating. . . .

The sound behind him so startled him that he dropped his hands and turned with a gasp. Elise had set the groceries down on the stoop and now sat beside them on the top stair.

She was laughing. Laughing so hard at first that she had cupped one hand over her mouth and made little sound until she got her first good lungful of air. And then it came out, clear and ringing. Her cheeks were bright pink; her shoulders were shaking.

Rolf stared, astounded. Nothing he had ever done had made his mother laugh—at least, not like this, with pleasure instead of derision. His jaw dropped. He began to giggle. Timidly, at first, then more confidently as Elise's laughter grew louder.

At last she stopped and wiped her eyes with the back of her wrist.

"Clever boy," she said. "Very clever boy."

Clever, she thinks I'm clever

". . . But you must learn to be more careful, so the adults don't catch you." She was still smiling.

At me, Rolf thought. *Smiling at me.* For the first time in his life he had done something to please her—not something she had ordered him to do, but something spontaneous, something *he* had thought of himself, his very own creation. Something that had pleased them both.

He had never felt so close to her, so overwhelmed by love for her. They shared a secret now: the experiments.

She had seemed very happy the entire week after. Perhaps it had something to do with the new man she was seeing, the lawyer. But in his child's heart Rolf hoped it had more to do with the fact that her son had pleased her.

He decided then to come up with an even better experiment, one that would make her laugh even harder, be even more pleased with him. But it had taken him an entire week to steal enough money to buy the firecrackers.

Today was a perfect day for it. Elise was still in a good mood, and kindly disposed toward him. He would lure an animal home, to the backyard, and—

—and yet, at the same time, he wanted to experience this particular experiment *alone.* The thought of it for the past seven nights had caused a strange physical ache that made him lie awake on his cot in a feverish state. He planned it over and over in his mind: he would go to the field, he would find an animal, he would perform the experiment by himself, where no one could see—

Even now the thought caused an unusual tightening sensation in his groin and abdomen.

He was halfway across the lawn when he heard a furious shout behind him. He paused, eyes focused straight ahead on the thick copse of oaks and maples that edged the Feinmans' property, and listened, his heart pounding in anticipation of punishment even though the shout had not been directed at him. Beyond the trees the sky was blue and cloudless. Wind stirred, making leaves undulate in slow, shining waves.

Elise!

Feinman's voice, coming through the open kitchen window, followed by his mother's voice, full of surprise. Background: whisper of leaves.

Jakob. What are you doing home?

Emergency surgery at the hospital. Never mind about that. What is this thing about Ralston, this damned attorney—

All innocence and protest. *Where did you hear such a thing?*

You're seeing him tonight, aren't you?

Words coming faster. Angrier now. Pitch rising.

I don't know what you're talking—

Don't lie to me, Elise. People have seen you with him.

People? Which people? I want to know who is accusing me!

You had dinner with him last night. I can't leave you for a minute, can I? You're no better than a—a common prostitute!

Silence. Then:

What do you expect me to do, Jakob? Live for the rest of my life as your servant while that lazy drunken bitch gets your money and your property and your name? I'm more of a wife to you than she ever was. How can you speak to me like that? I'm trying to find a father for your son. . . .

I can't trust you anymore. How can I even be sure the little bastard's mine?

Shrill and screaming now. *How* dare *you—*

I want you out of the house, both of you. Get out. Feinman sounded suddenly calmer. *I want nothing more to do with either of you.*

Rolf stood very quietly, scarcely breathing, as he debated his two options: move forward, to the field, and freedom, and hopefully a stray cat or two . . . or remain here, to listen to the argument's progress and gauge his mother's mood.

A year or so ago he would have considered a third option: move forward, and not return. But running away only made things worse. He'd gotten hungry and had finally been forced to seek the company of adults. People, even the police, were kind to him when he was discovered, but they'd soon enough—too soon—figured out who he was and returned him to his mother.

Rolf tried running twice. Each time Elise beat him so badly upon his return that he'd crawled into his bed and stayed there. The second time, three whole days, with a blinding headache. Elise had told everyone the exposure to the elements had given the boy the flu.

He didn't run away anymore.

Rolf sank down and sat on the grass, cool against the bare skin of his calves. Best to listen and learn his fate. Feinman's threat distressed him, but not unduly. He'd heard the same words said before in precisely the same tone. He had no reason to think

Feinman would make good on them this time. But predicting his mother's mood afterward—that was impossible. Sometimes the fighting left her exhilarated, elated, convinced she'd finally gotten one up on Feinman; sometimes she cried for hours after. Sometimes she and Feinman went into the bedroom and locked the door.

Go ahead, Elise screamed. It was very nearly a sob. *Go ahead. Throw me and the boy out. And I will go to everyone in this city, including your wife and brat, and tell them that Rolf is your son. Maybe I should go to your patients, hah? Maybe the newspapers?*

That's ridiculous. They won't believe you. They wouldn't care even if they did, Feinman said, but his voice sounded weaker.

Enough people will believe me to hurt your practice, Jakob, and you know it. What am I supposed to do? Wait for Verna to die?

She'll drink herself to death soon enough. We've been through this before. I can't risk a divorce. I can't risk the scandal—

We could move. To a different city. New York, maybe. Or Washington. No one would have to know. . . .

I'm old, Elise. Too old to be moving around.

You're not even forty-five, for God's sake—

I have roots here. Do you know how long it takes to build up a practice? I couldn't move. It would kill me. . . . I take good care of you and the boy, don't I? I've never tried to run away from my obligation to you—

The boy needs a father.

Just what does that mean? He knows I'm his father.

I've never denied it in front of him. What more does he want?

And I need a husband. How do you think I feel, playing servant to Verna, seeing her with her big house and fancy clothes and jewelry, while I clean the shit from her toilet? Those fancy things should be mine, *Jakob. Those things belong to* me.

Warning tone. *You forget yourself, Elise—*

Loud, hysterical burst of sobbing. *Get out. Get out, you bastard. Get out and leave me alone!*

Low muttering. The vehement slam of Elise's bedroom door, following by more weeping.

Rolf sat fingering the firecrackers in his pockets and staring at the distant trees. Feinman would not make them leave, of course. But his mother was crying, and that was bad. Very bad. A beating—or worse—would be waiting for him when he went back inside, unless he could devise a strategy for avoiding it.

In that moment he hated Feinman. Hated him for making Elise cry, for making things difficult again. Life had been good. His mother hadn't struck him once, all week, but now—

A soft mew made him turn his head. The Feinman family cat, Edgar Allan Poe, stood crying at the back door. Despite the name Edgar was a female white Persian, and very fat, or so Rolf had thought in those days, before he was old enough to realize she'd been continually pregnant.

"Edgar," Rolf called softly. Sobs still filtered

through Elise's open bedroom window. "Edgar. Here, kitty, kitty."

Edgar turned her head to regard him with dark blue eyes, very like Elise's, and the same decorous disdain as any other member of the Feinman family.

"Here, Edgar. Here, kitty." He rose to his feet and proffered the soda cracker. Edgar continued to eye him mistrustfully, and kept her place by the door. Rolf had never before approached the cat, had never offered it a tidbit or tried to pet it. He had never been much interested in animals, outside of the experiments. At best he and Edgar tolerated each other's presence in the house like polite strangers.

Cautiously, he advanced on the cat until he had crossed to the foot of the steps. He held the cracker at arm's length and continued to call Edgar softly.

Edgar mewed once, as if to complain of the dilemma presented her, then moved forward. Smiling, the boy let her take the treat. Her movements were dainty, like Darla's; it took her some time to dispose of the cracker. As she finished off the last of it, Rolf picked her up. To his surprise she did not resist, but began to purr as soon as his hands were upon her.

She was light in his arms as he carried her to the grass outside Elise's bedroom window and sat down. He could not remember ever touching anything as soft as her fur. With one hand he held her and, with the other, slowly removed the string and firecrackers from his pockets.

Her friendliness took him aback, as did the pleasant surge of fondness he experienced upon touching her and feeling her warmth settle trustingly against his body. The sense of affection mingled with his anticipation of the experiment, combined with it in such a way as to increase his arousal rather than detract from it.

He felt no regret for what he was about to do.

Edgar sat sphinxlike in his arms and closed her eyes in drowsy appreciation of the sunshine. Her tail curved around her body so that it rested atop one front paw. Stroking her back with his left hand, Rolf used his right to position a firecracker against the tail's tip. Then gently, very gently, he held it in position while he wound string—not too tightly—to keep the firecracker in place. It took him several tries to get it secure enough, and it was awkward work. By the time he finished, Edgar had opened her eyes and was staring suspiciously at him, though she still purred faintly.

Rolf stroked her until she closed her eyes again, then went back to work.

Clever boy. Very clever boy

There was something thrilling about forcing himself to move so slowly, so deliberately, when he was this excited about the experiment. Better to move seductively, with finesse

(Feinman would have done it this way)

than to use force. His breath began coming more

quickly; he became aware of his heartbeat. Slowly, yes. Very slowly. This was the way Feinman would have done it. He had another firecracker positioned against her hind leg, now. He began to wind the string.

Edgar opened her eyes and stretched. Instinctively, the boy reached for her leg and held it still. A mistake. Edgar began to struggle, pulling the leg away. But Rolf held on firmly, and continued winding the string around the firecracker.

Edgar unsheathed her claws and tore at Rolf's shirt, his suspenders, his hands. Long, thin rills of blood sprang from his bare forearms, but he continued stoically, ignoring Edgar's cries, and reached for the other hind leg and the last firecracker.

With a sharp movement of her white head Edgar sank her teeth into his thumb, then writhed free with a surge of strength that surprised him. She would have leapt clear except that the boy managed at the last second to clamp both hands around her. He could feel her heart pounding wildly, could feel her rib cage contract and expand with her panting. Her voice had lowered to a constant, deep-throated yowl.

The third firecracker and string had fallen to the ground. No matter. The matches, at least, were still in his pocket. Holding his flailing trophy at arm's length, Rolf rose unsteadily to his feet. There were tears in his eyes, blood on his arms and hands, but he smiled.

(Clever boy, very clever boy)

Only two firecrackers attached. The experiment would not be perfect, but it would have to do. And he could save the third firecracker for when he was alone. . . .

Over Edgar's desperate cries he could hear that the weeping in Elise's bedroom had stopped. He wasn't tall enough to peer into the window to see what she was doing, so he stood on tiptoe and called up.

"Mother?"

A soft moan in reply.

He set Edgar down and used a foot and hand to hold her, struggling, against the ground. With his free hand he fumbled for a match.

(Very clever boy. But you must learn to be more careful)

He raised his voice. "Mother? Mother, come to the window, please. There's something I want to show you."

Her voice was hoarse. "What do you want? Go away and leave me alone."

He was trembling desperately, eagerly. "It's for you, Mother. A present for you. . . ."

A pause, then steps approaching the window, then her swollen face. Her blond hair was tousled, her eyes red and dull. "What is it? What present for me?"

Rolf smiled up at her and struck the match against the sole of his shoe. It flared audibly. "Look, Mother. . . ."

(Clever boy)

Elise let go a screech that made both boy and cat cry out in terror. Rolf dropped the match. In a whirl she came bursting through the back door, down the steps, across the yard, and had Rolf by the arm.

He stood sobbing from sheer surprise; Edgar took advantage of his distraction and dived from his arms, then fled squawling across the lawn.

Elise jerked him so hard that his chin snapped against his chest.

Bad, filthy rotten boy! What did you think you were doing?

Tears coursed down his cheeks; his nose ran. Feinman would never behave this way. Feinman would never let anyone see him cry like this.

"I wanted—I just wanted to—to—"

Speak up! She slapped him square across the face; one of her nails grazed his eyelid. *What were you doing?*

He drew in his breath. "I w-wanted to make you h-happy, that's all. I thought you would laugh. I thought you'd think it was funny—"

Stupid, stupid boy! You can't be mine. My son would never be so stupid! That was the Feinmans' cat. The Feinmans' cat, stupid boy! It's one thing to have fun with a stray dog, but the Feinmans could catch you! What if someone sees you trying firecrackers to the cat's tail? What if Doctor Feinman were to see you? What would happen to us then, hah? What do you think would happen?

"I d-don't know. . . ."

Slap, square in the middle of the face.

They would be angry, that's what. They would throw us out onto the street and we would starve to death, that's what. And it would be your *fault. Do you understand?*

"Y-yes."

Slap.

Your fault. Do you understand, stupid boy?

Slap. Slap. Harder slap, almost a punch. He was sobbing too hard to catch his breath; he felt as if he were drowning in tears and snot. Feinman would not cry like this. Feinman would not— "Yes. Yes. I understand."

Do you understand that someone must be punished?

He sucked in a deep, gurgling breath, and an instant later expelled all the air from his lungs with a single shriek. "No!"

You'd better come with me, Rolf

Her eyes had taken on that strange light, that strange, horrible light. Rolf had learned to fear it. It was the light of inspiration; it meant that his mother had just devised an ingenious new form of punishment. The same light shone in his own eyes, when he dreamed of new experiments.

Rolf, come with me

Elise turned and yanked his arm, forcing him to stumble after her. She dragged him across the yard, up the steps, into the kitchen, filled with faintly unpleasant cabbage smell.

Stupid, stupid boy

Her face was contorted with hellish rage.

Someone must be punished, mustn't he?

He was babbling with fright. "Please, ohno-Ipromisel'llbegood, pleaseohnoGodohno. . . ."

She gripped him with a single hand, but her strength was so terrible he could not escape, even though he was flailing, as Edgar had, fighting with all his might to break free. One handed, she pulled a short wooden stool from under the kitchen table. She used it to get to the higher cupboards (and Rolf, unbeknownst to her, sometimes used it for exactly the same purpose). She jerked it screeching across the floor until it rested in front of the stove. In front of the pot of boiling cabbage.

With a thrill of terror he saw what she intended to do, and renewed his struggle, kicking, clawing, yowling, like the cat.

"Nooooo . . . !"

Elise pushed him onto the stool. Not an easy task; she had to use both hands and considerable force. She stood beside him, one arm wound around his chest, subduing his left hand, the one farthest from her. With her free hand she took his right forearm, so tightly that his fingers began to tingle.

The stool was just the right height. He could peer down into the heavy pot, into the roiling combination of water and faded red cabbage. Steam caught him full in the face. He tried to turn away, but Elise's sharp shoulder was pressed against the back of his head. From the corner of his eye he glimpsed her face, flushed in the rising steam. Her eyes glittered.

Someone must be punished

The same phrase, always the same phrase. It augured an inventive punishment, always worse than a beating. She'd said it the time she caught him stealing one of Feinman's double-edged razor blades, and used the blade to carve the words BAD BOY across his palm. She'd taken him to the bedroom and tied him down, because he'd struggled so.

(but he didn't build the guillotines anymore)

Elise drew his right forearm down so that his hand hovered inches above the churning water. The boy screamed. His knees buckled and he sagged, but the woman held him firmly in place. He flattened his hand, palm down, and spread his fingers wide in an effort to keep as far as possible from the water. His hand brightened to a cherry-red shade; he already had a first-degree burn from the steam.

For your own good, Rolf. I'm only doing this so you won't forget

(Clever boy. But you must learn to be more careful, so the adults don't catch you)

She plunged his hand into the water and held it there for just a second.

The pain was electric, stunning, worse than anything he'd known, far worse than the razor cuts. Too horrible for tears. He must have swooned, for after the initial flare of pain came blackness. And then he was vaguely aware of voices, and of being held firmly against Elise's wiry body. He kept his eyes squeezed shut against the steam.

Feinman's voice behind them, at the kitchen door. He must have been upstairs, listening.

Elise! What's going on in there? What are you doing to the boy? I heard screaming. . . .

(He must have screamed, then, before he fainted.)

Her voice was shrill, ferocious. *Get out, Jakob! I'm trying to teach the boy a lesson!*

A long pause followed. Then Feinman said, calmly, *I don't want to hear any more screaming. For God's sake, the windows are all open.*

I'll see to it, Jakob. Now get out!

Sound of a door closing.

(sound of help retreating)

Then the hiss of gas in the burner, of steam rising from the water, of Elise's rapid breath. She spoke softly into Rolf's ear, almost crooning. *Someone must be punished, yes, someone must be punished, mustn't he?*

She plunged his hand down into the water again. For a second, only a second, but it was long enough. This time when he began to scream, she slapped him breathless and whispered, her cheek pressed against his:

Quiet, stupid boy! Quiet! You must learn to tolerate punishment. It's for your own good, don't you see? For your own good. . . .

Someone must be punished, after all. . . .

* * *

It was a long time before he could use the hand again. When it was healed up enough, he caught Edgar and took her to the abandoned field,

(you must learn to be more careful, so the adults don't catch you)

where he strangled her. He buried her there, under a juniper bush. The Feinmans assumed she had run away and, after a month of posting signs around the neighborhood and scouting for her in the doctor's car, gave her up for dead.

Tampa

AUGUST 1990

15

"Mama?" Avra whispered. She was still back in her old room in New Orleans, nestled under the rose print bedspread, with Magdalen asleep in the next bed. Mama was standing over her, trying to speak; Mama had been trying to tell her that something was *wrong*. . . .

If Avra could just get Magdalen to wake up, Maggie would understand. Maggie would be able to tell her what Mama was saying. She called out softly.

"Maggie?"

No answer. She fought to wake. Maggie was in trouble. Mama had been talking about Magdalen needing help, and now Maggie was gone. . . .

Her eyes snapped open. Walls. Nothing but bare walls, and a ceiling. As Avra stared, tiny red and yellow squiggles began dancing on the ceiling. She closed her eyes. The ceiling disappeared, but the colors remained.

Wherever this was, it was not New Orleans. For a while she could only lie quietly and feel her heart race. The thing with Mama . . . had it been a dream? It had seemed so real, so vivid, that even now she had trouble believing it hadn't happened.

If it hadn't, then what *had*?

She opened her eyes again and slowly pushed herself to a sitting position. As she did, dizziness overwhelmed her. She lurched to one side and threw up a small amount of bile and fluid. When the spell passed, she crawled to a nearby wall, away from the warm, nauseating smell of her own vomit, and propped herself up, then gingerly peered at her surroundings again. She must have become sick at work. There was dried vomit down the front of her dress and someone had removed her shoes. Sick, that was it. She ran a hand over her face; it was hot and moist with sweat. The chopstick had been removed, and her hair had fallen onto her shoulders in heavy, damp tangles. But where had they taken her?

Because of the excruciating dizziness she had to turn her head very slowly to examine the room. Four bare walls and a ceiling, no furniture. She'd been lying on thickly padded carpeting. The overhead light was on and the window was covered with some sort of external blinds, so she couldn't see outside, but she got the impression that it wasn't quite dark enough to be night. Beyond the window, the tinny sound of rain against metal.

Not a hospital or a doctor's office, so where . . .

She released a low, wrenching sob as memory returned. Not sick. Not sick. Drugged. The Catacombs—

(the Shadow)

His face. Even in the darkness of the Catacombs she had recognized him, known Bruner. He had drugged her, then brought her here.

She hadn't been imagining things. He was alive, after all, and he had recognized her too. Had followed her to work, and now . . .

She hugged the wall, staining it with tears and saliva. Behind her closed eyelids little pinwheels of color twirled. She did not cry long; it made her head hurt fiercely, and the nausea worsen. She clung to the wall, eyes shut, gasping, and forced herself to concentrate.

Bruner had recognized her. Had brought her here, wherever this was. Knew that she had recognized him, and now he would have to kill her to silence her. He was going to come back soon.

She began to sob again.

Okay. It's bad. But you can't cry about it now. Think about a way out. Think.

The light hurt her eyes and made her head ache worse, but it allowed her to study her options. She studied the room again. The four walls, the ceiling. The covered-up window. The door was plywood, but she doubted that in her current state she could break it down. Haltingly, she rose to her feet, flattening both palms against the wall to steady herself. The dizziness was still bad, and she had to stop and wait a couple of times, but she managed to stand without throwing up again.

She staggered over to the door and turned the knob. Locked, as she expected. She gave it a test kick and succeeded only in hurting her toes; bare feet weren't designed for breaking down doors.

The window didn't look promising either. On the other side of the glass were horizontal metal slats—hurricane blinds, built to keep out high winds and vandals. Even if she managed to break the glass, she'd never get past the thick metal.

He had her and there was nothing she could do about it. With her back against the door she slid down onto her haunches.

And noticed, between the door and the window, the white photograph album placed conspicuously in the middle of the gray carpet. Atop it rested a black-haired rag doll in a blue dress.

They had obviously been left there for her to find. She sat staring at them for a full minute before she gathered the energy and courage to crawl over.

She felt compelled to pick the doll up. The Avra doll Gran had made, right down to the embroidered gray eyes. It was worn and bedraggled looking, easily twenty years old. And yet—

It couldn't possibly be the same doll. She didn't remember exactly what had happened to the original; she didn't remember seeing it after the night Mama died. Gran had probably thrown it away because of the bloodstains, or else it had been impounded as evidence. . . .

There were no bloodstains on this doll. And there hadn't been time, that awful night, for him to return to the house and retrieve it.

Had there?

No. Impossible. Only one explanation: the sick bastard had remembered, and had had a replica made. Looking at it, she became convinced. After all, the doll's dress was too dark to be the right shade of blue. She set it down gently and looked at the photo album.

From the outside it looked like a wedding album. She sat down, lifted it into her lap, and opened the faux leather cover.

On the first page was a photograph of herself at age five, taken only a few weeks before Mama died. She remembered when the picture was taken, remembered the favorite blue velvet dress she had posed in, remembered that Dr. Bruner had taken the photo. He must have taken fifty shots before he felt he had captured the pose he wanted. She had grown restless and thrown a tantrum, but the doctor had handled her with infinite good humor and patience. He had distracted her with candy and toys and jokes and ultimately the Avra doll, which she had thrown at him in a burst of temper. Right at the camera lens. He had lowered the camera and smiled at her.

She remembered because Mama had given her a

spanking. *You should be ashamed of yourself, acting like that,* Mama had said. *Why, the man is a saint!*

So there was her photograph, and beneath it, her name. In *his* handwriting. She could not remember what his script had looked like, but she knew all the same that it had to be his.

Under the picture were two yellowed newspaper articles. Her hands shook badly as she fumbled with the cellophane, but she managed to remove and unfold the clippings without tearing them. A reverse image of the newsprint remained on the album page's gummy surface.

Both articles had been clipped from the *States Item*, the now-defunct New Orleans newspaper. The first one, dated December 29, 1965, read:

LOCAL WOMAN SLAIN; SUSPECT ESCAPES

Mrs. Marie Jarulzski, 28, of Rue de Ste. Claire, was found murdered Friday night in her home. According to police she had been stabbed repeatedly, though they have divulged no motive for the slaying. Her two children were apparently eyewitnesses and are in the care of relatives. Police are currently seeking a local pediatrician, Dr. Rolf Bruner, for questioning. Anyone with knowledge of his whereabouts should contact Detective Waters of the New Orleans Police Department immediately.

Mrs. Jarulzski, a native of Florida, was a long-time employee of Morrison Insurance Co. She is

survived by her two daughters, Magdalen and
Avra, age 5, and her mother, Mrs. Isobel K.
Johnston.

The second one was dated January 30, 1966.

MURDER SUSPECT STILL AT LARGE

Police are still trying to locate the killer of
Marie Jarulzski, mother of two young dauthers.
The primary suspect in the case remains Dr.
Rolf Bruner, a local pediatrician. Dr. Bruner apparently fled New Orleans on the night of December 28 and has not been seen since. Police
are offering a reward for information regarding
his whereabouts. Those with such information
should contact Detective Waters of the New Orleans Police Department immediately.

Never captured. Free all these years, and Mama
dead. Bruner free and rich and laughing all these
years, taking women with little girls out to dinner.
The universe was a very sick place.

No wonder Gran hadn't told the truth. The
thought of it must have killed her.

And so he had recognized her at Selena's. Found
out somehow where she worked, and brought her
here. There was no statute of limitations on murder, was there? He'd have to silence her. He'd have
to kill her.

And Maggie.

With a start she realized that he had her purse. Her driver's license. He knew where she lived. Where *Maggie* lived. Maybe he wasn't here because he had gone to Willow Street to get her. . . .

Breathe. Breathe. Relax. If you let yourself become hysterical, you're dead. You've got to think. . . . Pretend you're Maggie. What would Maggie do if she were in this situation?

(She might be in it sooner than you'd like to think. . . .)

I don't know. When I feel better, I can try to find a way out again, but it's not going to work. . . .

You've got to do something. Maybe when he comes—

He was going to be coming, wasn't he?

—Stop it. When he comes, you can try to talk to him. Reason with him. He loved you, once—

Nausea, but not from the drug.

—in his own sick way. That's what Maggie would do. Pretend to sympathize with him. Feed him some line of bull, tell him Mama's death wasn't his fault. That you don't blame him for what happened. Talk your way out of it. When he comes in, be friendly, not hostile. Don't threaten. After all, he hasn't killed you yet. He could have killed you in the Catacombs. Could have killed you without anyone knowing, but instead he took the trouble to bring you to this place.

Why?

(Not that. Don't even think of THAT, of him touching you)

More deep breaths until the dizziness passed. She was huddled over the album with her cheek pressed against the sticky page; the newspaper articles rustled beneath the air-conditioning vent. She lifted her head.

What would Maggie do?

Turn the page. Maggie would turn the page. Maggie would see what else was in the album.

She expected to see more photos of herself, maybe of Maggie and Mama. Maybe all of herself —the first page clearly showed the degree of his obsession with her, but she was trying not to think about that at the moment.

She did not expect what she saw.

Two June 1966 snapshots of the same dark-haired girl—a portrait, like the one on the first page, showing the shoulders up. She must have been right around six or seven years old. Her name, RACHEL BERNSTEIN, was carefully lettered beneath the pictures in the same handwriting that graced Avra's page.

BEFORE: Rachel was wide eyed and somber in the first photo. She wouldn't look at whoever was holding the camera. Her long straight hair was pulled back in a ponytail, and she wore a pink plastic headband to prevent any hairs from straying onto her forehead.

And in the second—

(Our eyes see this, but we do not understand. We *will* not understand.)

—in the second, labeled AFTER, Rachel lay flat against a floral background. The ponytail and the pink headband were gone. Her long hair was

fanned out against the bedspread, as if someone
had taken great care to arrange it. Her head lolled
at an unnatural angle to her shoulders. There were
red, puffed marks on her neck. Her eyes were open
but unseeing.

On the same page, a small newspaper clipping
and a lock of straight dark hair tucked under the
plastic.

1966. She would have been close to Avra's age
now.

(We are not seeing this. We will not understand
this. NO.)

Pages and pages and pages. The album was filled
with pages, arranged in exact chronological order
beginning with December 1965 and ending April
1989. Different children, but every page the same.
BEFORE and AFTER. The name, the date, the hair, the
newspaper article. All the same, except for Avra's.

Avra's page had no swatch of hair, no AFTER
photo.

She shivered at the cool breeze from the air-conditioner against her damp skin.

*That's why he brought you here, my dear, and left this
where you could find it. Because he wants you to know he
intends to complete his fucking BOOK—*

With sudden vicious strength she hurled the album across the room.

Jangle of keys at the door. Slide, then click of a
dead bolt turning.

From where she huddled, arms resting on her

knees, face buried in her arms, Avra glanced up. Not much time had passed since she had discovered the secrets of the album; minutes maybe, or maybe an hour. She had been in too much misery to notice the passage of time.

The door swung slowly inward.

The first thing to appear was a gun—

That's it, kid. You're going out now. Just like that, and you can't even try to tell Maggie what's going on. Dammit, Maggie, if he does anything to hurt you, I'll—

You'll what?

I'll feel like shit, that's what. The ridiculous thing was, she was worried about Rasputin too. She'd feel like shit if anything happened to Raz or Jason.

(You won't feel like shit, stupid. You won't know about it. You'll be dead)

—and then a sleeved arm, and then he was standing with his back to the door, looking at her, pointing the gun at her. She blinked, trying to focus her blurred vision. He'd lost most of his hair on the top, but he was still slender and very handsome. He looked closer to fifty than sixty. He smiled suddenly at her with hideous fondness.

"Amazing," he said. His tone was as gentle as a lover's. "How you resemble your mother. Quite a beautiful woman, Marie."

She could not answer.

He continued smiling at her until he saw the photo album, resting spine-side up on its spread leaves. The *States Item* clippings were scattered on the floor beside her. The smile faded; his eyes narrowed.

"This will never do," he said disapprovingly. "Avra, pick that up."

He spoke as if to a child, as if the past twenty-four and a half years had never happened, as if their relationship had remained exactly the same as before Mama died.

For a moment she could only stare. *Reason with him, remember? Pretend to sympathize. Promise him you'll tell no one—*

Right. Reason with the monster who took those pictures. She thought she'd known who and what she was dealing with; she hadn't known at all. The amazing thing was how *normal* he looked; no, better than normal. He was meticulously dressed in cream-colored linen slacks. A handsome, well-groomed, *attractive* man.

The better to lure women and little girls, my dear.

"Avra," he repeated. His tone was one of affectionate exasperation, of a father trying to deal with an unruly but beloved child. Yet there was a steel edge buried there. He would only tolerate so much disobedience, and no more. He gestured with the gun. "Pick it up."

She crawled over to the album and lifted it.

"Good girl," Bruner said. "Now put the newspaper articles back where they belong, please."

She obeyed, crawling with the album in one hand back to where the clippings lay. She carefully refolded them, then replaced the plastic over them and closed the album. Her hands felt numb, unresponsive, as if they belonged to someone else.

He smiled again. "Better. Much better."

She threw it at him.

You should be ashamed of yourself, acting like that. Why, the man is a saint!

The act surprised her as much as it surprised him. She was immediately glad and sorry that she had done it. She hadn't intended to do such a stupid thing; she'd intended to do as he said, to talk to him, to convince him she was on his side. Now she was going to get herself killed . . . but maybe getting it over with would be a relief.

She hated him.

He stepped aside, but the album was too heavy and she too weak for it to come close to hitting him. It struck the carpet in front of him with a thud; the metal ring popped open, and laminated pages began to slide out.

For an instant Bruner's features contorted with fury . . . and then eased into a more benevolent expression. He sighed. "Avra. You'll just have to pick it up again."

Careful. You don't know who you're dealing with.

Her head reeled, but she fought the nausea and picked the album up again. She slipped the laminated pages back onto the metal rings.

(He touched these pages after he killed them. He pressed the plastic down and put the new photographs in, just like this.)

She snapped the rings shut. It took her some

time because there were so many pages that they kept slipping out. Once she managed to get the binder shut, she closed it and set it down, then slid it across the carpet toward him and crawled back to lean against the wall.

Through it all he stared intently at her. When she was finished, he said, very softly, "Good." He was looking at her with that strange light in his eyes.

(the Shadow's eyes)

She turned her head and rested her cheek against the cool wall. For a time neither spoke. She could hear the faint sound of his breathing.

"Did you look at it, Avra?" he asked quietly. "Did you read it, and do you understand?"

"I saw it," she said. Tears spilled onto her cheeks. She hated him with more intensity than she'd ever experienced; at the same time she hated herself more for being weak. For being a victim. She should have refused to pick up the album and let him kill her.

"You saw it. Do you *understand*, Avra? Do you *understand*?"

His voice, though quiet, became so impassioned that she tilted her face to look at him. His eyes burned; the question clearly had some deep secret significance for him. If she answered incorrectly . . .

"Yes," she whispered.

"Rolf," he said suddenly. "Say: Yes, Rolf."

Rolf. Rolf. Ugly name, ugly wolf name. *Why, Rolf, what sharp teeth you have. . . .*

"Yes, Rolf. I understand." *I understand: You killed those children. You mean to kill me.*

Relief flitted across his features, which then became illumined with saintlike rapture. "Good. Good. Then you know. *Someone* must be punished, after all."

Her body tensed at this ominous reply. She had given the wrong answer.

He took a step toward her, the gun in his hand still aimed directly at her skull. "I cannot be blamed for any of this, of course. I am merely an agent. I did not start this, Avra—though we both know who did. It must end somewhere. With you."

"Oh, God," she said, pressing her face to the wall and squeezing her eyes shut so tightly that the red squiggles reappeared on the backs of her lids. He was going to shoot her. Probably in the head, scattering blood and brains all over the clean white wall. She wondered whether there would be time to feel pain.

And then he would go after Maggie.

This was fear: a horridly cold, tangible thing, felt more with the body than the mind. It made the dreams of the Shadow seem like a joke.

She felt him move closer. The voice of a stranger seized her memory, uttering a phrase at once meaningless and terrifying:

Oh God Amelie

She waited miserably for the click of a trigger.

Nothing. Only the sound of his breathing, now in her ear.

She wanted to leap up, catch him off guard, fight. To die struggling, not cringing like this. But her body would not respond.

The soft fabric of his shirt brushed against the skin of her arm. She jerked and opened her eyes to see him leaning over her with the pistol. He had switched it to his left hand, and pressed the cold barrel firmly against her right temple.

"Don't move," he said.

She obeyed, but her eyes tracked the movement of his right hand. It held a hypodermic syringe. With his little finger he caught the hem of her dress and drew it back until her left thigh was exposed. With a quick, deft motion he thrust the needle under the skin and slowly depressed the plunger. It stung, but she didn't flinch, didn't move.

Was he killing her by injecting her with poison, or an overdose? Then why not just use the gun? And if he wasn't going to kill, why drug her again? None of it made sense. . . .

Sense. You're asking a madman to make sense. . . .

He slid the needle out, then stood up and backed away from her.

She retained vague memories of the encounter in the Catacombs. Her right thigh still ached where he had jabbed her. Then, the drug had acted quickly; she expected the same swift, numbing sensation now, but it did not come. He had used a different drug.

Bruner stood by the doorway and watched her. She closed her eyes and turned her head toward the wall again, waiting for the shot to take effect.

Minutes passed. At last she became drowsy. Bruner and the empty room and the terror receded, became unimportant; the only thing that mattered was sleep. Avra began to sink toward the floor.

She was distantly aware that he caught her, held her in his arms, but the realization brought no fear. She opened her eyes briefly and saw a flash of metal near her face.

At first she thought it was the gun. And then she felt the tug on her scalp and heard the crisp sound of scissors cutting hair.

16

Shortly after nine o'clock that evening the phone rang. Maggie tore the receiver from the cradle in the middle of the first ring.

She'd been pacing for the past hour and a half alone in the house on Willow Street. Murray had taken the van to Hyde Park to search for Avra—they'd both agreed someone had better stick around the house, in case she showed up or called—and the longer Murray was gone, the worse Maggie's anxiety became.

Anxiety. Radar. Whatever you wanted to call it, it'd been very bad around six-thirty, then tapered off into a dull, steadily growing fear. She'd begun to pace: up the stairs, into the bedrooms (somewhat guiltily into Avra's, looking for a clue as to where she might have gone), down the stairs, into the living room, into the kitchen, out onto the porch. Jason followed, at first keeping up with her, padding patiently behind her on the stairs. After half an hour he gave up and curled, panting, on the porch to better catch the humid breeze. Although the sun had set and the air was cooling slightly, the house was hot and stuffy, and in no time she'd worked up a sweat. The windows were open wide, admitting the sounds of Hyde Park's Saturday-night crowd.

It was her fault, of course. Avra had known Maggie was going to move in with Murray. But Ave had been doing so well the past few years; Maggie had honestly believed Ave could handle life on her own.

And I deserve my own life, too, dammit. I love you, Ave, but do I really have to spend the rest of my life looking out for you?

For an instant she'd been honestly angry. What if Ave really had choreographed this on purpose, as Murray'd suggested? What if this was a stunt to make Maggie feel guilty about leaving?

Well, it's working. But I don't need any help with that. I'm perfectly capable of feeling guilty all by myself, thank you very much.

But no. The radar had said no. Something bad *had* happened; something very, very bad. As bad as the time when—

(Not now. Not Mama and New Orleans again. Let's not think about that right now. We're already upset. Talking to Murray about it didn't help; it just made things worse. It just made me remember.)

She just happened to be in the kitchen when the

phone finally rang. The sudden sound made her jump. Heart pounding, she picked up the receiver.

"Hello?"

Please be Murray, calling to say you've found her. Or Ave. Be Ave. Ave, you little shit, you've had me worried sick—

An unfamiliar, mature male voice. "Yes, is this Ms. Magdalen Kallisti?"

She drew in a breath. The police didn't call, did they? They were supposed to knock on the door. If Ave was dead, wouldn't they come to the door?

Get a grip. Maybe this has nothing to do with Avra. Maybe it's just a damn telephone solicitor—

Suspiciously: "Who is this?"

"Ms. Kallisti, my name is Doctor Jacob Feinman. I'm calling in regard to your sister, Avra."

Her knees went weak; she gripped the kitchen counter to keep from sinking. "Where is she? Is she all right? What's—"

"Please don't be alarmed, Ms. Kallisti. Physically, Avra is quite well."

"Thank *God*—"

"She's here in my office. I'm afraid she's a little too woozy to come to the phone right now; I've had to administer a tranquilizer. That's why I wanted to speak with you."

Quite well. Physically. Which meant—

"What's wrong? What's happened to her?"

He paused as if searching for the gentlest words possible. His tone was warm and full of sympathy. "I have a psychiatric practice downtown. This evening I received a call from my answering service about an emergency. One of my former patients, it seems, found your sister—"

"Found her?"

He sounded apologetic. "Wandering the streets in a very distraught condition. Near the Hyde Park area, I believe."

"Yes, yes. She works there. I was worried because she hadn't made it home. Her shift ended at five—"

"I see. You must have been quite concerned."

"Yes."

"At any rate, rather than take your sister to an emergency room, my patient contacted my service, which contacted me. It's just as well. As I said, your sister is dazed and anxious—near hysteria, actually, when Mrs. Barstow brought her in—but by no means psychotic. She was able to tell me she had a sister named Magdalen, and give me your phone number. We even talked for a little while about what was bothering her. In my professional judgment she does not need the stress of being processed through an emergency room, and from there into the psych ward at Tampa General—"

"No. God, no, she doesn't need that. . . ." Heavy guilt. She'd been right—Ave had been totally freaked about her moving out, and had been trying *not* to show it. But Maggie had never realized how bad off Ave had been. She should have seen this coming—

Maybe she had, and had forced herself to ignore it.

"My sentiments precisely. What she *does* need is rest and professional counseling. Is she currently seeing a psychiatrist? I'd like to contact—"

"No. She's not seeing anyone, not right now."

"Ah. Well, I'd be happy to offer my services, or recommend a colleague. As for tonight, she needs rest. I thought it best to send her home in care of a relative instead of calling a cab, since she's quite drowsy."

"Yes. Yes. Thank you so much, Doctor . . ."

"Feinman."

"Doctor Feinman. Where's your office? I'll come get her."

"Good. Are you familiar with downtown?"

"Yes."

"Good. I'm at 2323 South Franklin."

She grabbed a pencil from the mug, found a scrap of paper, and started writing. "Twenty-three twenty-three South Franklin. I have a fairly good idea where that is—"

"It's the white high-rise next to the FloriBank Building. Just pull right up into the parking garage. There's no attendant this late, so you don't have to pay." He paused. "Will you be alone?"

"Yes."

"Then it's best to be cautious this time of night. Go all the way down to level P6. Park right by the elevator—I think it's all right this once to ignore

the no-parking signs. Just wait in your car. I'll
come down for you."

"That's awfully thoughtful of you. But will Ave
be all right alone?"

"She's drifting off to sleep now, and I'll lock her
inside the office until we return. Don't worry. I'll
take good care of her."

"Doctor, I can't thank you enough—"

"Don't thank me, Ms. Kallisti. Avra is fortunate
she has a caring relative like you to come get her.
Not all my patients are so lucky." Another pause.
"I'll be seeing you shortly, then."

"Yes. It shouldn't be more than ten or fifteen
minutes."

"Good-bye, Ms. Kallisti."

"Good-bye." Maggie returned the receiver to its
cradle. She should have felt some sort of relief. Ave
was alive, not lying dead in a traffic pileup or in a
gutter. She was quite well. Physically.

Then why the anxiety still? It didn't ease after
the phone call; it got *worse*.

*Because Ave's having another breakdown, and you
can't face that. Can't face not being with Murray. Because you feel guilty. . . .*

Maybe. But there was no time to worry about
how she felt. She found a Post-it by the phone and
scribbled:

SWEETHEART—
I FOUND HER! GONE DOWNTOWN TO

PICK HER UP. WILL EXPLAIN WHEN WE
GET BACK.
     LOVE—

She stuck the note to the microwave, locked Jason inside, then got into the Datsun and headed
downtown.

She had no trouble finding the building at 2323
South Franklin. The rain had let up for a while,
and the trip took ten minutes at most. She didn't
think, instead settling into a mindless state of
dread. She drove carefully, with cold, mechanical
efficiency, and did not speed.

By the time she spotted the white high-rise and
pulled into the parking garage, the Datsun's steering wheel was slippery with sweat. She kept wip-
ing first one hand, then the other, on the side
seams of her shorts.

*If you'd just talked to Ave this morning when she came
down for coffee. You could see how upset she was; you
knew it had nothing to do with the guy who supposedly
stood her up. She saw you with the paper, looking for
apartments. She knew. And you knew she was hiding
something from you. You should have talked to her about
it. . . . But you chickened out. . . .*

Ave's voice in her head. *Oh, Maggie. For once, stop
feeling so damn guilty.*

(This has nothing to do with guilt, the radar
said. This has to do with something else. Something much worse. . . .)

The underground garage was darkly shadowed
in some areas, garishly lit in others. As instructed,
she made her way down to level P6, the lowest
level.

(Why was that supposed to be safer?)

(Never mind. Not important now. Need to get
Avra.)

Actually, it *did* look safer. The lights by the elevator were bright, throwing harsh shadows against
gray concrete walls. Only one other car had been
parked on the same level, in a handicapped space a
few steps from the elevators: a silver Mercedes.
The doctor's car, of course, which was why he'd
specified level P6. He probably intended to help
Avra down into her sister's car, then leave from
here.

Thoughtful man. Thank God the woman who
found Avra brought her here instead of leaving her
in some awful emergency room. . . .

She pulled the Datsun right up beside the Mercedes, alongside a curb painted red and ominously
proclaiming NO PARKING. A white metal sign on the
wall perpendicular to the elevator stall read: VIOLA-
TORS WILL BE TOWED.

She turned off the ignition and waited. With the
air-conditioner off and the windows up, the Datsun's interior quickly became stuffy. Through the
rolled-up windows she could smell the lingering
odor of automobile exhaust. She had her fingers on
the keys, ready to crank the engine and get the air
running, when the elevator doors opened.

An older man stepped halfway out, keeping one hand inside the elevator car to hold the doors open. He spoke clearly so she could hear him through the glass.

"Ms. Kallisti? I'm Doctor Feinman."

She'd known before he said it who he was. Clearly the owner of the Mercedes. His clothing (a linen suit), like his coloring, was pale, and as expensive and elegant as the silver car. His demeanor suggested education and wealth.

He was also a strikingly handsome man. Yet the sight of him disturbed her vaguely, struck her as odd, like a picture hung slightly askew. Was it the clothes? The posture? She couldn't pinpoint it, and repressed the feeling immediately. Terrible of her, to think negative thoughts about the man who was trying to help Avra, the man who had already done so much.

She tossed the keys in her purse, slung it over her shoulder, and climbed out of the Datsun. Smiling faintly, his expression the precisely appropriate mixture of welcome and sober concern, he waited for her to step onto the elevator before releasing the OPEN DOOR button. The steel doors closed over them.

The air inside the elevator car was only slightly better than that in the garage—it was warm and stale and stank of cigarettes. The building's air-conditioner had obviously been shut off, probably since noon because it was Saturday. The heat and

anxiety combined to make her queasy. She hoped
it was cooler up in the doctor's office.

His eyes were blue and very bright. He seemed
to be studying her carefully; like a psychiatrist, she
thought. *Probably thinks I must be crazy, too, if I'm
Ave's sister.* And then it occurred to her that perhaps Ave hadn't mentioned they were identical
twins. That had to be it—he was surprised to see a
carbon copy of Ave. The intentness of his scrutiny
embarrassed her; she shifted her weight and
glanced away, at the control panel, and watched as
he pressed the button for the top floor.

"I hope I didn't keep you waiting long," he said.
The elevator rose upward with a slight lurch that
made her grab the wooden rail. Doctor Feinman,
however, gracefully kept his balance.

"No, not at all. I'd just pulled up."

"Ah. Good."

She finally looked back at him and saw he was
still watching her with that curious expression.
His smile had widened; his hand moved to the la-
pel of his expensive jacket.

Not right, the radar said. This is not right.

A wave of claustrophobia washed over her. She
did not like being on this elevator alone with this
man in this deserted office building. Something
about his expression, his eyes, was growing increasingly *not right*. She tried desperately to remember if she had seen any other cars in the parking garage.

She glanced back at the control panel and tried

to keep her sudden uneasiness from showing on her face. He was a psychiatrist; he would notice such things quickly. She was wrong about him, of course—just having an anxiety attack because of what had happened to Ave. After all, a stranger wouldn't make up a story like this, call her at home. A stranger wouldn't have known how believable it was for Ave to have a breakdown, wouldn't have known that Maggie would drop everything to come and get her sister.

Still, she wanted off the elevator, to be away from this man. *Please, God, hurry. Let the doors open. Let me OUT OF HERE. . . . Just let me off, and I'll never ask for anything again.*

He must have sensed her discomfort, because he said, "Please forgive me. I'm afraid that in my profession I'm accustomed to scrutinizing people rather closely." His hand moved to the jacket's inside pocket. "It's just that you look so very much like your sister, Magdalen."

Magdalen. That was what was wrong: he kept calling her Magdalen. On the phone:

Is this Magdalen Kallisti?

No one called her Magdalen anymore. No one had called her by that name since . . .

Since the day Mama died.

She looked up at him sharply, and, in that brief, ugly second as she met his gaze, knew who she was looking at. *Knew.*

(For God's sake RUN)

And saw from his face that it showed on hers.

At the same time she knew it was impossible; he had been dead almost twenty-five years. Dead, yet here he stood, smiling at her.

Ave had been hiding something. But not this. Please, not *this*. . . . This was only a dream, an incredibly convincing dream.

A waking nightmare.

Oh, God, Ave—what has he done to you this time?

His hands moved in a blur. The left pressed the STOP control, the right pulled something from the pocket. She caught an impression of a shoulder holster beneath the jacket, but the weapon he held in his right hand was too small to be a gun.

She didn't wait to see it clearly. She lunged at him, clawing, trying to knock whatever he held from his grasp. All instinct. It didn't occur to her until the weapon went flying that, had it been a gun, she would have been killed. By then it was too late to think of cooperating.

The plastic syringe sailed past her, struck the steel wall, then rolled on the floor near her feet. She stooped down and grabbed it, wary of a needle, but the syringe was unlike others she'd seen. The needle was retractable.

Wielding the syringe like a switchblade, she turned to find that he had freed the gun and aimed it at her chest.

His face was flushed and he was breathing very hard. He no longer smiled.

"Magdalen, you little bitch," he gasped. His

voice had turned harsh. "You were always causing trouble."

"Where is she? Where's Avra?" she demanded, refusing to lower the syringe. Ridiculous, to point it threateningly at him. He had only to pull the trigger to be done with her. She shook violently with anger and fright. "Is she here? Here in the building?"

"Little bitch," he whispered. "Sneaking little *bitch*. Give that to me." He thrust out his empty hand.

She drew back, keeping the syringe just beyond his reach. Had he wanted to kill her, she would already be dead. He wanted her alive, which hopefully meant Ave was still alive somewhere.

She shook her head. "Not until you tell me where my sister is."

His face contorted; he spread his fingers for emphasis. "Now. You're a fool if you think I won't kill you. Give it to me *now*."

(Take Avra. Run. For God's sake RUN)

(I can't. There's no place to run to—)

"NOW." A pause. His voice lowered, softened, and somehow that softness was far more terrifying than if he had screamed. "*You* were the one who woke Marie, weren't you? You woke her. . . ."

"Yes," she whispered. "Yes, it was me." *And if I can, you son of a bitch, I'll stop you again now.*

Her answer made his eyes blaze with a curious excitement.

She moved as if to surrender the syringe, and at

the last moment, as it was almost in his grasp, she charged him with it.

She came close to injecting him with its contents, but he jerked his arm away instinctively. The momentum threw her against his chest; if she remained close to him, she reasoned, it would be harder for him to aim. For a few seconds they grappled. From the corner of her eye she saw the gun in his hand, waving wildly, cutting through the air. Up it went—

Then came down. The impact against her skull sent a sickening jolt of pain traveling downward through her jaw, her teeth, down the length of her spine. She dropped to the floor.

In the second before she lost consciousness, she was vaguely aware that they had begun to descend.

17

As the elevator headed down to level P6, Bruner retrieved the still-loaded autoinjector and slipped it into a jacket pocket. He dared not administer the ketamine now. His right hand still gripped the .22; he turned the weapon to examine the butt. Impossible to see in the elevator's dim light, but he guessed there might be hair and blood stuck to it. He was right. When he wiped the gun on a cotton handkerchief, the evidence became more visible: one dark tendril and a tiny deep red smudge stood out against the white cotton. Very incriminating, especially once she was dead.

He wrapped the gun in the handkerchief, then withdrew another handkerchief and wrapped it again before replacing it in the shoulder holster.

Another worry, yes. But for the moment violence had provided a release which helped to steady him.

He crouched over Magdalen's still form. Her brazenness had infuriated him, and at the height of his anger he'd struck out with unintended force. At first he thought she was dead, but as he watched, the barely perceptible rise and fall of her rib cage showed that she still breathed. Her head was turned to the side; one cheek and her open lips pressed against the dirty carpeting. Blood pooled at the hairline above her temple.

"Magdalen," he said sternly. "*Magdalen*. If you can hear me, open your eyes."

She did not stir.

Her unresponsiveness distressed him. It indicated a serious, perhaps potentially fatal, injury. He slid a hand beneath her shoulder and carefully rolled the upper half of her body over. Against the dark frame of hair,

(Marie, after all these years, how young you remain!)

her face was ashen. Gently, he parted her hair—thick and soft as Avra's, though sadly cut much shorter, falling midway between shoulder and chin—and examined the surface wound left by the gun. The scalp was lacerated and bleeding; a skull fracture was likely. He probed tentatively for depressed bone fragments with no success. Other than an X ray there was no safe way of knowing. Serious, very serious. Shards of bone pressing against the brain could cause swelling . . . and death.

Yet it could have been worse. Two inches lower, and the butt would have struck her left temple, rupturing the middle meningeal artery, in which case she would have suffered an intracranial bleed. His hands came away bloodied.

(Not on the suit, stupid boy. Wipe them on the hand-kerchief. . . .)

Using the middle fingers of both hands, he lifted her eyelids. The irises were the same color as Avra's: dove-gray, the color of snow clouds. Her pupils contracted only slightly at exposure to the dim light. He studied them carefully. Were they the same size, or did he imagine that the left pupil was a fraction larger than the right?

That would not be good. It would indicate increased intracranial pressure from a bleed or edema, prognosis poor. Untreated, she would most likely die. And if she died . . .

The plan would be ruined. Ruined. She was absolutely pivotal. Without her there could be no re-enactment, no one to take the place of Marie.

The calm brought on by the release of aggression vanished.

(Celia, how could you forsake me? After all I've done for you and the others, after all I've risked. . . .)

After his last encounter with Celia he'd determined his only course was to find the sister, then continue with the plan. His resolve not to give up had seemingly met with the children's approval; a few minor successes had restored his faith in Celia's help, in the plan. After carefully removing all traces of his and Avra's presence, he had abandoned the white van in a mall parking garage in nearby St. Petersburg and walked the half mile to another garage where the Mercedes waited. All had gone smoothly; he had made excellent time, had not been noticed, had aroused no suspicion.

And after twenty-five years of waiting he had at last added a lock of Avra's hair to his scrapbook. Now almost complete, it rested in the safe along with the items he would later dispose of.

His confidence bolstered, he had been exceptionally brilliant and convincing on the phone with Magdalen. There was a chance that Avra had told her sister about the encounter in Selena's restaurant, in which case he was prepared to use threats, if necessary.

But Magdalen had not known, had not recognized his voice. He, in turn, had recognized hers; it had taken his full concentration to call her "Ms. Kallisti" and not "Marie."

He had used the name Feinman on purpose— after all, he would be dispensing with it soon, and he had wanted to test her reaction to it, to see how much she knew.

No reaction, and from her tone she clearly was not acting. She believed his every word; she had fallen cleanly into his trap.

He had been so sure then that the children were helping him. So sure. But now . . .

He forced himself to subdue the hysteria that threatened. There was work to be done, a great deal of it, if he was to keep Celia and the others at bay. He had to maintain control more than ever now, if he wanted to survive.

The elevator stopped at level P6; the door slid open. Through an agonizing effort of will Bruner forced himself to act. He lifted Magdalen—clumsily, because like her sister, she was a tall woman—and carried her out to the Mercedes. He propped her against the car, letting her upper half lie on the hood, and pressed against the lower half of her body with his own to keep her from sliding onto the oil-stained asphalt. He did not want her in his car, bleeding on the upholstery—as much from distaste at seeing his beautiful Mercedes sullied as from fear of evidence—and so he put her in the trunk. It was an awkward manuever, and as he unlocked the trunk, his hands were shaking so badly that he dropped the keys. At last he got the trunk closed and crawled into the car.

He was on the verge of grasping the steering wheel when he looked down at his hands. Traces of her blood, dried red-brown crescents under his fingernails. Her blood on his hands. Her blood in his car, on the gun, the handkerchief. Helen's body, Helen's blood, spattered in *his* garage. Blood on the jumpsuit, home in the safe—

(Had he gotten blood on his clothes, on the linen suit? It would be painfully noticeable against the light cream color—)

Work to be done. For now, just get her to Riverhills.

He turned the key in the ignition and drove out

of the garage. Too quickly at first; the Mercedes's tires squealed, echoing in the empty garage.

Slowly. Slowly. The roads were slick from the intermittent rain, and this was Saturday night. The cops would be out in force, looking for drunks and speeders. He had been speeding the night Celia died. The night the policeman stopped him.

The night his life began to fall apart. . . .

As he pulled onto Franklin Street, he was careful to observe the signals and the speed limit. The drive back to Temple Terrace seemed interminably long. Several times he grew disoriented and imagined he was back on Route 123, with Celia's body in the trunk. Halfway home on the interstate he saw flashing lights in the rearview and careened off to the roadside in a panic. But the cop had been in a hurry to get somewhere else, and passed on.

If she died in the trunk before he got her home—

Without medical intervention she would most likely die anyway. He did not have the means at his office or house to help her, yet he dared not take her to a hospital. He would have to take her home, risk her death.

Hope that she would regain consciousness in time to play her role in the plan.

And if she did not . . .

Celia, how could you forsake me? I'm doing this all for you—

(For your own good)

When they finally arrived at Riverhills, Bruner

pulled the Mercedes into the garage, beside the Volvo—he had driven it into the garage and placed Helen's body in the trunk; later, when Amelie joined her mother, he would dispose of it—and closed the garage door before carrying Magdalen into the house. He placed her on the floor of the second guest bedroom.

She was so still at first that he thought she was dead, and reached down to press a finger against her neck.

(So white, her skin, for one who lived in Florida. Marie had always been pale.)

Her pulse was thready and rapid. As he touched her, she stirred.

"Magdalen? If you hear me, open your eyes."

She murmured something unintelligible, but her eyes remained closed.

He had purchased another dead bolt with the thought of installing it while Magdalen was drugged, but it was clearly unnecessary. Even if she regained consciousness, she would be disoriented and weak, unable to escape.

Too weak to play Marie. He should have killed her on the elevator and disposed of the body, should have admitted to himself that the plan was crumbling.

Even so, he closed the door when he left. In the living room he stopped at the wet bar and poured himself a cognac. His anxiety was growing, and he filled the snifter two thirds full, then sat down on the low couch and stared at the dull silver shutters on the other side of the sliding glass door and the picture window.

The sense that Celia and the children were watching had grown unbearable.

Yet they did not appear. They were watching, all right, but they were *waiting* for something. For him to act.

But what was he supposed to *do* to placate them? Silence.

He drank the cognac in huge, careless swallows. Within minutes he had drained the contents of the snifter and poured himself a second drink, this time filling the glass to the rim. He was too tense to become as drunk as he should have, but he soon became drunk enough to cry. A tear spilled down his cheek, into his mouth; the taste of salt mingled with that of cognac.

Exhaustion—he had not slept since Thursday, and then only fitfully—and self-pity overwhelmed him. He had worked so *hard* . . . not only the past few days, on the children's behalf, but his entire life. All that Feinman owned, all that Feinman had *earned*—the medical practice, the identity he'd worked so hard to construct, the house on the river, the Mercedes, the expensive clothes—he would have to surrender them all.

He could not face losing these things, could not face starting over. He had done so too many times in his life, and now he was tired. *Old.* To lose all those things . . .

Worst of all, to lose Amelie. All the time and effort spent courting her, wasted.

No. He drew a hand across his face and stood, swaying. Cognac sloshed over the rim of the snifter, staining the sleeve of the linen jacket, but he did not care. He stumbled through the living room, spilling liquor as he went, into the kitchen, into the hall toward the master bedroom. Toward Amelie. He would not be cheated of this one last pleasure.

He opened the door to his room and stood in the doorway, admiring her. She lay asleep on top of the comforter, in the center of his bed—*his* bed. Her blond hair lay spread out on his pillow. Her mouth hung open; her breath came and went in gusty little sighs. Perfect beauty, perfect innocence. No woman in the world could intentionally have been more seductive.

He set the snifter on the mahogany dresser and moved unsteadily toward the bed. As he did, illumination graced him: he saw what Celia and the others had been trying to tell him. The strength of the revelation dropped him to his knees. He reached out and caught hold of the bed, his posture that of a child kneeling for bedtime prayers. He rested his forehead against the comforter and sobbed aloud, but his tears were ones of gratitude.

The sister was unnecessary. The sister was unnecessary. The sister was unnecessary.

Helen's death and the sister's injury were complications, yes. Intentional ones, to test his strength. But Amelie's presence was a sign of intervention and favor.

Of course. A child to play Avra's role. The seduction would be more authentic, more appealing. A just reward for him—he would have Amelie at last.

And Avra to take Marie's part. She had played the child; time now to let her play the woman. The notion satisfied him. It smacked of completion, of events coming full circle.

The children had merely been testing him, and had judged him worthy. With their help all complications—Helen, the sister—would dissolve. It was futile to worry about such unimportant details now. He needed only to have faith, to hold to the plan unswervingly.

He ceased weeping and pulled himself up to sit on the edge of the bed.

Amelie still slept, the perfect child-goddess. He leaned forward to stroke her hair; the sensation never failed to thrill him. How sublimely different from the touch of an adult's hair—how infinitely finer and silkier the texture. Avra's

(Darla's)

hair had felt like this years ago, though now he had to admit it had undergone subtle, disappointing changes. The lock he had cut this afternoon and carefully placed into his album had seemed peculiarly unsatisfying.

He closed his eyes as he continued to run his fingertips through Amelie's hair, out onto the rougher surface of the cotton pillowcase. For an instant the years receded, and in his mind's eye it was five-year-old Avra lying there, dark hair fanned against the pillow.

And then time fell away altogether, until they were both children.

Baltimore

AUGUST 1936

18

He had loved Darla desperately, from the first moment he was old enough to be aware of her.

At least part of his infatuation was due to her physical attractiveness. She was tall for her age, and slender, with angular, arrestingly beautiful features, and her hair—

Her hair. It was glossy dark, almost black. When she went out in the sun, a reddish-violet cast became visible. Mrs. Feinman never permitted her daughter's hair to be cut, and by the time she was nine years old, Darla's hair fell below her waist. On summer Sundays, when the Feinmans went for a ride (usually just Darla and the doctor—Mrs. Feinman was often indisposed on Sunday mornings), Rolf would run to watch as the big black Ford pulled out of the circular driveway and the wind teased strands of Darla's hair out the rolled-down car window.

He spent his boyhood dreaming of touching it.
He could imagine no greater pleasure. Since Mrs.
Feinman could not be bothered, the task fell to
Elise, morning and evening, to brush out the girl's
hair. Darla would report to the servants' quarters
and submit stoically to Elise's energetic brushing.
Sometimes before parties Elise would spend hours
trying to create ringlets with a curling iron,
with little success; Darla's hair was determinedly
straight. In summer Elise would often braid it, but
most times Darla wore it brushed back, with a ribbon headband to keep it from falling into her face.
Rolf watched these twice-daily encounters from a
safe distance, imagining himself in Elise's place.

Yet he adored more than just her hair and her
features. Like her father, Darla possessed a quiet
inward grace, an aura of elegance. She was a serious child with the poise of an adult, and though
she was always having parties (from which Rolf
was banned) and inviting schoolmates over to the
house, she had few friends.

Elise often watched the girl, as Mrs. Feinman
was far too busy with her social commitments to
spend her time raising a child (and, according to
Elise when no Feinmans were present to hear, the
woman was usually too drunk). Even so, the children were kept separate as much as possible, and
Elise discouraged them from playing together. To
Rolf the message was clear: Darla was his superior.
Darla was *different*.

Certainly, Elise never dared raise her voice or

hand to the girl; such privileges were reserved for her own flesh and blood. No one mistreated Darla; in fact, no one punished her (indeed, as Elise often pointed out, there was never any need). Darla had been born to wealth and comfort. She had never known want or cruelty or fear, and she would never know them. Rolf's admiration of her was surpassed only by his envy.

He was, after all, Doctor Feinman's son. And Darla was Feinman's daughter. As he grew older, he came to realize that he and Darla were brother and sister.

The secret tormented him. Not because it was unfair that Darla should have her own magnificent bedroom upstairs, filled with toys and expensive clothes, while Rolf had to share the downstairs servants' quarters with his mother (though Elise reminded him of the inequity often enough). By age seven Rolf had already come to understand that *fair* was a useless concept in life. The things that really mattered were who had the most money and who could hit the hardest.

No, the secret tormented him because he desperately wanted to share it with Darla. More than anything he longed for her to direct her compassionate gaze at him and *know—know* that he was her brother. Her reaction to the revelation constituted one of his dearest fantasies.

He imagined that she would embrace him. She would kiss him solemnly, her hair sweeping forward to brush his cheek. The news would move her deeply, perhaps to tears. She would proclaim her love for him. Most importantly, she would lead him upstairs and present her bedroom to him, insisting that he take his rightful place with the rest of the family. Elise, naturally, would stay downstairs.

He was six when it first struck him that Darla had to be his sister. No wonder he so loved her! He questioned his mother timidly on the subject.

Yes, it was true. Darla was his sister. And if he dared mention it to her, or to anyone—*anyone at all*—his mother would kill him.

He knew Elise well enough to understand that the threat was meant literally.

He did not want to die, yet he promptly went outside and found Edgar Allan Poe, sunning herself in the backyard. He crouched a few feet away from the cat and whispered:

Darla is my sister. Darla is my sister. Darla is my sister.

And then, with a happiness that sent a warm flush to his neck and cheeks:

I am Darla's brother. I am Darla's brother. . . .

By mid-August the burns were mostly healed and he could flex the hand without pain, though the flesh was shiny and scarred. Because school was out, the temporary loss of his right hand had presented an inconvenience only to him. The most upsetting part was that it left him unable to continue the experiments.

Eventually, the story evolved that Rolf had incurred the injury himself, though he and Feinman and Elise all knew it was a lie. Still, they pretended, even among themselves, that the boy alone was to blame. After a time, Rolf knew, Elise would forget it had all been a lie, and would fervently remember it as true.

Surprisingly, Doctor Feinman took it upon himself to treat the boy's wound. Up to that point he had never taken the slightest interest in Rolf's health. The doctor dressed the burns with ointment and wrapped them in thick white gauze. Every evening when Feinman came home, he changed the dressings. It hurt, but Rolf enjoyed the sessions; they were the only attention he'd ever received from his father. He looked forward to the chance to sit in the patient's chair in the doctor's office, a dark cavern of a room used on those occasions when Feinman received patients at home. The office was filled with expensive Oriental carpets, crystal lamps, leather furniture, and books—shelves and shelves of books. And a real human skull atop the bookcase, far beyond a seven-year-old's reach. Elise had said it was the mortal remains of a disobedient young patient, and let that be a warning to him, but it looked like an adult's skull to Rolf, and he had already begun to learn that he could not always believe his mother. Sometimes she was downstairs cooking dinner, and sent Rolf upstairs to the office alone. He valued those times most, for they forced Feinman to speak directly to him, albeit in the falsely cheerful, impersonal tone he used with all his patients:

And how are we today, my boy? Better, hmm?

(*My boy.* . . . Did he realize what he was saying, *my boy?* Was the casual phrase a secret signal, an acknowledgment of their relationship?)

Rolf would search Feinman's eyes, which were quickly averted; he never found what he sought in them. Even so, he was sorry when the nightly visits to the doctor's study stopped.

A week after the bandages came off, the weather turned warm and humid. Early on a Friday afternoon Elise walked to the grocery, leaving Rolf to play out in the backyard. Normally, he would have raced to the abandoned field, eager to try out all the new experiments he'd dreamed up while the hand was healing. But today he was overcome by a vague malaise—he was in the first stages of catching a summer cold—and so he sat in the shade of the trees, out of the strong sunlight, which hurt his eyes and made him queasy.

Nearby, Darla's ten-week-old puppy, desperate for company, whined forlornly at the sight of him. It was a black Labrador named Jack Armstrong, brought home by the doctor to ease Darla's grief over the disappearance of Edgar Allan Poe. In Darla's absence (she was attending a birthday party), Jackie was chained up in his doghouse on the edge of the copse of trees. Neither Elise nor Mrs. Feinman allowed the dog in the house when the girl was gone.

The pup was almost cute enough to arouse Rolf's affection: it was loose skinned, gangly, with feet disproportionately large for its body and intelligent cinnamon-colored eyes that reminded Rolf of Darla's. Jackie was far more gregarious and eager to please than Edgar, and had actually approached Rolf on a few occasions wanting to be petted, which the boy had done with a sense of detachment. He would never hurt Jackie, of course, because Darla loved the animal, but he often dreamed of how amusing it would be to use the pup—so energetic and comically uncoordinated—in an experiment. Today would have been the perfect opportunity, with Elise at the market, Mrs. Feinman shopping, Darla at a party—but no. He would not, for Darla's sake. . . .

Besides, he was feeling too ill to take advantage of the opportunity. His head hurt, and he did not feel like moving from his soft grassy seat under the trees, even though his bladder was urgently full. After several moments' indecision (Should he bother to go into the house? He lacked the energy. If Elise caught him outside, she'd thrash him—but then, she had left for the store only moments ago), he stood up and wandered to the far edge of the trees and unbuttoned his knickers.

The movement caused Jackie to renew his pleas for attention. The dog strained until his choke collar was pulled taut, then sat in the shade cast by a nearby maple. The noise, Rolf decided, made his head hurt worse.

"Shut up, Jackie!" Having to shout above the dog's whining irritated Rolf further. He picked a spot at the base of an old oak and aimed for it.

The dog's whines grew more insistent, became frantic barks. If someone passing by heard and decided to investigate . . .

"Stupid dog!" Rolf snapped. "Stupid, stupid Jackie. Shut *up*!" He glanced back over his shoulder and saw the cause of the puppy's unrest.

Darla was walking across the lawn toward the doghouse. She wore a bright red-and-white party dress, stiff organza with puffed sleeves; her hair, pulled off her forehead with a red ribbon, fell unfettered down her back. She crouched down on one knee and stroked Jackie, whose tail wagged madly.

Rolf dared not breathe, but held perfectly still, praying she had not seen him.

Too late. She caressed the puppy one final time, then lifted her face and stared directly into his eyes.

A dizzying wave of humiliation swept over him. He closed his eyes until he no longer felt faint, then opened them again. He could do nothing but gape at her, his fly open, his penis in his hand, and wait for her to turn away from him in disgust.

Instead, she rose, leaving Jackie to whimper after her, and walked toward him under the trees until she stood barely an arm's length away.

Her boldness left him too shocked to move, even to swallow. His heart began to beat sickeningly fast. The situation horrified him, yet there was something vaguely exciting about it, something which reminded him of the experiments. He should have hurried to button up, but instead stayed as he was.

She studied him, her face solemn, her eyes bright with curiosity.

He found his breath and whispered, "You're not supposed to be here."

"Judith threw up," she said matter-of-factly, "so her party ended early. I got tired of waiting for Mama to come so I walked. It wasn't far."

"Your mama will be mad."

She shrugged. "No, she won't. She doesn't care what I do." Her eyes focused on the hand clutched at his fly; her voice lowered. "Can I see it?"

He hesitated, but her manner was so entirely free of embarrassment that he finally dared unclench his hand.

Her voice lowered further still. "*Oh,*" she said, and leaned closer for a better look. Her hair fell forward, sweeping gently over his open palm, his exposed genitals.

He shuddered at the unbearably ecstatic sensation.

"It's *growing,*" she whispered, at the same time that he felt himself stir in his hand.

A flood of feelings welled up in him. He was bursting with the need to tell her *now* that he was her brother, that he loved her, that when he grew up and became a doctor, he would marry her. It was worth risking Elise's wrath, worth risking death. The familiar daydream returned, of Darla kissing him, leading him upstairs to take his rightful place as a member of the Feinman family. . . .

He tried to tell her all those things, but could not find his voice. For a moment the two of them stood silent. It was Darla who spoke next, in an uncharacteristically timid tone.

"May I touch it?"

Except for a declaration of undying love nothing she could have said would have moved him more deeply. She was not disgusted by him; no, she *revered* him, as he revered her. There could no longer be any doubt—his feelings were returned.

He nodded and withdrew his hand.

She bent even closer, draping her beautiful dark hair behind her ear with her index and middle fingers so that it would stay out of the way, so that she could better see him. With those same two fingers

(that had touched her hair, her glorious hair)

she reached for him and drew them with excruciating gentleness along his length. He moaned with surprise and pleasure and locked his knees to keep them from buckling. Her pale, radiant face hovered a mere foot away from him now; her forehead puckered with the intentness of her scrutiny.

"It's not like mine at all," she murmured.

Hope entered him. He had shared a secret with her; now she hinted that she might be persuaded to reciprocate. "Could I see?" he asked, startled to find that he could speak.

She flushed scarlet and glanced quickly at his eyes, but there was no shock, no derision in hers. He could see her struggling to decide: Was it safe outside, here in the trees? Could he be trusted with such a tender revelation?

The most important revelation of all still burned within him. "You can trust me, Darla," he breathed. "I am—" He broke off. He yearned to tell her, yet he knew if she did not keep the secret, Elise's retaliation would be swift and dreadful, and Doctor Feinman would put him and his mother out onto the street. . . .

I am your brother, Darla. You are my sister. . . .

Her head turned sharply. There came the sound of a vehicle turning into the circular driveway, the slam of a car door.

"Mama!" she exclaimed, and turned back to him. They shared a look of dismay and—did he only imagine it?—love, then she pulled away from him, graceful as an animal despite her panic, and bolted across the lawn, into the house.

For a few seconds he stood dazed, looking after her. And then he stuffed himself back into his knickers, buttoned his fly, and found a clean spot on the cool grass to wait for Elise.

The feeling of malaise developed into a bout of influenza. He forgot that he had been feeling ill before his encounter with Darla; his memory edited the event so that he saw a direct connection between her touch and his sickness. Elise had dragged him to enough sentimental movies at the Rialto Theater for him to know that people got sick and died because of unrequited love.

A high fever filled his mind with bizarre thoughts. At times he became convinced that he would die because he had been too cowardly to reveal himself to Darla as her brother. That idea, combined with the tearfulness induced by the fever, overwhelmed him with self-pity and made him weep until his pillowcase was soaked. Feinman did not come to visit him, but gave Elise foul-tasting cough syrup and instructions for its administration. Whatever guilt or paternal obligation the doctor felt had healed along with Rolf's burns.

In his semidelirium he scripted all the things that he and Darla had not said under the trees, all the things he knew Darla had *wanted* to say, but had not been able to, from timidity or simple lack of time. Rolf became convinced that she knew of their relationship, that she had long ago arrived instinctively at the truth, but was shyly waiting to hear him proclaim it aloud. He no longer doubted that she loved him—hadn't she touched him *there*, in the most private of places? And she would have revealed herself to him, in turn, had they not been interrupted by Mrs. Feinman's arrival.

The thought of her made him weak, made him long to recover so that he could see her again, could touch *her*. When he was well, he would go to her and tell her the truth. She would get Doctor Feinman to protect him from Elise, and even if she could not—well, then, the two of them would run away together. He dreamed fitfully of a world without pain, without punishment, without Elise, a beautiful world filled with no one but Darla. He grew certain that a happier time would soon begin; he did not realize it was about to end.

The event that crushed his dreams of life as Darla's acknowledged brother came one summer's dusk, though he was too adrift in a sea of fever and codeine to remember the exact day. Certainly, it had been less than a week since their fateful encounter under the oak.

He dozed restlessly on the small cot in the room he shared with his mother. The window was open, and the parted floral print curtains breathed in and out against the screen. Outside, banished to his doghouse, Jack Armstrong whined fitfully, at times giving a tearful yelp to protest the absence of his mistress, who had gone to spend the night at a girlfriend's. A warm late summer evening, but the boy shook under sweat-dampened sheets. He was miserable from the fever, sore throat, and coughing, and had risen, shivering at the painful caress of air against his skin, only once that day, to pee. The act brought Darla to mind, and he used the thought of her, of her touching him, to sustain him through the worst of the illness. He replayed the moment a thousand times:

May I touch it?

The look on her face, so pale and then so flushed, the unbearable tide of sensation that swept him, the feel of her hair, soft against his skin. . . .

Each time he enhanced the memory, added details, subtle changes of expression to her eyes, her lips, her face, so there could be no question that she *knew*, and had been waiting these seven years since his birth for him to tell her himself that he was her brother. He reasoned it to be a test of sorts, to prove his worthiness. Only if he was brave enough to speak the truth, to risk his mother's anger, would he be rewarded, recognized as a member of the family.

His mother had entered the room twice, at lunch and sunset, to dose him with the doctor's bitter syrup and ask if he wanted food. He did not, so she left him with a sweating glass of cold water that quickly went tepid.

The door stood half ajar, and the kitchen's brightness cast a long, thin triangle of light into the gloomy bedroom. He heard his mother working in the kitchen, heard the clatter of dishes and the quick, sure sound of her steps as she served Feinman supper. Feinman ate in the kitchen only when his wife and daughter were gone. Rolf distracted himself from his misery by listening to the rise and fall of their voices, sometimes understanding snatches of the conversation. The incident with Rolf's burns seemed, strangely, to have improved relations between them. Feinman's voice sounded uncharacteristically distraught, Elise's (impossibly) comforting.

Feinman spoke first. *Can't bear it much longer . . . passed out again in her room . . . thank God Darla . . .* The rest was muffled by the sound of Elise running water at the sink.

Elise replied, at first too low for Rolf to hear, then her tone grew bolder, more impassioned. *. . . not good for her . . . not good for any of us, Jakob . . . How much longer? How long?*

Can't do it . . . would ruin me. . . .

. . . sick . . . woman's sick . . . institution or something *. . . no one would blame you . . . think of yourself . . . of the girl . . . more of a mother to her than Verna has ever been. . . .*

Murmured agreement. And then a very strange noise, one that Rolf thought he must have dreamed. A dry, hoarse sound: Feinman sobbing. *Not fair . . . Darla . . . Darla. . . .*

Creak of floorboards. Scrape of a chair pushed back from the table. Murmurs, low and comforting at first, then growing increasingly passionate. A moment of intense silence. Then Elise, too softly to hear distinctly. But from the cadence, Rolf recognized the words he had heard so many times before:

Not here, not here

Approaching footsteps. By the time the light from the kitchen fell across his face, he had squeezed his eyes shut.

He's asleep. The medicine. . . .

Click of the door as it shut; semidarkness again.
More silence, then the soft sound of fabric brushing against fabric, against skin. Rolf peered
through the filter of his blond lashes.

Back pressed against the closed door, Elise stood,
dress and apron gone, full slip pulled down to her
waist. Her bare skin gleamed pearl in the twilight.
As Feinman struggled free from his unbuttoned
shirt, she drew his head to her breast with one
hand.

The boy closed his eyes, desperately wanting
and not wanting to see what followed. He listened
to Elise's little moans, to Feinman's ragged breath.

In a far corner of the house the telephone rang.
Abruptly, all movement and noise stopped. Rolf
could hear his own breath. Two, three, four rings
in the tense stillness.

. . . *still passed out cold*, the doctor whispered.
Don't answer it
But it could be a patient
Don't answer, Elise said firmly. Feinman's pro-
tests were muffled as she pulled him to her, then
quickly ceased. Footsteps. The groan of Elise's bed
as it took their combined weight. More rustling as
the doctor rid himself of the rest of his clothes and
Elise drew back the spread.

The boy watched from under half-closed lids,
fighting to keep his breathing shallow and regular
as Elise, freed now from the slip, pushed Feinman
down on the bed and bent her face low, between
the doctor's legs—as close as Darla's face had been

to him, to Rolf—and then Elise bent closer, closer in the shadows, until there was no distance between the two of them at all.

Suddenly, it was no longer Elise and Feinman at all, but Darla, himself and Darla, Darla's hair brushing against him, Darla bending low to kiss him *there*. . . .

He closed his eyes again, unable to bear more. Beneath the thin flannel blanket and the sheet, beneath his cotton pajama bottoms, he felt himself stir with an ache as strong and sweet as the moment Darla had touched him. The fever seemed merely an extension of the yearning; he was sick for her, his entire body ached for want of her. He had to tell her of his love, or die.

He longed to touch himself, but dared not move. Instead, he watched for a while as the adults grappled in the darkening shadows, first Feinman in ascendancy, then Elise. Tonight it seemed to go on for a very long time, until the twilight gave way to total darkness, until at last his desire yielded to illness and even this half-welcomed distraction tired him. He wished only for the doctor to finish and leave, for his mother to fall asleep. For quiet, and the chance to dream of Darla. He finally dozed, despite the sounds of their increasing passion.

He was startled awake by a sudden sweep of light as the bedroom door was thrown open. He frowned, confused, until he remembered Feinman and Elise on the bed. The doctor, then, had finished and was finally leaving.

But no. Feinman and Elise clung to one other on the bed, trying to hide beneath each other's body. In the doorway, framed by harsh yellow light, stood a small, familiar silhouette: Darla. Her face was eclipsed by darkness. Rolf could only see the sharply delineated outline of her form, perfectly straight and still for an amazing length of time. Years afterward he would be able to recall, as if gazing at a snapshot, Feinman's face captured in a pane of light and contorted with horrified recognition.

And then Darla gave a hoarse wail that began deep in her throat, reminding him of Edgar Allan Poe's death cry. The wail rose steadily in pitch; it followed her as she turned and ran back into the kitchen, out into the living room, and up the stairs, to Mrs. Feinman's room.

She had taken ill at the girlfriend's house during dinner—a sore throat and fever, no doubt contracted from Rolf. Clearly, the best thing was to get her home, where her doctor father could look after her. The girl's parents had telephoned the Feinman residence and were distressed when they received no reply.

Darla was not. She pointed out that her father had probably gone on a house call, and her mother often fell asleep early. Yes, she was such a sound sleeper that she hadn't heard the phone. Yes, she

was certain her mother was at home. Darla wanted
to go home; she wanted to go home *then*. Even if
her mother was gone, a servant would be there to
let her in.

(Then why hadn't the servant answered the
phone? the girl's mother wanted to know, but by
then Darla was on the verge of tears and further
attempts at reason seemed pointless.)

No one answered her faint knocking at the door
to let her in, either, but it didn't matter. The door
had been left open, although Elise usually made
the rounds and locked up the house as soon as it
turned dark. Darla had entered with her little suit-
case and gone upstairs looking for her father. She
knew that he was home because she had seen the
black Ford in the garage, but she did not call him
because by that time, her throat was so inflamed
that even whispering was painful.

Her mother was sprawled out on her bed, fully
dressed as if she'd intended to go out, then been
overcome by narcolepsy. Mrs. Feinman lay on her
back with her coat on, mouth open, snoring, in
that heavy, sodden slumber that Darla had come to
hate. Her father was not in his bedroom, not in his
study. Sniffling with self-pity and frustration,
Darla made her way back down the stairs. Her
head throbbed, and she ached with fever. She was
desperate for an adult to minister to her, to settle
her into a soft bed with clean, sweet sheets, dose
her with medicines and speak in low, soothing
tones.

She saw that the light was on in the kitchen, which meant Elise was there. Even if the doctor was not with her, Elise would know where he was, and would take care of Darla until he arrived. But as she pushed through the swinging door, she saw that the room was empty, and she began to weep fervently. In her desperation it did not occur to her to knock on Elise's door before opening it.

It was for Darla's sake, Feinman said, that Elise and Rolf had to go. Not for his wife's, not for his, but for Darla's. The girl had insisted. She was filled, or so Feinman said, with a passionate hatred for Elise, and there was no longer any chance she could accept the woman as her stepmother. Elise railed, screamed, threatened, pleaded, but Feinman held quietly firm.

Elise and Rolf had to go.

Feinman was an honorable man, of course. He agreed to set them up in a tiny apartment across town. Elise got a job selling tickets at a movie theater. Until she was mysteriously beaten to death many years later, Doctor Feinman came at least weekly to visit her. After Feinman's death Rolf learned, to his amazement, that the doctor had made provision for his bastard son's medical education in his will.

When Elise told the boy they were leaving, Rolf had but one thought: to see Darla, to tell Darla the truth. Certainly, he could understand how the girl had come to hate Elise, but he could not believe that hatred extended to him. This was his chance to reveal himself, to win acceptance, perhaps finally to escape from Elise forever.

Early on his last morning in the Feinman house, two weeks to the day after Darla's fateful discovery, Rolf stole up the stairs. Elise would have thrashed him had she caught him doing so without permission, but she had been up late the night before, sobbing and packing the last of their belongings, and so was still asleep in bed. Doctor Feinman had already left for the hospital; Rolf had waited in bed until he heard the Ford pull out of the driveway. Mrs. Feinman, of course, was no concern at such an early hour.

His hand trembled as he clutched the polished oak banister. He had only been upstairs a handful of times when he helped Elise carry folded towels or trays of food up to Mrs. Feinman. Once or twice he had glanced at the inside of Darla's pristine white bedroom, but those brief glimpses had sustained his imagination for years.

Too quickly, he found himself standing before her white door. He raised a clenched fist to strike the painted wood . . . and began losing courage. He wanted to turn, to run back down the stairs to his bed, to lose himself beneath the covers.

The thought of life alone with Elise, without the hope of ever seeing Darla again, renewed his resolve. He swallowed a gulp of air and rapped on the door with his knuckles, flinching at the sharp sound it made in the silent house. He was half convinced it was the sound of his own heart.

She had been asleep. He heard her murmur thickly on the other side of the door, heard the rustle of bedclothes being pulled back. She opened the door in midyawn, eyes squeezed shut, mouth wide open. Her white floor-length nightgown had a red satin ribbon and lace at the throat. The first rays of sunlight streaking through the open window behind her shone through the gauze-thin fabric, so that he saw the two small dark nipples of her childish breasts. Alas, her beautiful hair was in a thick coil atop her head, to keep it from tangling as she slept; the fact made him wince with longing. This time, of all times, he had wanted to see it down.

Aquiver with joy at the prospect of morning, Jack Armstrong wormed his small body past her, scrambling over her bare feet. With puppy awkwardness he half climbed, half fell down the stairs, then ran to the front door and gave an expectant bark.

"Jackie! Come back, it's too early!" she called in disgust, then rubbed her eyes and blinked at him. After her recent bout of flu she still sounded as though she had a cold. "What do *you* want?"

The clear note of hostility in her tone took him aback; he stammered in confusion. "I—I . . ."

"Go away," she said crossly, "and let Jackie out when you go down." She moved to shut the door.

"No!" he cried, made desperate by her reaction. This was not the radiantly loving scene he had envisioned. He thrust an arm toward her, plucked at her sleeve. "*Please* . . . I've come to tell you a secret."

"A secret?" She hesitated; a thin gleam of curiosity brightened her eyes, and lit a spark of hope within him.

His voice dropped to a whisper. Its quavering embarrassed and infuriated him. "Darla . . . don't you know who I am?"

I'm your brother, Darla. Darla, I am your brother. . . .

"You're Rolf." The blankness of her eyes, her expression, tore at his heart, but he forced himself to speak the words he had so often dreamed of telling her.

"I'm your brother, Darla. Your father . . . he's my father too. You're my sister."

She took a step back from the doorway. For an instant her face went entirely slack, then she grimaced with rage. "That's a lie!"

His face burned as if she had slapped him. Her behavior seemed insane, impossible, violated the rules of his inner reality. She seemed *angry,* but surely he had misunderstood. "It's the truth, I swear. I'm your brother. You're my sister. Darla, I love—"

She did not let him finish. "You know what my mother says?" Tears began rolling down her cheeks, but she seemed too furious to notice. "My mother says *your* mother is a whore. She says your mother doesn't know *who* your father is!"

He did not entirely understand the words, but

the hatred behind them stunned him. "But, Darla," he whined in a small shaking voice, a baby's voice, stupid Rolf's voice. "Darla, I *love* you. Brothers and sisters are supposed to love each other."

"You're not my brother," she said nastily. "And I don't have to love you back. You can't tell me what to do! You're just a little servant boy, and I hate you *and* your mother!"

He released a loud, gasping sob. The sound seemed to fan her anger; with a swift movement she jabbed both arms, palms flat out, at him, and pushed so that he lost his footing and stumbled backward into the hallway. Before he could get up, she had slammed the door.

Stupid, stupid boy. Did you really think she could ever love something as stupid as you?

He stood outside her room for a moment, trying to decide how to react to the total destruction of his imaginary world.

Jack Armstrong's barking drew him back into reality. He went downstairs and let the puppy out the front door, then on second thought went out himself.

He did not discourage the little Lab from following him to the abandoned field. Jackie's eyes were moist and brown, and reminded him very much of Darla's.

Tampa

AUGUST 1990

19

Avra opened her eyes. In that first instant she thought she was home on Willow Street and expected to see the ceiling fan revolving above her, but the room was too dark. For once the blackness didn't frighten her; she felt tranquil and enjoyably drowsy. Normally, she would have kept the window shade up and the curtains parted so that the glare from the streetlamp outside could serve as a night-light.

(Almost thirty years old, and here she was still afraid of the dark, and too embarrassed to use a night-light)

Didn't matter. Nothing mattered anymore. . . . She let her eyes close slowly, wanting only to sink back into bliss, into sleep.

And opened them again at the faraway sound of a child crying.

No. Only her imagination. She held her breath, trying to hear. Nothing, just the drone of the air-conditioner cutting on. At night she heard the strangest things as she drifted off, especially when Maggie was gone. She'd swear she heard someone trying to break into the house, or someone being strangled in the backyard, or (most often) someone standing at the bottom of the stairs, calling her name. And it would just be the refrigerator making its weird nighttime noises—(why did it never make sounds like that during the day?)—or the air-conditioner. . . .

The air-conditioner was running.

But the air-conditioner on Willow Street was broken.

The realization startled her into waking consciousness, brought back the unwanted memory of where she was. She pushed herself into a sitting position. The movement made her slightly dizzy, but the earlier nausea seemed to have passed.

She remembered: Bruner had been here, in the room. She had thrown the photo album at him. He had pointed a gun at her and she had been sure she was going to die, but instead, he had given her a shot.

(The Avra doll. Had she dreamed it?)

The drug, whatever it was, kept her heart from pounding, kept her breathing regular, but beneath the calm overlay of its effect she was cold with panic.

Maggie. Why did she keep thinking of Maggie? There had been a dream (or a vision; it had seemed too real for a dream). . . .

You can't cry now, honey. You've got to help Magdalen

He had drugged her again, then left her alone. She was still wearing the same dirty clothes she had worn to work that morning (centuries ago). The cotton gauze of her dress was stiff where the vomit had dried, and her skin was sticky with old sweat. The observation triggered self-pity and an odd tug of homesickness. She wanted more than anything to get up, drive herself home, and take a nice long soak in the tub. Her muscles ached as if she'd slept in the same position for days. It was hard to be sure after the drugs, but it seemed that hours had passed since he'd given her the shot.

If he wasn't going to kill her, why was he keeping her here?

Not knowing was the worst part. If she knew what he intended, she could prepare herself. . . .

(Stop lying to yourself. You know what he wants. You saw the photographs. You just don't know when.)

She raised a hand to her hair as she dimly recalled the flash of scissors near her face, the sound as they cut—

He had taken a lock of her hair for his album. All he needed now was the AFTER photograph. He'd be coming back, all right.

But she couldn't just sit and wait; she had to find something to *do*. She rose, unsteady on her feet at first, made her way over to the wall, and fumbled for the light switch. She gave it a flip. Two flips. Three.

Nothing. The storm must have caused the electricity to go out. But no, the power was still on; she could hear and feel the air-conditioner. He must have thrown the circuit breaker. But why?

Son of a bitch remembered after all these years how afraid I was of the dark.

With one hand against the wall to guide her, she walked around the room. No chance of breaking through the window, but the closet gave her a glimmer of hope. The door was wooden, the slatted folding kind without any knobs. She pushed it open, looking for the rod where clothes were hung —a potential weapon. But Bruner had anticipated her. The rod had been removed, and the overhead shelves were secured so she couldn't pull them down.

She could have wept with frustration, but instead forced herself to keep making her way around the room's perimeter. As she moved her hand along the wall and onto the bedroom door, she felt the wood give under her hand. She drew back, certain that the drugs were playing tricks with her perception. But when she pressed on it again, it *moved* forward, away from her. He hadn't pulled the door all the way closed.

Knowing it was too good to be real, she found the knob and drew it toward her.

Open.

The whole time she'd been moving around the coal-black room, the door had been ajar.

She moved to open it wide, but stopped, suddenly afraid. What if Bruner was standing on the other side, leering in the darkness? Easy to imagine, over the hum of the air-conditioner, that she heard his breathing. Maybe that was what he'd been waiting for all this time, for her to make her escape.

She stood for several seconds with her hand on the knob, straining to listen.

Nothing.

Holding her breath, she pulled the door open. There was no way to tell if anyone waited at the end of the hall, nothing to do but risk it. That's what Maggie would do.

(See, Ave? Nothing there. No rotting corpses, just a bunch of old cardboard boxes.)

She ventured forward cautiously, a step at a time, one palm flat against the wall. Her hand came to the wall's edge as the hallway opened to the right. She had a choice: continue straight ahead, toward the main part of the house, or turn. She turned. Maybe the side hall led to an exit, to outside.

Her guess appeared correct. The hall continued several feet, then ended in a door which probably led to a garage or utility room. Avra ran her hands over it, turned the knob—no success—then fingered the dead bolt. Locked, and the key had been removed. She jiggled the handle a few times out of frustration, then retraced her steps back to the main hallway.

As she rounded the corner, she heard it again: a child crying.

Unmistakable this time. Not her imagination, and not the air-conditioner, which had cut off moments before. The sound traveled clearly from the end of the hallway.

On the other side of the house a child wept as though her heart were broken.

Her heart: a little girl.

Abruptly, the sound stopped.

There was nothing in front of Avra, nothing her eyes and brain could register. But she became convinced that something—*someone*—was standing several feet in front of her, where the hallway seemed to open onto a larger room. In the darkness a shape coalesced.

A child. Before it formed completely, Avra knew it was Rachel Bernstein, the girl whose photo followed hers in Bruner's album.

Impossible. She saw nothing, only an absence of light, and yet—

Yet she saw Rachel Bernstein standing at the end of the hallway as clearly as she had seen her in the photograph, the one marked AFTER: Rachel's brown-black hair flowing straight down, onto her shoulders, no longer restrained by the ponytail and the pink plastic headband, the skin of her neck mottled with dark purplish bruises. She stared back at Avra with the same reproachful expression she'd worn in the BEFORE picture.

The sight sent a jolt like electricity traveling from Rachel across the floor, up Avra's legs, her spine, into her limbs, raising the fine hairs on her arms. A purely physical message, registered by her body before her mind could make sense of it. Not the overwhelming terror of the Shadow dream, but a subtle eeriness.

Avra snapped her eyes shut, but Rachel's image remained. Not real. And not the first time Avra's mind had played a trick on her. One Saturday afternoon when the twins were eleven, they had watched *The Wolf Man* on TV. That awful moment —when Lon Chaney, Jr., began changing into the wolf man before their eyes, sprouting hair and claws and teeth—had scared Avra out of her wits. Maggie had spent the rest of the day trying to explain how it had all been done with makeup, and for the afternoon Avra believed.

But by nightfall logic went out the window. She'd had a bad dream, and when she'd wakened in a cold sweat just as the wolf man was leaning over her bed, his hot breath on her face, his yellow fangs dripping saliva, she'd opened her eyes—

—opened her eyes and *been wide awake*, and still seen him there, as if the dream image had been imprinted on her retinas forever. Not until Maggie had wakened beside her had the horrible image faded.

That was what she saw now, with Rachel Bernstein. A dream image, like the wolf man. Sure enough, when she opened her eyes again, the girl was gone.

But unlike the wolf man or the Shadow, Rachel Bernstein had not seemed malevolent, had not wanted to hurt her. The girl had simply been watching, waiting for something. . . .

Very quietly, Avra began to laugh, a shuddering, unpleasant sound uncomfortably close to sobbing. Her seeing Rachel Bernstein—which, of course, she *hadn't*—meant that none of this had happened at all. None of it: seeing Bruner in the Catacombs, finding herself trapped in the empty bedroom, seeing a ghost in the hall. . . . It had to mean that she hadn't seen him at Selena's either. That had just been some poor old bastard out for dinner with his daughter and grandchild.

I must be really *crazy; I'm not just seeing the ghost of a murdered person—I'm seeing the ghost of a murdered person who never existed in the first place.*

It didn't seem funny at all, but her giggling grew louder and hoarser, until she clamped her teeth down on her tongue and forced herself to stop.

Rachel Bernstein—whether she was the imaginary ghost of an imaginary person or not—was gone, but the darkness and the hallway were still there. Even if it was all a delusion, she had to try to escape.

She began moving again, very slowly. Within a few steps her palm ran over some molding, and a closed door. Probably a bathroom or another bedroom. A bathroom would have been welcome—her bladder wasn't urgently full, since she'd had nothing to drink for several hours and had been sweating profusely. Still, it would have been nice to pee, splash some water onto her sticky face, wash her hands—

Right. Take a leak with Bruner somewhere nearby. Talk about getting caught with your pants down. . . .

She jiggled the knob, pushed in hard a few times. Locked. She gave up and continued on. Farther down, to her left, she got the impression of an open doorway, and crossed to the other side.

Her impression was correct. She found molding, then the edge of the wide-open door, and stepped inside. Even in the darkness she could tell that this room also lacked furniture.

Part of her knew she should have been frightened—after all, Bruner had left *this* door open, not the other; obviously, he wanted her to enter. Yet she felt no fear, only an urgent need to explore the room and discover what lay inside.

A soft moan came from the far corner.

This time Avra didn't ask herself if it had been the air-conditioner or her imagination. In four quick steps she was across the room, on her knees, bending over the dark form lying supine on the carpet.

"Maggie? Maggie, my God, has he *hurt* you?"

Her voice shook with an odd mixture of relief and terror: relief that Maggie was here, and alive; terror that Maggie was here, and injured. Avra listened as her sister stirred and released another groan.

"Magpie? Can you hear me?" She groped gently and found her twin's shoulder. "You've got to

wake up, Maggie. We've got to get out of
here. . . ."

(Do you even hear me, Maggie?)

No answer. Maggie was hurt, apparently seriously—the thought made Avra feel physically ill
herself—but she had no way, here in the dark, to
be sure how bad, or even to know *what*, Maggie's
injuries were.

She touched her sister's face. The skin was cool
and moist. Avra crouched forward and cocked her
head to listen. Maggie was breathing, but so softly
Avra could barely hear. She straightened and ran
her hand across Maggie's forehead.

"Maggie," she said.

And cringed when her fingers touched something wet and sticky. Leaning close so that their
faces almost touched, she could just make out Maggie's pale skin, framed by dark hair; but some of
the black streaks on her sister's forehead, down the
side of her face, weren't loose strands of hair at all.
Avra ran shaking fingers lightly over Maggie's jaw,
up her temple, along her hairline. In some spots
the blood had crusted, causing the hairs to stick
together in stiff clumps.

He had shot her in the head.

She pressed spread, bloodied fingers to her face
and sucked in air with deep, gasping sobs, no
longer worried that Bruner might hear.

He had shot Maggie in the head, and she was
dying. No wonder he hadn't bothered to lock the
door.

Had he shot Murray too?

"Poor Magpie," she whispered, not really aware she was speaking. "I'm damn sorry to get the two of you messed up in this. It should just be between me and him. . . ."

"Ave?" Maggie's voice was high pitched, weak, childlike. "Ave, is that you?"

She gathered herself instantly and found her sister's hand; it was damp, cool. "I'm here, Magpie. I'm right here."

An indistinct murmur. Ave leaned closer to hear. "What is it, hon?"

"What's going on?" The words were slurred slightly, as if Maggie were tipsy.

Overwhelmed by the need for comfort, Avra opened her mouth to say:

Maggie, you've got to help me find a way out before he kills us both. I can't do it by myself—please don't die and leave me here alone with him. . . .

She closed it, ashamed of her own selfishness. Maggie was hurt; she might be dying. There was nothing to be gained by frightening her with the facts. Avra swallowed and said, in a falsely bright tone, "You hurt your head, hon. Don't worry about it now. Just rest."

"But where *are* we?" Her tone became faintly petulant.

"Home," Avra said. "We're home now."

"This isn't home. . . ." Her whisper trailed to silence.

"You're confused, hon. You're going to be all

right, but the doctor says you have to lie still and keep very quiet. Try not to worry about anything."

She felt Maggie tense beside her.

"The doctor," Maggie rasped. Her breathing quickened. "The doctor. He called me, Ave. Bruner called me. He . . ." Her voice faded, then strengthened again. "What *is* this place?"

Avra gently touched her sister's cheek. "It's all right, Magpie. We're home, but you hurt your head and you're very confused."

"Bruner . . ." Her breathing grew ragged. "He said you were at his office. We didn't know where you were. The radar . . ."

"Hush. You're not making any sense. You had a bad dream, that's all. Hush now." Avra stroked Maggie's cheek lightly, fearful of causing more pain. She had always been the one to receive comfort, never to give it; now she heard herself speaking with her mother's voice, her mother's words, soothing with her mother's touch.

"He wants to hurt you, Ave. He tried to hurt me—"

(Raz, did he hurt Raz?

No, don't ask. It'll just upset her—)

"He can't hurt us, Magpie. He's dead. You hit your head and you've had a bad dream, but you're going to be all right. It's okay now. I'm here. I'm not going to let anyone hurt you. . . ."

(liar)

Her sister's voice, dreamy. "He's not alive?"

"No, sweet. You had a bad dream. The head injury did that. You're safe with me now."

"Don't leave me, Ave. I'm scared."

Avra answered, hoping her sister wouldn't notice the slight catch in her voice. "I'll be right here beside you, hon. You just go to sleep, okay? I'll stay here so the bad dream doesn't come back."

A deliberate falsehood, but it had the hoped-for effect. Maggie relaxed with a sigh. Avra crouched next to her, waiting for Maggie's eyelids to close, for her breathing to become regular.

She *had* to leave. She couldn't just stay and wait for Maggie to get worse. Or die. As much as she hated leaving Maggie alone, moving her might make her injuries worse.

He had kept them both alive when he'd had ample opportunity to kill them. He already had a lock of her hair for his album; why set her free now? Why leave the door open so she could find Maggie?

He was planning something. She had to figure out what it was if they were both to stay alive.

Avra stayed huddled next to her sister for a few minutes until it was clear Mag was asleep. She rose slowly so as not to disturb her sister, then stole on her bare feet into the hallway. This time she made her way more quickly.

Within seconds she made it to the very spot where she'd imagined Rachel Bernstein stood. The hall ended, opening onto what was probably the living room. No doubt all the windows here were covered with hurricane shutters as well; it was as dark as the rest of the house.

On an impulse she decided to bear left, feeling her way with one hand against the wall. If she could just find an unshuttered window, she might be able to find something—a lamp, a chair—to break it with. No point in searching for a phone. He could listen in on an extension, and by the time help finally arrived—

Without warning she lost her footing and fell forward. When the adrenaline rush eased, she got to her knees and reached behind her to discover what had caused the fall: two steps leading down. A sunken living room. She'd have to remember where the steps were.

From the unexplored wing of the house came the thin, sharp wail of a child.

Avra froze, listening. This time the sound continued. It was not an aural hallucination, not the air-conditioner, not the imaginary weeping of Rachel Bernstein's imaginary ghost. It was a real child, crying.

She got to her feet and followed the sound, careful not to stumble over the steps again, careful to avoid running into furniture. As she passed from the living room into the kitchen, the carpet changed to vinyl. At the threshold her foot struck something hard and sharp, sending it clattering dully across the floor.

She grimaced with pain. Her right big toe was cut, probably bleeding, but she was far more concerned about the noise she'd made—and the source of the weeping. She bent down and cautiously felt for the object; perhaps it could serve as a weapon.

Her fingers grazed something sharp. Gingerly, she examined the object with her hands, then picked it up by its thick wooden handle and straightened. For an instant—no more—she was amazed and grateful at her good fortune.

It was a knife, a large butcher knife.

With a gasp she dropped it.

(Did you see it, Avra? Do you understand?)

The knife had not been left at the kitchen entrance by accident. It was there for a reason, just as the door to her prison had been left ajar for a reason.

To follow the child's crying she had to enter the kitchen. When she did, she would literally fall over the knife. He *wanted* her to have it.

She took a staggering step forward. The other end of the kitchen opened onto another hallway, from which emanated faint, flickering light . . . and the sound of crying.

His room lay at the end of the hall. Of that she had no doubt. He had a little girl in there with him.

(Don't cry, darling. Sometimes it hurts, but you want to get better, don't you?)

"No," Avra whispered, and sank to her knees. The veil separating past and present lifted.

He was waiting for her to come to him. For the child's weeping to draw her. As it had drawn

Mama. He was making it happen all over again, and wanted her to know it.

But twenty-five years ago Avra had escaped. This time she would take Mama's place.

(*Amazing, how you resemble your mother. Quite a beautiful woman, Marie*)

The girl continued to cry steadily, pitch slowly rising to a crescendo of pain, then dropping low to begin the cycle again.

Avra clapped her hands over her ears, but the child's weeping carried through. The sound mingled with that of Avra's sobbing, but she heard only one voice, her own of twenty-five years before.

Her crying had wakened Mama and Maggie.

I did not start this—though we both know who did

She hugged the floor, pressing her face against the cool vinyl, only dimly aware of the large steel blade an inch or so from her cheek. How could she stay here, knowing what he was doing to that child?

Images formed beneath her closed eyelids: Bruner, dapper and elegant at the restaurant, the charming tableau of him and the mother and the little blond girl exchanging smiles as they waited for a table. . . . It had been her birthday, hadn't it? Her sixth birthday. She had looked so pretty, like a little porcelain doll in her green velvet dress.

Patience, Amelie. When we get home. When we get home

Amelie. He had called her Amelie. She remembered because it was such an unusual, pretty name.

A woman's voice, shrill with fright, crying out in a dream: *Oh, God, Amelie.* . . .

"I can't," Avra whispered. "I'm sorry. I *can't.* . . ."

It was a moment of revelation: she had seen down to her very core, and found nothing but fear, as hideous as the Shadow Itself. She was weak, evil. She could not help the child, could not help herself, could not help Maggie.

Her self-hatred was so intense that she held herself and began to rock in a surrender to madness.

20

A half hour before Avra regained consciousness, Bruner woke with a start to find himself on his bed beside the still-sleeping Amelie. With a thrill of disoriented panic he struggled up to glance over her motionless form at the glowing readout on the alarm clock.

Ten twenty-seven P.M. For a moment he sat unable to make sense of the time.

Ten twenty-seven. He had fallen asleep and napped barely thirty minutes. Not a serious transgression; it would not affect his plan. Avra and Amelie were still heavily sedated, and there was time to do everything that needed to be done. Bruner sighed and sank back against one of the cool down pillows, then reached out idly to stroke Amelie's shining hair.

He would have her soon enough, and she would help him fulfill the plan. For that he was grateful. So gently that he scarcely touched her, Bruner swept his fingers over her flushed face, over the turquoise-blue denim that covered her flat little girl's chest, her abdomen. Scarlett O'Hara lay cuddled in the crook of her arm.

It was difficult to leave her, but he forced himself to rise and take the .22 from the nightstand. He tucked the gun into the waistband of his pants. Amelie would continue to sleep until roused. Before the plan was set in motion—once done, there was no stopping it—he wanted to check on the sister.

He moved stiffly through the unlit rooms. To test his grace in the dark he did not turn on the lights. Before he released Avra, he would throw all the circuit breakers except the one for the air, and burn a single candle in his bedroom. Just enough light so she would see, and understand.

She had always been so terrified of the dark. And Bruner was wise enough to know that such deep terror could never really be outgrown. We might pretend to be adult, to be beyond our childhood fears, yes. But add a little stress . . . and how quickly we remember.

Earlier—he was not sure exactly when, or how —Celia and the others had communicated to him that it was *essential* Avra die in fear; afraid, as all the others had perished. The more terror she experienced, the more satisfying, the more just, her punishment would become.

When he arrived at the second guest bedroom, he snapped on the overhead light. Magdalen stirred and moaned as he did so, but she did not attempt to rise. Clearly, she could not be used for the re-enactment. Still, he was curious to see whether she was close to death.

When he bent over her, he realized he did not need to examine her at all. What did it matter if she died? She was no longer critical to the plan. It now required only Amelie and Avra.

Her skin was wan and cool to the touch; her thick hair formed Medusa-like tendrils against the carpet. The left side of her handsome face was streaked with congealed blood.

Bruner sat on his heels beside her. "Magdalen," he commanded sternly. "Magdalen, wake up. Open your eyes."

Her eyelids fluttered. Had he been her actual physician and interested in her recovery, he would have been pleased at her improved response. She peered at him through half-open lids, then lowered them and turned her face away, groaning at the pain caused by moving her head.

"The light," she muttered peevishly. "Turn off the light."

He reached out and rolled her face toward him. Holding her head firmly so she could not pull away, he quickly lifted first one lid, then the other. The pupils contracted in the overhead light, and they seemed perfectly equal in size. His initial uncertainty about that had probably been due to an attack of nerves.

He took her hand and, in the same commanding tone said, "Magdalen, squeeze my fingers."

She squeezed—weakly, briefly—but she squeezed. All very encouraging for her prognosis. Then she pulled away from him irritably and closed her eyes.

So she would not die immediately after all. But she was so weak that any thought of utilizing her was out of the question. He would have to deal with her himself, just as he would have to deal with Amelie and Avra.

Another body to dispose of; four bodies total— *You must not be concerned about that, remember? It's only a test; Celia and the others will help you when the time comes.*

The brief rest had sharpened his mind. He did not need her; he should have killed her on the elevator. No matter: he could remedy that now. He smiled faintly as he drew the .22 from his waistband.

It might prove useful, having her corpse here. He could leave it for Avra to stumble over in the dark. A beautiful way to heighten her fear—since it was important for her to feel as much fear as possible.

He pressed the gun barrel to Magdalen's forehead. Eyes closed, she drew away and murmured fretfully.

Yet if he killed her now . . . He knew how close the twins had been. If he killed Magdalen now, would Avra sink so deeply into despair that she would refuse to participate? It would be best if she came to him, as Marie had come to him that night. Would her grief render her insensitive to Amelie's cries?

He withdrew the .22 and contemplated this.

Perhaps it would be better, after all, to let Magdalen live. To leave the door to her room open, so that Avra would find her, bloodied and dazed and helpless. It would be enough to increase her fear, enough to give her even more reason to confront him, to fight him. He had been gambling on her sympathy with the child to draw her to him, to force her to act; yet the sister provided another reason for her to cooperate: to try to save three lives, instead of only two.

Celia's wisdom, again. Magdalen had been provided him so that the Plan could not fail. He bowed his head, humbled by gratitude.

And the sister, if she improved, if she regained consciousness, could be made to understand what was happening. It would please Celia and the children if Magdalen knew *why* she was being punished. Better for her to die knowing, perhaps even to see how Avra had been dealt with.

After all, the sister deserved to die in fear as well. It was the sister who had brought Marie.

Bruner replaced the gun in his waistband and left the room, turning out the light as he went. This time he did not bother to close the door.

He returned to his bedroom, went into the walk-in closet, and prepared two more syringes, one adult and one pediatric dose of naloxone. The drug quickly counteracted the effects of Demerol. Once he administered it, he would have to act swiftly to set the plan in motion.

Before leaving Amelie, he took the Polaroid camera from the closet and set it on the night-stand, then lit the single taper on his dresser and turned off the lamp. The act evoked a deep sense of reverence in him. As he stared, mesmerized, at his candlelit reflection in the mirror, and at Amelie lying asleep behind him, he felt the room take on the hallowed feel of a sanctuary.

He went to Avra first. Since the naloxone brought a person back to consciousness rapidly, he did not want to risk giving it to Amelie and then leaving her alone. He took a flashlight with him and stopped in the garage to switch off the circuit breakers to all the rooms. It would take several minutes for the naloxone to bring her to conscious-ness, but he preferred to be safe.

He found Avra almost exactly as he had left her, pressed against the wall, near the corner farthest from the door. She was half sitting with her legs extended in front of her

(such long legs she'd had, even as a girl. He had always admired them)

with the skirt of her dress hiked above her knees. Her head slumped to one side, and she appeared to be barely breathing.

He propped the flashlight on the carpet beside him and bent over her. An eye-watering, sweet-sour smell of aged vomit and perspiration wafted toward him as he pulled up her dress to reveal her thighs. The left one, the one he'd injected with the ketamine, was swelling and bruised, so he injected the naloxone into her right.

Her breathing quickened almost immediately, but he managed to retrieve the flashlight and, holding the beam steady so that it illumined her face, backed out of the room before she opened her eyes.

He left the door ajar behind him and returned to his bedroom, leaving that door partially open as well. Sound would travel much better that way.

After he gave Amelie her injection—his ears straining the entire time to detect sounds of movement coming from the far wing of the house—he held her so she woke in his arms. As she looked up at him, her gaze wide and disoriented, he smiled tenderly. She responded with a faint, uncertain smile. His excitement at holding her, at the thought of having her, became so great (indeed, his physical response at merely touching her was immediate, that of a much younger man's) that he felt unable to restrain himself until Avra arrived. Somehow, he found the strength to transcend his impulse.

"Amelie," he said gently, his expression growing somber. "I'm afraid I have some very bad news about your mother."

Curled like an unborn child, Avra lay sobbing on the kitchen floor.

Get up, Mama said. *Get up and stop that crying*.

The sound in her head so startled her that she stopped and hugged herself, listening. Mama's voice in her head, as clear and unmistakable as if the words had been spoken aloud. The words seemed to come from outside herself.

Or did they?

So this is what it feels like to go insane

She began to cry again.

Stop that, Mama said sharply. *Magdalen needs your help. You've got to get up*.

The dream. She had forgotten. A dream, or else a drug-induced vision: They had been in the old house in New Orleans, and Mama had been trying to tell her to help Maggie, said that Maggie was in trouble. . . .

It had seemed so real. She could picture Mama clearly, her blue bathrobe, the way she wore her hair in that French twist. . . .

The skin on Avra's arms, her neck, her back prickled and turned to gooseflesh.

Maggie *was* in trouble. Mama had been right. . . .

Careful. Next thing you know, you'll start believing that she's really talking to you. . . .

When it came right down to it, she *wanted* Mama there. *Needed* Mama there so badly, and if the only way she could do it was to go crazy, then what the hell did it matter? She was going to die, and if the illusion brought her a few minutes of comfort . . .

Mama *had* been right about Maggie.

"Mama?" Avra whispered tremulously. A tear glided silently down her cheek, out of a deep sense of relief at the notion that Mama might really be there, might really be able to help—and at the same time, out of a deeper realization that Mama wasn't there at all, was only a pathetic effort of her imagination.

If madness brought peace, why resist?

Hush, hon. Get up off the floor. That's the first thing. Get up off the floor and stop that crying

Avra sat up and wiped her eyes. A sudden calm filled her: She believed. The alternative was too horrible to accept.

Pick up the knife, hon

She struggled to her feet, then bent down and felt carefully for the knife. Her fingers touched cold metal; gingerly, she ran them down the length of the blade, found the handle, and grasped it. She moved forward, hand out, searching. She needed to find someplace to hide it, so he couldn't use it against her. The refrigerator. She could throw it behind the refrigerator.

No, don't throw it away. You might need it

"No," Avra whispered. "Don't you see, that's exactly what he *wants*. If I go in there, he'll hurt me again. I'm so *tired* of hurting. . . ."

He can't hurt you anymore

Avra began to shiver as the air conditioning cut on. "He's got a gun and he knows I'm coming. He's *waiting*. . . ."

He thinks he knows. He can't hurt us, Avra. We're already dead

Dead. The word sent a shock tingling through her body, starting at her scalp and moving down her spine into her arms, her legs. Yet while her body reacted strongly, her emotions dulled.

Better to think of herself as dead, as the worst having happened. But he could still hurt Maggie, and the little girl. Whatever happened to her, she couldn't abandon either of them.

He can't hurt us, Avra. We're dead

We're dead. We. Us.

(Do you see, Avra, and do you understand?)

"Yes," she whispered. "Yes, I think I understand."

Clutching the knife, she stepped into the dark corridor. At its end stood a door, ajar and faintly outlined in flickering light.

21

As he cradled Amelie in his arms, Bruner became aware of movement in the flickering shadows that hovered on his bedroom walls. Not a person or a creature: no, the darkness *itself* seemed to move.

As a child he had lain awake in his bed and stared up into the blackness. He did not fear it; on the contrary, it fascinated him. He imagined that it moved, that he could see atoms of color—the shifting, iridescent colors of a soap bubble—swirling, colliding in the air above him. As he grew older, he quit looking at the dark and forgot that it moved, that one could see colors in it. But he never quite lost the impression that the darkness was an entity, that it was *alive*.

It was alive now. It pulsed with energy, and as Bruner stared, he began to see the colors again. Beneath the colliding, iridescent rainbow atoms the darkness was full, pregnant. Celia and the others—*all* the others—were here. The air was heavy with their presence, but this time Bruner was not afraid. They were merely waiting, just as he was, for the plan to be fulfilled, the punishment to be meted out. They were the silent witnesses, and he the executioner.

Amelie's weeping was crucial to the plan, but it distracted him; part of him listened with unbearable anticipation for Avra. With each passing second his anxiety increased. What if she did not come? What if, through no fault of his, the plan had gone awry?

No. Impossible. This was the last test, the very last; he would have Avra soon, and Amelie. He had to demonstrate that he could be patient a few moments longer.

Another part of him was aroused by the weight of Amelie's body against his, by the knowledge that he would soon possess her completely. The intensity of her cries fluctuated: a quick burst of loud sobbing would be followed by a long spell of silent tears. When Bruner had first told her of Helen's death, she had dashed the doll to the floor and released a single sharp wail, then wept quietly.

Her silence concerned him. Would Avra hear, and understand? Were Amelie's cries loud enough to direct her here, to this room?

Slowly, Amelie's weeping gained momentum and grew steadily louder; Bruner was comforted. She burrowed hard into his chest, pressing her face, her arms, her undeveloped breasts against him. He could feel the rapid beating of her heart. His excitement increased. Surely she knew the effect this was having on him.

"Amelie, darling," he whispered. He kissed her hair, fine and soft, pale gold glinting in the candlelight. It smelled of baby shampoo. Its silken feel against his lips overwhelmed him. He pressed her to him and bent his head lower so that he could kiss her hot, damp face, her cheeks, her eyelids, her eyebrows. He bent further to touch his lips to the incredibly tender skin of her neck. Thoughts of Avra and Celia receded, became unimportant. He felt pressure and movement in his loins, and squeezed her to him even more tightly.

Amelie let go a little cry that made his heart leap. Perhaps he had stirred her to passion; but she struggled against him, tiny fists striking his chest, and said, indignantly:

"You're *hurting* me."

The words excited him, but he paused. He realized that he was crushing her so that she could scarcely breathe. He eased his grip and pressed a hand to her forehead.

"You feel warm, darling. And you must be very tired. Here, let me help you out of those clothes and we'll tuck you under the covers. You can sleep in my bed tonight. Would you like that?"

She shook her head, then made an alarming choking noise. "No. *No.* I want to go *home.* I want my mommeeeee. . . ." Her mouth was filled with saliva; the last gurgling phrase was almost incoherent.

"You can't go home, darling. Mommy's dead." He loved Amelie, of course, and he said the words gently, but they brought an odd satisfaction, as did the look of horrified misery in her eyes. Grief angered her; she started crying violently and fought to push his hands away.

Stupid boy. Stupid, stupid boy. Did you really think she could ever love something as stupid as you?

Good. Good. Let her cry. Avra would hear, and it would not be long before she arrived.

"Poor child," Bruner soothed. "Poor, poor Amelie." With one hand he held her tiny wrists tightly; with the other he undid the metal fasteners on the shoulder straps of her overalls.

Click-click. Click-click. The straps fell away; the bib sagged. Amelie still wept, but she had ceased struggling. The surge of emotion had exhausted her. Cautiously, he let go of her hands, then pulled the bib down until the turquoise denim was bunched around her waist. Underneath, she wore a white T-shirt made of thin, clinging cotton knit.

Bruner undid the metal buttons at the waist. "Amelie, lift up," he ordered.

She put her arms on the bed for support and raised her bottom, then her legs so he could pull the overalls off. He draped them neatly on the foot of the bed, then turned toward her once more.

"Raise your arms," he said. The excitement made it difficult to catch his breath.

"But I don't have a nightie." Amelie wiped her nose with the back of her hand and snuffled noisily. "I get cold if I don't wear a nightie."

"I won't let you get cold, darling. Raise your arms."

She began to obey, then stopped. An odd expression crossed her face. She lowered her arms and frowned suspiciously at him.

I don't have to love you back. You can't tell me what to do. You're just a little servant boy, and I hate you. . . .

Stupid, stupid boy. Did you really think I could ever love you?

Her look of distrust filled him with unrestrainable rage. Roughly, he yanked her arms above her head. She screamed with surprise and pain. Blindly, savagely, he pulled the little white T-shirt over her head, tearing it. She sputtered as the lace collar caught in her open mouth. He tugged it off her, then her shoes and the little lace-trimmed socks, and threw them all recklessly on the floor.

She recoiled from him, drawing her knees to her chest and wrapping her arms around her legs. She began to wail again, this time from fright. Her body shook uncontrollably.

His own body trembled, though not from fear. He sat panting, inches away from her on the bed. The brush with violence had aroused him fiercely, given him a painfully taut erection. He wanted to take her now; he could no longer wait for Avra.

Quickly, he unbuttoned his shirt, pulled it from his waistband, and unzipped the fly of his linen slacks. He reached in and freed himself, revealing himself to her. He glanced up to see her, owl eyed, watching him; she still trembled.

(In anticipation? Perhaps she understood what she saw.

Surely she understood. Of course she understood.)

He took her by the wrist and dragged her toward him. She slid across the bedspread, resisting, smooth, chubby legs trying to push away from him.

He was too strong for her. He pulled her closer, closer, until she was pressed to him, until her warm young skin touched his own. He circled her rib cage with one arm and crushed her to him while his other hand worked frenziedly to lower his slacks, his undershorts. He felt her nylon underwear brush the tip of his penis, felt the soft flesh with the hard pubic bone beneath it. His body muffled her cries.

His passion was so urgent, so intense that nothing could have stopped him. . . .

Nothing, except small sounds, muted and faraway, emanating from the kitchen. Something

(the knife)

clattering to the floor, followed by a woman's moaning, sobbing.

Avra.

The ghosts that lined his shadowed walls stirred and spoke to him with a single voice, soundless and yet so loud that it thrummed painfully in his temples. The air vibrated with their words; atoms buzzed against his naked skin.

She's coming she's coming she's almost HERE

Unthinking, he loosened his grip on Amelie. She pushed away and nearly succeeded in breaking free, but he recovered and caught her, held her firmly in his lap.

The sounds from the kitchen stopped.

He did not move, scarcely dared breathe. Amelie seemed to sense that they were waiting for something and gave up struggling. Not his imagination: Someone was moving down the hall, toward the bedroom.

She's coming she's almost HERE

Gaze fixed on the door, Bruner groped with his hand and found the gun beside him on the bed. Clutching the unresisting Amelie to him, he took it in his hand.

Footsteps just outside.

She's HERE she's HERE

The door glided slowly inward.

He could not see her clearly at first—only a ghostly impression of a gray-white face—because the doorway was eclipsed by shadow. And then she crossed the threshhold into the room, into the candlelight.

He drew in his breath at the sight of her. It was Avra, hair wildly disheveled, blue cotton dress crumpled and stained, cheeks and eyes streaked with black mascara.

Yet it was Avra transformed. Never before had

she appeared so beautiful; never before had she so resembled Marie.

She did not move, only stared at him. Her pale eyes were wide and calm, though her chest heaved as if she had just run a great distance.

She held the knife. She understood the plan.

(Did you see it, Avra, and do you understand?)

Understood. And accepted her role in it. As obediently as Celia had accepted her fate. As Amelie would soon accept hers.

Tears of love and gratitude burned in Bruner's eyes. As he sat with Amelie pressed next to him, he sensed himself stirring; the feelings of desire triggered by his struggle with Amelie transferred themselves to a new object of worship. Never before had he been so intensely aroused by the sight of a grown woman. He determined then that he would take Avra before she died, would complete the act he had begun so many years before. He lowered the gun until it rested on the bed, but did not release it from his grip.

"Avra," he whispered softly. "Avra, darling. . . ."

(Darling. Darla. . . .)

(Darla, I'm your brother. I love you)

At first she did not respond. He felt a brief thrill of fear. Was she merely an apparition? Had she killed herself there in the kitchen, and joined the children so soon? Had she stolen from him his one chance at redemption?

And then she spoke. The voice belonged to

someone else, not the Avra-child of his memories, but to a mature woman.

(Darla, here you are, grown up at last)

"Rolf," she said quietly.

His name; she'd said his name! He remembered the pleasure that had once given him, hearing her utter his name aloud.

"Let the girl go. I'm the one you want. You did this all for me, didn't you?"

"Yes," Bruner answered, smiling. "Yes, all for you, darling."

(All for you, Darla. . . .)

"Then let the girl go. You don't need her now."

He pondered this and decided she was right. He could release Amelie without fear. She could not escape from the house, could not find a place to hide from him. He would do with Avra as he pleased, then go to find Amelie. Let the child go, then, if it hastened the moment he could have Avra to himself at last.

To love her . . .

Hurt her, *punish* her for what she had made him do.

He eased his hold on Amelie. For an instant she remained motionless, staring wide eyed, transfixed by the sight of the wild woman with the knife in the doorway. She did not seem to realize that she was being freed. Bruner watched the girl's thin chest heave, watched the play of ribs beneath her white child-soft skin.

A whisper crackled through the air. Avra, to the child. "Get out of here. *Run. . . .*"

Amelie scrambled from the bed and ran soundlessly past Avra into the dark hallway. Bruner watched her go with a sense of wistfulness, but it was outweighed by a growing desire, mingled with triumph. Celia and the others remained; indeed, their presence was solidifying. He began to see dark shapes in the shadows.

The thought of taking Avra in front of witnesses was intensely stimulating. He held out his arms, the .22 still in his right hand.

"Avra," he said. "Come to me, darling."

She took a step toward him, still keeping the knife low. If she saw the gun, she did not react to it. Her visage was serene.

"Not Avra." Her tone was gentle, soothing, curiously maternal. "I'm not Avra anymore. Don't you know me, Rolf?"

The darkness stilled abruptly; the swirling of atoms ceased. Celia and the children faded with Amelie's receding footsteps. The room was empty save for the two of them.

For Bruner there was no sight, no sound, but her. And as the silence and stillness grew, he saw her more clearly, saw that he had failed to recognize the woman who had crossed the threshhold.

Her lips began to move. With sudden conviction he knew what she was about to say, and raised his hands to his ears to blot it out. "*No. . . .*"

But she spoke over his protest. "It's Marie, Rolf. Don't you remember? Marie."

He did not want to believe, yet he trembled. "You're not Marie." He raised the gun. "Marie is *dead.*"

She did not react with fear, did not even raise the knife in response, but continued to speak calmly. "Do you remember the secret you told me? It was right before Christmas, a few days before I died. Before you killed me."

He shook his head, not wanting to hear, to understand. "No. . . ."

"In my room in the house on St. Claire. We stood by the bed, do you remember? I wore the dark blue dress with the polka dots, the one you liked so much. The girls were in their bedroom, playing."

"*No. . . .*"

"You talked to me about marriage, about the girls. About how important it was for them to have a father. And then you told me about *your* father. About being illegitimate."

He gasped.

"Don't you remember, Rolf? You said you never told anyone else. And I never told. The girls were certainly too young to understand."

He remembered. He stared into her gray, mascara-streaked face and saw Marie as she had been that day, her thick hair pinned up into her customary French twist, her features shadowed by the heavy drapes that hung in her bedroom. As she continued speaking in her calm, quiet voice, all became terribly clear. Helen's death, Magdalen's injury, were not tests, not fortuitous intervention, but warnings.

"You can't hurt me, Rolf," the woman said. "You can't hurt me because *I'm already dead.*"

He saw now. *He* was the intended victim. Celia and the others had used him as an unwitting pawn to engineer his own punishment. He nearly swooned. He had not experienced such terror since he was a boy, before he became too strong for Elise to physically overpower.

Marie, first of all his victims, now led the children. Appropriate; how very appropriate. Moaning, he closed his eyes and sagged against the bed.

She took advantage and came at him with the knife raised.

He struggled to his feet, almost tripping over the hem of his unzipped pants, and lifted the gun in his shaking hand.

His reaction was too slow. She slashed at him, once, twice. The second blow caught him. The metal blade hacked into the meat of his right forearm, then withdrew with a faint sucking sound. He cried out in amazement and pain as he dropped to a half-sitting position on the bed. A bright stain spread rapidly across the linen sleeve.

He was stunned that she could hurt him, could violate him so. He had not allowed anyone to do so —physically or emotionally—since he was a boy. Since Elise and Darla.

No, he was wrong. Marie had hurt him. Just like this.

"This time will be different," the woman said. "This time you won't be able to stop me, Rolf."

The gun fell to the bed and as he fumbled for it, she came at him again, going for his arms. She nicked the back of his left hand, but he managed to get the gun and pull the trigger. The .22 leapt in his hand.

The bullet sang past her. She drew back, then disappeared into the hallway before he had another chance to fire.

He collapsed against the headboard. The cut on his forearm was deep, into the muscle, and required sutures. He tried flexing his fingers, but the agony was too great. Cautiously, he let the gun slip from his fingers onto the bed. Gasping with pain, he managed to get his shirt off and wrap it around the wound. It bled through the loosely woven fabric almost immediately. Quite possibly she had severed

(BITCH little BITCH)

the ulnar artery. But there was no time now for a proper bandage; he hitched up his pants with one hand and fastened the belt, then retrieved the gun. He hurried into the dark bathroom and grabbed a hand towel from the rack. In the candlelit bedroom he rigged a tourniquet/bandage of sorts, tucking the towel's edges in so it would hold. In the process he left fat drops of blood on the bathroom counter, the carpet, the bedspread.

And to think how he had worried so about getting a drop of Helen or Magdalen's blood on the cream-colored linen. Now both shirt and pants were soaked with blood. Blood everywhere: Helen's, Magdalen's, his own . . . What did it matter? Celia and the others would not help him now. So many complications, and no one to help him.

All the complications had been sabotage. There was no way out.

As Bruner approached the bedroom door, he released a spasm of noise that began as nervous laughter and ended as a groan. He lapsed into a feverish swirl of memories, images: Celia, Avra, Marie . . . Darla. So many years since he had thought of Darla. . . .

(He thought of her constantly, saw her in every child, in Marie and her dark-haired daughters. . . .)

He remembered the day they had stood beneath the great oak, remembered the look of profound love in Darla's eyes, the feel of her hair brushing against his tenderest skin, the moment of rapture before his mother, Elise—

Elise. Oh, God, let him not think of her.

The oppressive weight of the past hung suspended above him by a precarious thread. At any moment it would descend and crush him.

Bruner bowed his head and wept. Mere seconds had passed, but he could not have judged how long he stood thus; the past and present had become so intimately entwined that the concept of time no longer held meaning.

The disorienting tide of memories ebbed. His mind emptied, save for one sharp, crystalline thought: Despite his injury he had to find Marie. Avra. Both of them together, in the one body. Had to find them, and punish them. Even if it did nothing to satiate the children—

(the children, how he despised them, every one of them, lying little temptresses, little sluts feigning innocence. The little bitches *deserved* to die . . .

little *bitches*

little *BITCHES*)

—he would punish Avra himself, for what she had dared to do to him.

(a second time)

He staggered through the open doorway. Beyond, the hallway was silent. Perhaps . . .

(Pleaseohplease, I'm doing this just for you, to please you)

Perhaps if he killed her, the children might change their minds and leave him alone. All they understood was death and blood. Her death might enable them to see the truth. It was his only hope of escape.

His attempt to play upon Avra's childish fear of the dark had backfired: the .22 would be practically useless. In the dark a knife seemed a far more dangerous weapon. To shoot her he needed to see her;

to cut him she needed only to hear him, sneak up on him, slash out blindly. . . .

He had to get to the garage and switch on the circuit breakers. With the lights back on it would be simple to find her and kill her. But he would have to risk going through the kitchen and the living room to the front door.

He took the house keys and a flashlight from the nightstand. The keys went in his pocket; he tucked the flashlight under his injured arm, since he needed the good hand for the gun. He only had to make it swiftly to the garage. In the dark he had the advantage: he knew the layout of the house, the position of the furniture. And once he got the lights on . . .

In the doorway a wave of dizziness overcame him and he paused to steady himself, resting his good shoulder against the frame. He was light headed, still bleeding, but terror and hatred enabled him to overcome the dizziness and pain. Avra had hurt him, and for that she had to be punished. A second time.

Not me, do you understand? Not me. . . .

Weeping, Bruner stumbled forward into the shadows.

22

Until the gun blast shattered Avra's trance, she had watched events with detachment, like a dreamer who takes on the identity of another in the dream: self, yet not-self. It was Mama, not Avra, who dared pushed open Bruner's door, Mama who saw what waited inside the dimly lit room, Mama who dared step inside.

But it was Avra who fled.

The noise of the explosion jolted her from the dream. She was Avra, only Avra again, and realized that she had just very nearly been killed. The next time Bruner took aim—he was fighting even then to hold the gun steady, level with her head—he would not miss.

Clutching the knife, she ran into the corridor, through the kitchen, through the archway into the living room. Instinct, not cowardice, propelled her. Dead, she was of no use to Maggie or the girl. In the bedroom he could see to aim the gun; there was no place to hide. The darkness would destroy his advantage.

She stopped just in front of the hallway leading to the guest rooms. Impulsively, she had headed for her sister. To protect Maggie? Or to comfort herself?

Magdalen can't help you now

If she went to her sister, she would be leading Bruner to her, hastening Maggie's death. He had to be stopped before he made it that far.

Avra returned to the kitchen and peered into the corridor beyond. Silence and darkness. The door to the master bedroom was half ajar. She could see no shadows, no signs of movement, in the flickering light. The wound must have slowed him down, but he would be following. Soon.

She became aware of the noise made by her gasping, and something more: the girl's sobs. They emanated from the center of the living room. Hoarse and weak, but loud enough to reveal her location.

Avra moved back to the entryway between the kitchen and living room and stood, one hand resting against the wall. Eyes still straining to see if Bruner followed, she called softly over her shoulder.

"Amelie?"

The hysterical weeping continued. If he fired at the sound in the darkness—

"Honey, please try not to cry. I'm here to help

you, but I need you to be quiet and not move a muscle. Do you understand?"

Do you even hear *me?*

No response, just steady sobbing, interrupted by an occasional hiccup.

"Honey, I need—" Frustrated, she broke off as Amelie's crying grew louder. That was it, then; she had to stop Bruner before he made it farther than the kitchen.

She stepped into the living room and stood beside the entrance, flattening her back against the wall. The darkness hid her, and even if he brought the candle, the angle was such that he wouldn't be able to see her until he passed by. She would take advantage of the surprise, strike out with the knife—

There's no other way out of the house

Alive, anyway.

She wasn't as strong as Bruner. She doubted she could wrestle the gun from his grasp before he killed her, but if she caught him off guard, wounded him badly enough—

Not wound. Kill. She would have to kill him.

Her legs weakened under her; she pressed against the wall for support.

Minutes passed unbearably. At first she wondered if he had bled to death—there had been a surprising amount of blood—or fainted; perhaps she should investigate.

No. No. Probably just bandaging the wound. And then the awful thought struck her:

He had gone to switch on the circuit breakers. Of course—the simplest solution to his problem. Just turn on the lights, and it would take only three bullets.

A wave of nausea clutched her; she turned and pressed her face against the wall's coolness until the sickness passed.

Think. Think. The fuse box would probably be out in the garage, if this house was like most Florida homes. She remembered the blind hallway outside the bedroom where he'd kept her prisoner. It had dead-ended in a heavy door that she guessed led outside.

Of course. He'd driven her here, then carried her from the garage into the house, so no one would see him bring her in.

She peered into the kitchen, checking for any sign of him. Nothing; only darkness.

Maybe there was another way to the garage. . . .

She saw something then, standing in the kitchen. Waiting for him, just as she was waiting. Something she knew she did not really see.

Some*one*.

Rachel Bernstein, with her long dark hair and unflinching gaze. Standing there as plainly visible as if she stood in daylight.

And then she vanished, swallowed by the black like an abruptly extinguished flame. Her disappearance was followed by a sweep of light, an easing of darkness. From the hallway a black, faceless figure emerged.

(the Shadow)

A beam of light shone from one side of his chest. Dazzled, Avra drew her head back before it revealed her. She could not see him as he made his way toward her, but she could hear . . . not crying, exactly. He was talking to himself or some invisible other. Crooning, punctuated by sharp little sobs and moans. Most of what he said was unintelligible, but she could make out fragments:

Not me, not me

. . . little BITCH . . . don't you understand?

. . . only wanted to make you ha-aaappy. . . .

His voice broke on the last word. He drew out the second syllable in a petulant, tearful voice; a little boy's voice.

But I love you. . . .

His speech became so rapid and garbled, she understood no more. If he'd possessed any shred of sanity before this moment, it was gone now.

She leaned harder into the wall and gripped the knife tightly. His rasping breath was louder; her own breathing quickened. She fought to slow it, so he would not hear, and oriented herself toward the spot where he would pass. Her mind emptied itself, became focused on one thing alone: She would have to try to kill him with the first plunge. It was the only way. If she missed, there would be no second chance.

As he neared the doorway, she raised the knife

high, above her head. Just inside the kitchen he paused. A wavering ellipse of yellow light appeared on the far living room wall opposite her. Gradually, the ellipse grew smaller, rounder, sharper along its edge. For a moment it lingered, then jerkily descended and traveled across the carpet, over an end table and lamp, a sofa . . .

Searching for Amelie.

If Avra attacked now, she would have to move into the entryway, directly into the flashlight beam. He paused for several agonizing seconds, and then the ellipse of light shrank again. One step away . . .

"Ave? Is that you?"

From the hallway to Avra's left Maggie's voice, groggy and feeble. Then Maggie herself, trapped in a harsh circle of light, eyes squinting in pain, shoulder slumped against the wall for support. Congealed black streaks ran down one side of her face, from temple to jaw.

She raised a hand to shield her eyes.

Bruner stepped into the living room and aimed the gun. It went off just as Avra, shrieking, rushed him, and Maggie fell back into darkness.

23

As he stumbled from his bedroom, Bruner felt an ominous presence surround him.

Presences. For they were all here, every one of them, every child he had ever loved, ever sacrificed —except the two he sought to sacrifice now. He cried out as he stepped into the heart of unspeakable coldness, but his voice made no sound. He turned to escape back into the bedroom, but the darkness had solidified into a barrier; they gathered behind him. He was spurred forward. He staggered down the hall, his shoulder grazing the wall, flashlight squeezed under one arm, gun ready at chest level.

Death. Bruner swallowed and tasted metal; the air stank of blood. They wanted death, more death, and he would give them two. His thoughts collapsed into a single mantra:

Kill Avra make them go away kill Avra

Reason no longer held sway. He was driven by two forces: the need to escape, and the need to punish.

Rolf

He turned with a startled cry, holding the gun at arm's length, absurdly threatening the dead. The presence behind him had spoken, thirty-six voices chanting as one in his ear. Close enough for a caress, a kiss.

Celia. Less than two feet away from him. Naked still, and frail, but her skin was luminous, the gleaming yellow-white of the full moon. Her eyes reflected light from an invisible source, so brilliantly that he winced at the sight.

The air buzzed with hatred. Celia's hatred, the hatred of the blond-haired girl beside her,

(Tabitha, wasn't that the name? He had only vague memories of her, Tabitha with the dreamy eyes)

and that of the child behind her, and the one behind *her*. . . .

The hallway was crowded with children, and their hatred was directed at a single point: him.

Bruner half ran, glancing over his shoulder as they followed. Their collective voice pounded in his head:

Someone must be punished

"Not me." Bruner sobbed. "Not me. You don't understand. *I* didn't start this. . . ."

Closer. Celia, the other children surrounding her, stood close enough to touch him now. Her eyes glittered with the iridescent rainbow colors of living darkness. She reached for him.

"Not *me!*" he shrieked. "It's that little BITCH who's to blame, don't you understand?"

Her fingers hovered above the bloody skin of his left hand. He turned, moved to fire the revolver, but his hand shook so greatly that he lowered it in defeat.

His voice quivered, became one he had not heard in years: the whiny voice of young Rolf, stupid Rolf. "I only wanted to make you *happy.* . . ." He made a sweeping gesture of appeal with the .22. "For you. I did this all for you. Risked everything for you. I loved you, all of you, and now you've forsaken me. . . ."

A child's venomous voice in his head.

You're just a little servant boy and I hate you

He looked at Celia, but she had disappeared. Darla stood in her place. Darla, beautiful Darla, hair cascading onto her shoulders, past her waist. His beautiful Darla, but her eyes were narrowed with contempt.

Just a little servant boy

"Darla," he moaned. "I *love* you. Brothers and sisters are supposed to *love* each other."

He yearned to touch her, to stroke that hair again, but as he reached forward, forgetting the gun in his hand, he felt a wave of unbearable cold. The Presence was centered here, in Darla. She took a step forward.

He turned and staggered into the kitchen. Blessedly, they did not pursue him, but hovered in the hallway, waiting.

Waiting for him to find Avra, kill Avra. He fought to steady himself. She might be waiting for him here in the darkness; he had to be careful, very careful, now. His breathing slowed.

A thin, steady sound coming from the living room. Amelie. Perhaps her death would satisfy them. Awkwardly, he squeezed the flashlight under his arm to be sure it would not fall and angled his shoulder so the beam swept across the living room, exposing furniture—hiding places—in its path. Controlling the beam was difficult; the pain made him grit his teeth, but he continued. From the sound of the girl's weeping he could tell the light was almost upon her.

A noise to his left made him jerk his head. A voice—*her* voice. Avra, Marie. He swung his body toward it and directed the beam. Fast, very fast.

In his confusion he saw her, Avra, Marie, exposed by the yellow light and he lifted the .22, aiming for her chest. Better chance of hitting the chest than the head, moving so fast. As his finger came down hard on the trigger, there was pain, metal lightning bolt searing his shoulder, deep in his flesh scraping bone: scapula, ribs.

He screamed. The agony flared through his upper torso, rained blue sparks onto the backs of his closed eyelids. He propelled himself away from the source of pain, into the living room. The flashlight dropped from under his arm and rolled beneath an end table, where it brilliantly lit up the side of the white sofa. His foot caught the edge of the carpeted step leading down into the sunken half of the living room and he pitched forward.

He could not hold on to the gun. It came to rest in the darkness a few feet beyond his head. The bandage on his arm had come loose and he was bleeding copiously, but he knew the shoulder was far more serious. How bad, he could not say; the pain made him cling dizzily to the floor, on the verge of fainting.

He had failed. Fallen and failed, just as he had twenty-five years before. All that Feinman had been, all that he owned, all that he had achieved, was lost.

Open the trunk, Mister Feinman
Mister Feinman, please open the trunk

Time expanded. In the millisecond before he re-covered, he sensed Darla standing by his head. She had brought the others with her. They circled him, stared down at him like vultures patiently await-ing a feast. The worst of it was Darla's expression of utter contempt. The horror of it broke his heart: she was beautiful beyond his ability to bear; he was consumed by love for her. Yet to see the loathing in her eyes, those eyes that should have been brim-ming with love for him, those impossibly brilliant blue eyes—

A cry caught in his throat. Darla's eyes were not blue. *Darla's eyes were not blue, that unusual dark shade of cobalt blue—*

Her face metamorphosed: her dark hair short-ened, lightened to pale gold. She was still lovely, but it was a cheaper, harsher beauty.

Treacherous fingers were upon him; the sensa-tion restored time with a jolt. Driven beyond pain, he dragged himself forward, sweeping the carpet with his palm in search of the .22.

Someone was beside him in the darkness—a live, warm body. Avra. Marie.

He no longer feared the knife. But no cuts came now; she, too, was intent on finding the gun. He moved quickly until his hand touched it—and then became sandwiched between metal and warm skin. Her hand upon his. He fought with power born of insanity. Oblivious to the pain, he clung to the re-volver with both hands, one on the butt, the other on the barrel. The weapon was on its side; try as he might, he could not reach the trigger, or turn it upright to take aim.

He was aware of the children watching, disin-terested spectators.

A distant ache in his left hand and arm: she was cutting him again, trying to force him to drop the gun. Her other hand gripped the weapon and held it so he could not fire. He could not hold on to it much longer; he was dizzy from loss of blood and would soon pass out.

Desperate, he reached out, exposing the deep cut on his forearm. His right hand, already slick with blood, groped for the blade, found it, gripped it—

sharp edge slicing cleanly into his palm, but he
did not feel it—

and tried to tear it from her. His hand slipped,
came away empty. He was too weak.

He did not see her shadowy form before him in
the darkness. He no longer saw the children,
though he sensed their silent presence. He saw
only Elise, Elise's face before him, heard Elise's
voice.

Someone must be punished

He sobbed as he held on to the revolver.

Kill Avra please make them go away PLEASE

Sharp metal hacked into the flesh of his upper
arm. The pain was distant, muted. Avra cutting
him again

(Marie, trying to kill him again after all these
years)

The heat of Avra's body grappling with him in
the darkness, but he did not see her. He saw only
Elise. Mocking him, taunting him.

*Stupid, stupid boy! You can't hurt me. I'm already
dead*

One side of his mother's face swelled to ghastly
proportions, darkened to purple-black. The forehead above one white-blond eyebrow suddenly
caved in, spewing blood and splinters of bone; her
shut eyelid swelled grotesquely. She had died from
a single savage blow from a fireplace poker.

(Avra cutting him in the darkness, knife's blade
slashing into him. Killing him)

He had been in college at the time, and had not

seen his mother for three years when she had written to say her health was not so good anymore,
would he visit? The thought of seeing her again
had unnerved him. He arrived very drunk to find
Elise in her lounging robe, and a strange man leaving. Overcome by jealousy and liquor, he had tried
to take her. She had struck him—

*Stupid boy. Did you really think I would let you go
unpunished all these years?*

Cabbage cooking on the stove. The smell was
nauseating.

Give me your hand, Elise said. She held hers out to
him, beckoning. At the same time he felt fingers on
his wrist.

(Avra. Trying to get the gun away. Cutting him.
Flame-hot pain just below the collarbone. Lung
punctured; he could hear the gurgling, bubbly
noise in his chest, the same one Marie had made—

Not that. Not that. He refused to die at her
hands, refused to allow her the final victory)

Elise reached for him. Warm, strong fingers
hooking, winding, around his own. Tightening.
Pulling away the .22—

Come with me, Rolf

"No!" He tried to draw back. "Not my fault, do
you understand? Not my fault. I *loved* you. . . ."

You've always known. YOU *must be punished*

The children pressed closer. He glanced up and
saw that their features, once indistinct in the shadows, had sharpened with dreadful clarity. Each
bore the marks of death afresh; the bruises on Cel-

ia's white neck darkened from faded yellow-green to deep purplish red.

He met the child's unwavering gaze and for an instant, no more, reexperienced the moment of her death—not according to his recollection this time, but *hers*. He was submerged, drowning in helpless anguish, a sensation far more horrible than burns from boiling water, far worse than any pain he'd ever known.

Only an instant. He could not have borne a second more.

This was what Elise intended for him, had intended from the very beginning. The children were his punishment—thirty-six of them, thirty-six times to relive the anguished moment of death.

Only one way, now, to stop them, to escape torment at Elise's hands.

(to deny Avra the final victory)

With transcendent effort he tore the revolver from Avra's grasp and aimed as best he could.

"I only wanted to make you happy," young Rolf whimpered.

And fired.

An explosion of light and sound.

Avra fell back against the carpet and threw her arms up as a shield, too late; a furnace-hot blast seared her forehead, cheeks, eyelids, singed her lashes and brows. She saw the gunpowder flash with her eyes closed, saw it briefly when she opened them again to stare at the ceiling.

Flat on her back, trying to listen over the high, excruciating throb in her ears for the click of the hammer being drawn back. Silence. The air stank of sulphur and a fainter, more primitive smell.

Blood.

(This was how it felt to be shot. This was how it felt to die.

Shot. She'd been shot. *Where had she been shot?*)

No pain, except for the flash burns on her face, arms, and hands, the sharp, ringing ache in her ears. She'd heard that serious wounds, even fatal ones, sometimes didn't hurt because the person was too stunned to feel anything. Gingerly, she patted her cheeks, forehead, hair. Nothing there that felt like a wound. She ran her hands over her body, brought her fingers to her face. Her clothes were damp and sticky, but not blood soaked. Shot at such close range, and still alive. Too numb to move, she squeezed her eyes shut. It would all be over very quickly now.

She wasn't afraid. She had spent all her fear; there was none left. If anything, she was angry, frustrated: it wasn't fair that after all the struggling, she had failed. She'd been prepared to kill him. It had been sickeningly easy, to raise the knife up high and bring it down, again. Again. Again. So many times, he could not have lived, and yet he stubbornly clung to the gun.

She'd kept slashing until she heard the sound— the horrible gurgling she'd heard only once before

(a thousand times in her worst dreams)

She'd punctured his lung. She'd thought then that she'd won—and then there had come the shot, and the realization that she'd lost. And Maggie was dead or dying, and the little girl would die. If Raz was still alive, he had every right in the world to be pissed at her for getting Maggie killed. If she hadn't been so childishly jealous—

How ridiculous it seemed now, to be afraid of living alone.

Anger. Her life, all of it, had been a meaningless exercise of fear, guilt, and pain. Mama had died for nothing

(Mama, was that really you? Or just me all along, pretending to be someone else because I thought I couldn't face him alone?)

and now she, Avra, would die. For nothing, except to satisfy a madman's twisted desire. Just as Rachel Bernstein and all those children in the photo album had died.

(Had Rachel been angry like this, her last moment of life?)

Their suffering existed, but there was no logic, no meaning, to any of it. The universe was empty of justice: fair or unfair did not matter. The strong devoured the weak, nothing more.

She was tired of it and wanted it to end.

For God's sake RUN

No. No more running. Let the Shadow win. She waited for the second blast.

Nothing. She rested several seconds, trying to overcome the paralysis that froze her. Her eyes were still dazzled, though the image of the flash was fading. No movement, no sound in the darkness. Not even his breathing. Had he left her for dead? Couldn't be that easy, no. But if he had gone, she had to try to get to Maggie.

Something ominous about the silence: Amelie had stopped crying.

The thought of what might have happened to her, and to Maggie, gave Avra the strength she needed to move. Haltingly, stiffly, she rolled on her side and got on all fours.

She bumped into him before she made it even a foot. Her hand brushed fabric, and his body beneath it. His hip. He was lying face up, motionless. She was too dazed to comprehend, but it didn't stop her from searching for the gun. She ran her fingers over the skin of his chest, over the gaping wound on his bloody arm (she grimaced), his shoulder . . .

Fingers at the top of his face, across his forehead, down his cheek, grazing his ear. Her fingers contacted something slick, slipped down. Gingerly, she felt the base of his skull, felt the opening made by the bullet's exit. Felt sticky-wet bone and something warm, moist, gelatinously firm.

Her hands were covered with his blood. And not just blood. She swung away and retched bile until her throat and eyes burned.

Through it she was dimly conscious of someone speaking. When her stomach stopped heaving and she caught her breath, she heard it more clearly—

not in her head this time, but a real voice, calling her name.

"Ave?"

"ThankGodMaggie, are you all right? Did he hurt you?"

Pause. Her voice was weak, unsteady. "I dunno. What happened?"

"Take it easy, Magpie. Are you lying down?"

"Uh-huh."

"Stay like that a minute, okay? I'll get the flashlight and come there."

The flashlight rested under a glass end table only feet from where they had struggled. Avra crawled over and retrieved it, careful not to hit her head on the table's edge.

Much as she did not want to see, she forced herself to look at his body, to *know* he was dead.

(*Nothing at all, Magpie, see? Just an old bloody corpse, that's all. Nothing to be afraid of.*)

She felt extraordinarily calm, though her body shivered feverishly while she examined him. He lay on his back crucifix style, arms thrown out to either side. His blue eyes stared glassily at the ceiling. The back of his skull had exploded when the bullet exited; chunks of bone and brain and hair studded the blood, which was already thickening in a halo around his neck and head. His mouth, black with gunpowder, hung open.

He had put the barrel between his lips and fired.

The chest and sleeves of his cream-colored shirt were soaked deep red where the knife had torn the fabric. The arm with the gun was flung out to one side; the knife lay next to his leg, where she'd dropped it. She took both weapons. The dead could not reanimate, but she breathed more easily knowing he did not have them. There was a ring of keys in his hip pocket, and she took those too.

His death should have brought her happiness, or at least some measure of satisfaction. But staring down at him, she felt only sorrow. There was no joy in revenge, only the remembrance of pain.

She would have killed him had he not done so himself. In his final act of selfishness he had taken that from her, to her deep disappointment and relief.

She rose and walked on unsteady legs over to where her sister lay. Maggie pressed her arms against the floor as if to push herself up, then thought better of it and relaxed with a moan. "This isn't home, Ave."

"I know." Ave knelt beside her. A discreet sweep of the flashlight—careful, not in her eyes, don't want to make her head hurt more—revealed dried blood on the side of Maggie's face. Not fresh, thank God, but then Maggie said:

"Here," and touched her upper arm, almost the shoulder. A bright stain on her cotton blouse, but not much. Probably just grazed. Her eyes widened briefly as she looked up at Avra. "I heard a gun. Doctor Bruner—he wasn't a dream."

Ave drew in a breath and let it go. "It's okay. He's dead now. I made sure."

"Good," Maggie whispered, with quiet bitterness. Neither spoke for a few seconds.

Mouse-soft rustle at the far end of the room. "Look," Avra said, "there's a little girl in here somewhere, scared to death. I think her name's Amelie. I've got to find her."

"Um." Maggie raised a hand to her forehead and grimaced. "Damn. . . ."

"I'm going next door for some help. I'm leaving a gun here next to you. It's okay—no one's going to hurt you, but I didn't want to leave it where the little girl would find it. Be careful. I think it's still loaded."

Maggie closed her eyes and sighed in response, but as Avra rose, her voice suddenly sharpened. *"Shit."*

"What's wrong, Maggie?"

"Murray. Jesus, he must be frantic—"

She was too bitterly exhausted to feel glad, but in the part of her brain not dulled by fear or drugs, she felt the distant stirrings of relief. "Don't worry, Magpie. I'll call him myself."

For Maggie and the girl's sake Avra decided against finding the circuit breakers. No point in lighting up the corpse and frightening them. She put the knife in the kitchen and rinsed her hands with hot water, then went out and called to the child, taking care as she moved through the living room that the flashlight's beam revealed nothing but furniture and unstained carpet.

She found Amelie cowering under a coffee table. The girl refused to speak, but came to Avra easily enough and clung to her side.

She let the girl out the front door, and together they walked across the expanse of manicured lawn to the neighboring house. The night air was warm and heavy with moisture, but the rain had stopped, and the grass was soft and level beneath their feet.